This page is intentionaly left blank.

Published in the United States of America by
341 Enterprise
Georgia, USA
https://www.bellbookandclaw.com
Copyright 2019 by Victoria Winters
ISBN-978-0-578-65661-8
Vickie Sanford -other

ANDI UNDONE

Victoria Winters

ANDI UNDONE

VICTORIA WINTERS

CHAPTER 1

Someone shoot me, please...

Andrea took a bite of her pizza as the girl sitting across from her droned on excitedly about the latest Ariana Grande song to make the charts. *How does she manage to eat and talk at the same time without choking?* Her eyes drifted to the clock on the wall, wishing she could somehow make the hands move by staring. Not that her date wasn't cute, she was actually pretty damn hot, but Andrea could only pretend interest in the latest pop drivel for so long before her evil side began to slip through the invisible walls of her consciousness. She began to imagine her date with a duck's bill, and then her tinny voice became a quack, kind of like Donald's.

After a few minutes, she had given up watching

her bright red lips move; instead of imagining how they would feel crushed beneath hers. It didn't help. She had been looking forward to this mini-date. Now, about thirty minutes into the meal, her socially correct walls were falling like coconuts in a hurricane. The longer Serena talked the more Andi knew she didn't ever want to go on another date with her. It was a shame; they were a perfect match on the college's *It's Just Lunch* profile. Of course, so were the last three disasters.

Serena finally stopped talking long enough to take another bite of the double ham and pineapple calzone she'd ordered.

Andrea sighed. If she had to sit there and hear one more word about a stupid pop singer, she was going to get herself banned from her favorite pizza joint. Which would really screw up her life, since she depended on the money she made waiting tables, to pay her bills, and no woman was worth that. A dine and dash was out of the question, Misty would charge her double and take it out of her already meager salary. Resigning herself to at least fifteen more minutes of drivel, she picked a spot on the wall behind her head, locked her eyes on it and zoned out.

"So? What do you think?" Serena asked, startling Andrea out of her self-imposed zombie state.

She stalled, having no answer for a question she didn't even hear her ask.

"Sorry, what? I was watching a car chase on the television. Some people have no sense." It was weak, but the best she could come up with on the fly.

Serena pulled her full lips into a thin line. "I asked if you might be interested in going to the concert a week from Friday. Muna is headlining."

Andrea wavered for a moment, running a hand through her short black waves. Muna was supposed to be a killer trio and she had already considered going to check them out. But she couldn't imagine spending hours trapped in a car driving to and from Atlanta with Serena. And the prospect of a hookup did not outweigh the misery she would need to endure. She searched desperately for an excuse with no luck and finally mumbled something about having to work that night.

Serena wasn't impressed, nor did it get any better

as Andi fumbled her way through a few more excuses. Finally, she gave up kicking a dead horse.

"Sorry Serena, but this is not working. I appreciate you having lunch with me but let's just leave it at lunch, Ok?" She stood up and started putting on her jacket.

"Obviously, I made a mistake," Serena stated as she pushed herself back away from the table. "I won't bother you again." She began gathering her things, sliding on her coat and zipping it almost to her chin. Andrea could see by the way her lips were trembling she was upset. It tore her up to hurt the girl's feelings like that but there wasn't much she could say to make it better.

She was sure Serena thought she was a complete dick and she wasn't exactly wrong. Since she and Katie broke up, she'd perfected the act of pretending she was having a great time on a date, when she would really rather be anywhere else.

"Look," Serena finally said. "It's cool. Sometimes people click, sometimes they don't."

Andrea suddenly felt like shit.

"Goodbye, Andrea."

She heard the buzzer above the door buzz before her mind registered that her date had just walked out of the Pizzeria. The third time in the last two weeks. She let out a deep breath and sat back down. Misty came over, picking up Serenas half-finished calzone, tossing it into a trash can near the table.

"Wow," she said, "I thought the last two were bad. This one takes the cake. Where do you find them?"

That was the question. Andi really needed to reconsider her dating options. Obviously, *It's Just Lunch* wasn't working. She needed to expand her dating pool somehow. Unfortunately, unless she drove to Atlanta or Chattanooga, the available pool was pretty shallow. Really, almost non-existent. She'd been lucky to find the college dating site, but so far no one had clicked. That was the problem with living in a small town, you knew everyone by the time you graduated from high school. She loved living in Subligna, but it was almost an hour to Kennesaw State and at least half an hour farther to Buckhead. Heading north to Chattanooga was just as far. And if there were any lesbians in the area, they were not publicly coming out.

Cooper, her best friend through high school and the only other openly gay kid in the small town, flopped down the empty seat across from her. He was Misty's younger brother and she adored him, even if she struggled to understand his attraction to other men. When Cooper was ten, their mom had run off with her boyfriend one night and never came back. Misty had quit school and taken a job at the pizza parlor, so Cooper could stay in school. Marco, the owner was ten years older than her, but he had fallen hard. The attraction was mutual. They had been married for five years now and had a beautiful little boy, the spitting image of his father. She'd never seen Misty happier. Well, except when she found out she was pregnant again.

Resigning herself to another weekend alone, Andi folded her arms atop the table and slumped forward to let her forehead rest against them. "What is it about me that attracts all the freaks? Do I have a neon sign saying dumbass or something?"

"It wasn't so bad. At least you remembered this one's

name." Cooper said as he slid into the booth opposite her.

She kicked Cooper under the table.

"What was that song you were singing the other day? The one by Meathead?

"Two out of three ain't bad? That's Meatloaf silly." Andi wondered how he made it through the day sometimes.

"Yeah. Maybe you need to stop looking for perfection and make do with what's available."

She lifted her head to meet Cooper's eyes and tried to smile. It didn't work. She settled for sticking out her tongue. He returned the gesture, then broke out laughing.

" Look, you're going to be late for class if you don't take off. This conversation can wait." He started gathering the empty glasses and dinnerware. "I'm just saying that this isn't the end of the world. You're obviously not over Katie yet and you can't force it. One day you will meet someone your type. If you ever figure out whatever your type is since it's changed so many times since I've known you."

She grinned; it was times like this that reminded her how glad she was to have Cooper as a friend.

"Maybe you're right," she replied reluctantly. "Wanna catch a movie later?"

"Cant. I have a date. And don't wait up, I hope it's gonna be a long night."

" Where do you keep finding them? You are such a slut. Be careful."

"I always am," he called back as she passed through the door.

Chapter 2

Cooper watched as the last couple left the table by the window heading for the cash register. After ringing up the final customer, he was starting to feel anxious about his upcoming date that night. Lately, his luck had been going against him, especially when it came to online dates.

The last guy he'd hooked up with was a fucking disaster. Trent was so damn cute; he'd been blind to some of the more obvious indicators of potential problems to come. Like the guy's hygiene. He'd had no idea you could get ringworm from jock itch and the little round fungus blisters itched like hell. He had been certain Trent had given him aids or something equally as deadly. Andrea had sprayed him down with the anti-fungal spray and it cleared up in a couple of days, but it had opened his eyes. He had been taking unnecessary risks and it had to stop. He'd sworn a pact that unless it could be covered by a condom, it did not come in contact with his body. Even the hint of a sore or a fever blister was a red light. No exceptions.

At least his families' pizza business was making a killing. He made it a point to meet all his potential lovers at the Pizzeria, using the excuse that he loved the food. What he really liked was the cameras that got several shots of each one throughout the meal. Since they were trying to impress him, they usually ordered one of the deluxe pies which made Marco happy. Misty liked it that they all over tipped. Only one had caught on to the family connection and he'd been cool with it. In fact, he and his new boyfriend had become regular customers.

Cooper passed the two big boxes across the counter and thought about Andrea. She was starting a new semester and today was her first evening class. They had spent most of the morning sorting through piles of used textbooks in the back room of Renaldo's College Bookstore. Georgia's Hope Grant would only cover new books so Renny had a buyback program for the new textbooks he sold. He would pay between 30 and 50 cents on the dollar for any used textbook in good enough shape to be used for classes. He always got swamped with returns at the end of each semester, but they usually sold out within a few days of the start a new one.

Sometimes the books the students brought back were in really bad shape. Renny couldn't buy them and the student didn't want to keep it. They would usually trash them on the way out. Before closing each day, Renny would dig them out and toss them into the bargain bin figuring they might be too battered to be resold but if you were on a really tight budget, they still good enough to use in class. A lucky few got a chance to dig through the bins without charge. Andrea felt no reluctance about using the freebies and made it a point to show up with a large double cheese with all the meats and black olives in hand.

He glanced at the clock on the wall. Four-thirty. His date would be there in less than an hour and he had at least an hour of side work to complete before he could slip upstairs to the shower. It had been a slow afternoon and there were only a couple of tables still in use. Maybe he could get Misty to pick them up and he could duck out sooner. He had already dropped the pie off at the table and was now refilling their drinks.

"Is she always such a shitty date?"

"Huh?" He glanced up, finally noticing the young woman standing at the counter. He'd never seen her before.

"Your friend. Is she always such a bitch?"

"Sorry. My brain is on the fritz today. Do I know you?" Cooper looked her up and down but there was nothing about her that seemed familiar. Cute, if you went in for tiny blonde girls with soft curves and big doe eyes, which he didn't. She was possibly about as far from the tall, dark, and ruggedly handsome guys he drooled over as it was physically possible to be. But she was asking about Andrea and she was Andrea's type, so Cooper wanted to make sure he wasn't screwing something up.

Then he noticed she wasn't alone. That was when he realized he had seen her before. Misty had been seating them in the back-dining room as Andrea's date had stormed out. He doubted Andrea had noticed them at all. The tall redhaired girl with the glasses looked like the kind of girl Andrea would have doing her homework. Tall, lanky and wearing an outfit that cost more than he made in a month. Old money and a total bitch. Unless Andi walked into her on the way out, she would never give her a second glance.

The cocky bitch was different. He'd thought she was heavier when he saw her following Misty to the table. Without that heavy coat, she appeared twenty pounds lighter. And she looked several years younger than her companion. She'd removed the Gawd awful horn-rimmed glasses that had hidden those soulful brown eyes. If she unbraided her hair and put on something tight, Andrea would be all over her. Definity hot enough for his bestie to hit. Even better, she looked like the kind of girl who would encourage her.

She laughed at the bemused expression on his face, and he felt his jaw tighten.

"Come on, you have to say something. That was a classic dine and dump. It seemed like it went pretty well until the last few minutes. Then blamo… your girl blew her away. She was holding back tears on the way out."

After her comment, Cooper leaned over the counter toward her. "Tell me, do you always go around spying on perfect strangers?"

He rested his elbows on the counter and tried to look intimidating. He could tell it didn't work when she let out a boisterous laugh. Her devilish grin suggested she might be considering calling his bluff. He had not noticed her extending her arm to wiggle her credit card between two fingers, and she grinned when he noticed it in her hand.

Whatever. Doing his best imitation of Andrea's resting bitch face he quickly took the card and slid it through the reader on the counter and rang her out, hoping to get rid of her as soon as possible. He figured he had already screwed up Misty's tip. Red-faced, he slid the receipt and the card back to her.

She calmly signed the receipt and then smiled. " I do when they look like her. Trust me, anyone who wasn't shitfaced drunk or passed out from eating too much of the delicious pizza would definitely be watching her soap opera drama unfold. It was the most entertaining lunch I've had in weeks."

She reached back to slide her wallet into her back pocket and Cooper noticed the Rainbow necklace she was wearing. Definitely Andrea's type.

"Tell her I said she's too hot to waste her time on losers like that." She was gone before he could think of anything to say back.

He turned around to pull a to-go-order off a shelf as the next customer in line handed over a twenty and almost dropped one of the pies. His irritation must have shown because Misty sent Marco over to help the remaining customers. As he stomped away from the register, Misty motioned for him to follow and headed back toward the kitchen. She must have seen the entire exchange and was curious about what had been said. He didn't feel much like talking to her about it. After he mumbled a few irrelevant answers to her questions she gave up and let him escape to get ready for his date.

Chapter 3

Andrea raised her three middle fingers in a silent salute to the idiot who cut her off in traffic as she pulled forward and flashed her ID card to guard at the entrance to the student parking lot. As usual, she was running late. There was not a vacant spot to be found anywhere close to the Medical wing of the building. She circled around to the back, hoping to find one near the Automotive department. The walk to class would be longer, but the chances of finding one near enough that she would not drown during her dash to the building were much greater. Of course, there was nothing empty. Torn between wasting time looking for another spot and being late for the first day of the semester, she settled for the closest available spot. She didn't waste time looking for an umbrella that probably still in the ceramic vase beneath the coat rack at home. Instead, she gathered her things and stepped out into the storm.

Books clutched over her head to keep off as much rain as possible, Andi sprinted across the crowded parking lot. *Why was it every time it rained, she was late?* She kept one eye on her watch as she ran, determined to make it to her class before the final bell.

A flash of blue from the corner of one eye was all the warning she got before the rear bumper of the car slammed into her body, throwing her to the wet ground. She lay there gasping for air, happy that the driver had enough sense to stop backing up before he did more damage.

Jerry smashed his fist on the steering wheel, took a deep breath and opened the car door. His neck hurt; he must have tweaked it when he slammed on the brakes to avoid backing over whomever he had hit. The hard-plastic steering wheel had snapped his forehead back when he'd slammed on the brakes, stopping his forward momentum before he hit the windshield. His pants had a red stain where the edge of the cruise control had scraped against his leg, cutting his shin. He could still feel the warm blood trickling down his leg. *Please let her be alright. His insurance was canceled.* All he needed was the cops to be called. He made herself a promise to be more careful in the future and shoved the door open, hoping to bluff his way out of trouble.

"Why the hell don't you watch where you're going?" he yelled, uncaring that he had been the one who backed out without looking first.

Asshole. "I think I will be okay, thank you very much for asking." Of course, she had been carrying her cell phone in her hand and the impact had knocked it flying. She could see part of it under the back wheel of the pickup and another piece lying in a nearby puddle. There was no chance it was salvageable, but she grabbed the sim card just in case. Somehow, she struggled to her feet; then reached down to pick up her sodden textbooks and her now unreadable class schedule. Obviously, the grease monkey behind the wheel had no intention of checking to make sure she was unhurt. She debated calling the police to report it, decided that would be petty and make an enemy she didn't need, and decided to let it go. She threw her lab coat over her head and ran for the doors just as the bottom fell out again. By the time she'd made it the two hundred feet to the atrium, she was soaked.

Several students seemed to think it was hilarious. One particularly bitchy looking twit was laughing as she walked in the door, snug and dry in her polka dot raincoat and matching umbrella. Andi fought back the urge to smack that smirk right off her face and ducked into the bathroom to clean up as much as possible. Her hair was a sodden disaster, but it would dry fast. It was her new white lab coat she was worried about. She scrubbed at the three worse mud stains and hoped it would pass muster. The white coat was a required item and she did not have a spare one with her. Nor did she have the fifty bucks to buy another. Cursing herself for putting it on before she had made her run for the building, she hit the hand dryer once more in hopes of getting it wearable. At least her textbooks were safe inside her backpack. Money for replacements was not in her budget either.

She put it out of her mind and headed for the lab areas. Intro to Microbiology was one of those classes nobody seemed to know anything about, so she had absolutely no idea what to expect. On the way to the classroom, her eyes darted around, taking in the various students wandering the hall in their white lab coats. One, in particular, a tall redhead, was glaring across the student lounge area at me. *Did I know her?* She didn't look familiar, but a lot of people came in and out of the Pizzeria. Maybe she had been a customer. She only worked two nights a week, to give Misty a break and cover the cost of her pies but it was a popular restaurant and she may have seen her there.

More than once she had been told that she was one of those people— you know, the ones that were too unusual to put out of your mind easily. It was probably true; she loved tattoos and spent a large amount of her extra money at the Bears Den. She had started on a full sleeve last year and Bear was giving her a deal on the work. Bear was a health fanatic. His shop was spotless, and he refused to reuse a needle, so she wasn't worried about hepatitis. She had tested negative and had completed the required antiviral series necessary to enter the program.

The only comment the councilor had made was she was going to get sick of wearing long sleeves in the summer. Andrea doubted that. She'd never been inside a hospital that wasn't freezing, even in August.

If big red had a problem, it was something she'd developed without Andrea's involvement, so it wasn't worth dwelling on it. She finished her coke, tossed the paper cup and headed for the lab.

The first day of each semester is always the hardest. The most difficult thing was discovering which rooms your classes were in. Luckily, this school is set up like a giant H with all the administrative offices in the center while the classes radiated along the legs of the H. The Laboratory classes were along the right side of the north wing.

The bell began ringing as she passed through the door, and people are already settling in for the start of the class. Several of them looked up as she entered the classroom, but she stopped only long enough to add her name to the sign-in log on the front counter. A few latecomers rushed in before she thought about what to do next.

Of course, by now the room was full, and she had absolutely no idea where to sit. She noticed most of the students, the majority of which were women, we're gathered near or talking to this one guy; a tall muscular jock, with a face that would fill most women's night with wet dreams. To me, he looked like most of the football players back in high school. Big and dumb. No one can have that many muscles without lifting weights and taking steroids? He probably had balls the size of grapes.

She decided to avoid the crowd and take one of the back tables, sit down and glance through her first chapter while waiting for the teacher to arrive. No one bothered making any attempt to talk to her or join her at the table, which was perfectly fine with her. She was there to learn, not to get dates.

Just as the bell for the class started ringing the In-structor entered the class. Professor Anderson was a nice-looking middle-aged woman, mid-forties, tall and slim with short brown hair cut into an almost mannish style. Andrea instantly wondered if she was gay. She reminded her of a teacher she'd liked in high school. Unfortunately, her attitude did not match her friendly appearance.

"Everyone please take a seat. The class is about to begin. The chair you are sitting in will be your assigned seat for the rest of the semester. The person to your right will be your lab partner. I exp---"

The sound of the classroom door opening interrupted her speech. She turned and looked at the door as a final student rushed inside. Looking around for a vacant seat, he spotted the empty chair next to Andi and flopped down on it.

The teacher gave him a look that could freeze fire and continued talking. "As I was saying, the person beside you will be your lab partner for the semester. Get to know them, you will be spending a lot of time with them. Now turn to page 7 and begin reading the chapter."

Fuck. Andi turned to get a good look at the partner destiny had stuck her with. He had long black hair braided back into a skinny rat's tail, full sleeve tattoos, and gages in both ears like some kind of modern-day pirate. Surprisingly, he was also really cute, nicely muscled and when he smiled, some of the whitest, and possibly the straightest teeth she'd ever seen. Maybe it wouldn't be as bad as she originally thought.

"Yo! My name is Patrick. Friends call me Thumper. What's yours?"

She grinned. "Hi Thumper, I'm Andrea or Andi. I don't think the dragon lady likes you."

"Yeah, she can be a complete bitch at times but she's not as bad as she sounds."

"Sounds like you've met her before."

"Once or twice." He started laughing, "she's my mother."

Oh shit! "I'm sorry, I didn't know." Suddenly, the idea of Thumper as a lab partner didn't seem quite as attractive. She wondered if it was too late to look for another, then shrugged and accepted the idea that she was going to be his partner, like it or not.

"It's no big deal, she comes off rock hard but she's really a softy inside. I suppose she tries not to treat me any different from any other student."

"I'm surprised they let you take her class."

"It's not like I had a lot of choices. It is a required

class. But someone will probably be monitoring my work."

"I bet. What's your major?"

"Medical laboratory technology, I'm kind of a geek. What about you?"

"Same here. I guess will be together for a while."

"Well then here's to a great partnership.

With the basics settled Andi decided to take a better look at her fellow classmates. Of course, the first person to catch her eye had flaming red hair. The girl in the polka dot coat. "Just fucking great," she muttered.

Thumper raised one eyebrow.

"Not a biggie. The tall redhead on the other side of the room. I don't know what I've done to her, but she had been shooting daggers at me since I ran into her in the atrium."

"Don't let Cruella De Ville bring you down. You probably hit on someone she had her eye on in a club somewhere. She looks like the type to hold a grudge forever."

"What makes you think we would both like the same

type?" She thought about making some token denial to see how he would react but decided not to bother. She'd dated a couple of guys in high school, but it was soon apparent to her that her heart belonged to Katie. The breakup had almost destroyed her.

"Simple. You are the only woman in the room not falling all over themselves to impress Captain Caveman. Hell, even Pete is shaking in his seat and Pete knows the guy isn't gay."

She took a second look at Pete, wondering if he might be Cooper's type. Thumper was, but Thumper was straight. She had been around enough gay men to be able to tell within a few minutes of meeting them. She would chat Pete up some time and see where his head was. If he seemed okay, she'd get Cooper to drop by the school sometime. Call it an intentional chance encounter. Who knows, it could be a lucky chance. Of course, lately, she'd been avoiding anything that had to do with luck, since hers was all bad. But that had to change sometime… didn't it?

Chapter 4

"Andrea? Are you with us or are you a manifestation of my imagination?"

"Huh, Oh yeah. I'm here." Professor Mitchell was calling her name, and from the tone of his voice, it wasn't the first time he'd tried to get her attention. Somehow, she must have zoned out and missed the question. She looked around in desperation, hoping someone would come to her rescue and give her some idea of what she was sup- posed to be answering. She must have looked lost because he repeated his question again.

"What is the Pythagorean Theorem?"

Thank goodness, something she knew the answer too. "The Pythagorean Theorem is a formula used for finding the unknown length of a leg of a right triangle. "

He smiled. "I need a little more information than that."

Shit! What was that definition? "The hypotenuse squared is equal to side a squared plus side b squared."

"Close enough", he said. He moved on to another student. Jesse, please give me the formula Andrea just described.

I closed her eyes as Jesse rattled off *A squared plus b squared equals c squared.*

Of course, that was the answer he wanted. Once again, she'd over-analyzed the question and missed the point entirely. It was a math class. He wanted the math formula. Duh… It would have been a simple answer if her mind had been on math. Unfortunately, math was the last thing she was concentrating on. She turned back to her computer, tapped a few keys randomly, then gave up and closed the application and opened a card game instead. Moving cards around the board took little or no brain activity and it would make her look like she was doing something during the last ten minutes of the class. She had a solid A average in the class and was not re-quired to take the final Monday, so this was the last day she would be attending this semester. It was too bad she couldn't use her earbuds, loud music seemed to calm her nerves, making it easier to concentrate on the task she needed to accomplish. Instead, she was sitting in the class daydreaming about an unknown blonde in a warm shower. She could almost feel the soapy lather as her hands caressed her body beneath the spray. At least until the professor asked that damn question and everything vanished from her mind. When the bell finally sounded at the end of the period, she relaxed, shut the top of her laptop, and headed for the door. It was time to head for home to get ready to go to work. Fridays were always busy at the pizza parlor and with the weather warming up, she didn't expect it to slow down anytime soon.

***

"Whew. That's the last of them. Finally," Andrea said as she collapsed into a chair next to Cooper. It was after midnight and the restaurant stopped serving at eleven on the weekend. When she'd first started the job, she had received great pleasure out of giving the best service possible. After a year, possible had become giving the best service she could squeeze out after school drained her completely. She was spreading herself too thinly and something was going to have to give. Rolling her shoulders to release the tension that had built up over the past few hours didn't really help, but it was better than nothing.

Taking the summer off from school had seemed like the best solution to her problem at the time. Instead, she discovered she had to take at least one class every semester or drop out of the program. It was easy to look back and realize it might have been better to stay in school fulltime. She could have taken the class last semester and avoided the need to get up at six am. Between school and work, it didn't leave much personal time. Maybe she should consider a long-distance relationship? At least then she'd have some type of an excuse for not dating when one of her friends brought it up. Tonight, was even worse than usual, all she could think about was Kim laughing at her behind her back. And it was for such a stupid reason. Thumper had overheard a few of their other classmates talking about some so-called *hundred percent perfect match*. He had looked up one of the college's hookup sites and found her name. Evidently, Kim knew that the dating app had matched Andrea to her girlfriend. That explained why the girl had been such a bitch to her in class. Talk about insane melodramatics. It wasn't as if she had anything to do with it.

Maybe she needed to think about finding a new job? No. The job wasn't the problem. Granted, serving drinks and pizza to frazzled parents looking for a reasonably priced dinner out with the family was not the dream job she'd hoped for, it did pay the bills while she was in school. Attending College had not been within her grasp when she'd graduated from high school. Honestly, the fact that she'd graduated at all had surprised most of the people she knew. Most tended to underestimate her abilities, seeing the secondhand clothes from the thrift store and the tattoos as a sign of a misguided or poverty-ridden childhood. She couldn't understand why there was an issue. She liked tattoos, and while her parents had divorced, and her mother had struggled, she had never done without at any time. Maybe she had stretched her jeans a little longer than some of the kids, but that had been a choice, not a necessity. She liked digging through the bins at the thrift store, almost as much as she liked shopping at the Mall. It was like a treasure hunt.

Tonight had been especially tough. Dealing with assholes was kind of an unwritten part of being a server. Usually, if she could get the drinks out fast enough, the customers would be reasonably happy until the pizza came out of the oven. The last thing she ever wanted was to have a belligerent customer get rowdy and disturb the other customers. Unfortunately, this particular dip wad had not gotten the memo. He demanded his pizza be moved to the front of the line of orders and com-plained constantly about everything while waiting for his pizza. During the fifteen minutes required for his to bake, she refilled his drink twice, brought him a free order of cheese bread and dip and replaced the silverware he in-sisted was not clean enough. When she served the pizza, he had burnt his mouth on the hot cheese despite the fact that she had warned him to let it cool for a moment since it had just come out of the oven. Of course, he had left without leaving a tip.

As if the day had not been a series of disasters already, the toddler with the last party had eaten too much, got sick and threw up all over the booth and the floor beneath the booster chair. She scraped the last bit of regurgitated pizza and strawberry soda off into the dustpan and dumped it into the plastic bag hanging on the front of the bus cart.

Cooper knew she was exhausted. "Take off if you want, I can finish the last bit of cleanup."

"Thanks, Cooper, I'm in no hurry. I've got a lot on my mind."

"I bet. I wish I could have been a fly on the wall when you saw the ice bitch. The look on your face was priceless."

"True. Thumper said he could have bounced a ping pong ball off the table and used my open mouth as a target."

"Every time you tell me something about him, I find myself wishing he was gay. Are you certain he couldn't be swayed my way? Right now, being Bi is the way to go. Maybe I could persuade him to give it a try."

Andrea gave him a not so subtle eye-roll. "Not a chance in hell, bubba. He's so straight, it's a miracle he doesn't snap off in a hard wind. The man has zero flex in his sex life, its women all the way. Mary Ann is the only reason he's not considered a player. She's got a great personality and she'd hot as hell. I don't think he even sees other women. He certainly wouldn't risk losing her, especially over another man."

"Besides," she added, "you're too much of a player to have time to entice a straight guy into your boudoir."

"I know. But he has the dreamiest golden-brown doe eyes. You could fall into them and never hit the ground."

"You are a dog," she said. "Wanna grab a movie and veg out on my couch?"

"Can't tonight. I have a date with Donavan. We are going to hit the Boom-Boom Room. I intend to dance the night away."

"Hmmm, Donovan again. This is like the third time, isn't it? He's the personal trainer from the gym, isn't he?" She smiled, remembering Coopers' impulsive desire to get into shape after watching a movie about male strippers a few weeks earlier. He'd managed to go to the gym three times before he gave up. However, he had caught the eye of the handsome young man who had tried to help him work his way through the program. Cooper wasn't overweight. If anything, he was on the slender side, but he wanted to bulk up and tighten his muscles. It wasn't going to happen; Cooper was not the type to spend hours sweating while working out with weights or on a nautilus machine.

She pulled on her jacket and checked her phone, frowning when she realized she had several missed phone calls and three texts from her mother. Her mind went immediately to her brother, and she offered up a short prayer in hopes that nothing was seriously wrong. It sometimes seemed like he had a glowing arrow floating over his head, the tip pointing down at him with neon words saying *Dumb Fuck*. Opening the text, she grew quiet and her hands began trembling.

Cooper raised an eyebrow, waiting to hear what had made her so upset. "Is everything at home all right?"

"Yes. It's not one of them. It's my grandmother.

She's dying. And they don't expect her to make it through the next few days."

"Dang. I'm sorry. Is there anything I can do?"

"No. But thanks for offering. All I can do is wait. I'll call mom when I get home. Go! Dance the night away. " She gave him a quick hug and pulled her helmet off the shelf next to the door. Usually, she took the short cut in the ride home, tonight she thought she'd take the long route and enjoy the feel of the wind. Her grandmother was the one who'd paid for her to go to college. She'd paid the entire tuition in advance, claiming that was the only way she could guarantee Andrea would finish the course. Andrea had been looking forward to having her grandmother on hand when she graduated next year. Sometimes life sucked.

Chapter 5

Andi sat in class watching as Kim read her report on hemodialysis to the class. Mrs. Anderson was sitting on a stool to her left making notes on her tablet as she talked, waiting on her to finish before she passed judgment on her efforts. Andi wouldn't need to read hers today; the teacher went table by table and there were at the minimum three others that had to read before her table came up. This was great since she forgot to print a copy out to be read anyway. She had no idea how Thumper handled it. The pressure on him to succeed was enormous, his truck needed a motor, and someone had told his mother he was drinking beer at the pizzeria. She had a good idea of who the rat was.

Thumper took it all in stride, considering it all minor inconveniences when compared to the rest of his life. The doctors had recently put him on dialysis three days a week, a sure sign that his liver was getting worse. Not to mention his personal life was in tatters. MaryAnn was having second thoughts about being in a relationship with someone who could die any day. He had sunken into a deep depression and withdrawn into a monosyllabic moron who grunted his answers when he bothered answering them at all. Luckily, his mother seemed to realize he was going through something he didn't want to discuss with his mother and left him alone to sulk during class.

Andi wasn't sure how to help him. She wasn't clear about the details of what had happened, all she knew about it she'd pried out of her partner a word or two at a time. Basically, Mary Ann cheated, he found out, they had a big fight, she moved in with the side dude. So how do you tell someone with a broken heart it was doomed either way and he needed to move on. At least his ex didn't stay around to rub it in his face, the new couple had taken off for Miami the next day. That had lasted about a week; until he got busted and she was left alone in a motel with no money and no vehicle. Karma is a bitch.

As usual, under the white lab coat, he was wearing

a black button-up shirt and black jeans, his typical goth biker apparel. Today he seemed unusually pale, more like a vampire than a living person. She wondered if he was hiding something he didn't want her to know.

Thumper was sick, very sick. The doctors were worried about him surviving the year, much less living long enough to have any kind of normal life. He had AIDS. He had no idea which of the tattoo needles had been infected by the HIV virus. According to the doctors his liver was failing from cirrhosis. Even though he was on the waiting list for a transplant there was very little chance of finding a donor match to his AB negative blood type with his unusual genetic makeup The specialist told him that only one in ten million people were born with his unusual combination of genetic markers and most of them were not American. It was essentially a death sentence. She could not imagine being twenty-three years old and knowing you could die at any time. It had to be hell.

Andi wondered if his illness had been the blame for the breakup. Thumper would never admit it, even if it was true. But it had to be eating at him, knowing she didn't care enough to stay until he died. The reality was probably more along the lines of Thumper getting wasted and then telling her to fuck off because he didn't want her to be around to see him slowly fade away. Either way, he wasn't talking about it and she needed to give him his space

When the bell rang for the end of class, they both headed for the student break room. Neither had a class for an hour, so they usually grabbed a table and spent their time gossiping about the other students. There were only three days left to this semester and they were passing so slowly, it was beginning to get on everyone's nerves.

"Can you believe it. That bitch Professor Dawson gave me a C+ on my final. A stupid 84 on a paper I spent all week preparing."

"At least you passed. You got an 88 average. I made a 70 on the report. Can you imagine explaining to my mother the Professor, how her son ended up with a 74 overall in an English Grammar class."

"That's not right. That paper was a hell of a lot better than one of her boing lectures. It was all I could do to sit through one of them without falling asleep."

"At least you are through for the day, I still have to take my math final this afternoon. I can handle the algebra, okay, but the geometry formulas give me a headache."

"Speaking of headaches, her comes Kim and her little clique. I wonder what it is about her that they like?"

"Her money?"

"That's got to be it. I think she enjoys lording it over everyone. Maybe it makes up for something she's missing—like a soul." She had tried for weeks to make some kind of limited friendship with the snow queen, but she continued to freeze her out. Andi figured she must avoid anyone with half a brain, preferring her fawning sycophants that practically dropped to the ground to act as rugs to keep her feet from touching down. After several attempts to carry out some kind of civil conversation, she gave up and ignored her from that point on.

"Have you figured out why she hates you?"

"Nope. No idea."

"Maybe she feels threatened by you."

"Threatened?"

"Not physically, though that would be rad to watch. I meant sexually?"

"Sexually? You're still not making sense She is not my type."

"Maybe you are both interested in the same girl."

That made her stop and think. It had been a while since she'd been out on a date. Even longer since she'd been involved in a real relationship. She wasn't too into the bar scene, and there weren't many options available to meet a woman with a similar inclination in a small country town. Between school and working all the time, her days usually ended with a quick dinner, six hours of sleep and a shower to get her moving in the morning. Not that she didn't get hit on. At least once a week someone got drunk and made a pass. Most of the time it was a man. Occasionally it would be a woman, usually older, and often more than willing to take her out and spoil the hell out of her if she'd just give them the nod. In the last year, she'd taken only two up on the offers. Nether became a love match but both were now friends.

"It's possible, I guess. Maybe I went out with some-one she liked. Not intentionally, but without knowing she was even in the picture. I've never seen her with anyone I was remotely interested in, but I can't rule it out."

"Look at them now, talking shit and glancing over here like it matters one tiny bit what they get off on."

"True." Then Andi got quiet, staring as if her eyes were focused on something or someone over by the door.

Thumper gave her a puzzled look then turned his head to see what had caught her attention. The most amazing girl stood in the door scanning the crowd. She was of average height, slender, but curvaceous. Pale golden blonde curls cascaded across her shoulders and halfway down her back. When she smiled, bright green eyes twinkled, and her sun-kissed face lit up. She was about as close to perfection as any woman he'd ever seen. From Andi's reaction, she thought so too.

Andi's breath caught in her chest as her eyes locked with the unknown blonde. Then she smiled and began walking, heading down the aisle that led directly to her table. Her heart began pounding in her chest, and her blood was racing. What did she want? She began going over what she would say to the girl when she reached her. Then suddenly, she began to wish the floor would open up and swallow her.

Thumper saw her face pale and turned to see what had caused Andi's unusual reaction. Standing two tables down was Kim, her arm draped casually across the shoulder of the blonde girl. The final piece of the puzzle fell into place.

"Damn," he said, "that's one I didn't see coming. I wonder what she sees in her?"

"I need to go; my class starts in five minutes." Andi gathered her things together as quickly as she could. As she moved to slide out of the booth her phone slipped from her hand. When she caught it, she saw that she had swiped to open *Its just Lunch*, the popular dating app she'd started using a couple of months ago. She sneered at the screen, remembering how badly she had tanked her last date. She stared blankly at the few thumbnail photos of girls she'd had been matched with, going back once again. There was only one she scored a perfect one-hundred percent match to. A gorgeous blonde with green eyes and a smattering of freckles. Once again, she wondered why she had not accepted the invitation to lunch she'd received. Maybe she had thought the girl was too perfect? Maybe she was scared of taking a chance on someone she might really like. The truth was the ones who looking for a quick fuck-and-forget me were so much easier to deal with.

"Wait, isn't that the girl you showed me the photo of? The one you didn't go out with," Thumper asked as he rose to follow her back toward the Medical hall.

"Yes. She wasn't my type. Too pretty." *No. Stop debating the idea. You know how much you hate cocky women. She's not only not your type, she goes in for tall skinny redheads. Oh, god. Maybe she was her type!*

"Ugh. You sure she didn't turn you down?" Thumper looked at the girl once again and sighed. "Hell, I'd smash that in a minute. I can't believe you were matched with someone like her by that app, anyway. It had to be a mistake. Maybe the algorithm was sick that day."

"Fuck you. She isn't what I wanted, that all." Andi

stuffed her phone into a jacket pocket and made her way toward the exit door, leaving Ms. Perfection to Kim and all her cronies.

Chapter 6

There was no such thing as a good day for a funeral.

Andi waited as the final instructor signed her exemption from class. Just as she feared, her granny had passed the previous night. Now she had to make a trip down to the Georgia coast. She had received a pass from her English Lit professor for the class she would miss Thursday because she had already taken her final, but she almost wished she had that as an excuse not to go. Her grade was good enough to exempt the Microbiology final and Matt was done. She really should be happy it happened at the end of the semester, this way she would not have to make up missed classwork. However, her mother had already driven down, leaving Andi the option of flying down and driving back with her, or riding down on her bike. There was no way she was driving back with her mother. If it had been anyone except her grandmother, she would not have bothered going at all.

At least Misty understood her hesitation about being around so many relatives, a family she never saw and had little in common with when she did see them. Before the funeral even started, there would be overly melodramatic professions of grief, and at least one would faint or need to be taken to the hospital. Even though her mother was the oldest, and it was her responsibility to take care of the arrangements, each of her aunts would use the funeral as a way of testing their own power. They would argue over who sat where during the service and who would ride in what limousine to the gravesite. Yet, as soon as the ceremony was over, they would all gather back at Granny's house and eat and talk and visit as if it was some type of family reunion.

She would suffer through it and escape as soon as she could find an opening.

Cooper and Misty were raised in Savannah. After Andi mentioned having to go to Clyo, a small suburb in the next county east of her old hometown, Misty had gone on and on about some oyster bar by the park near the old city pier in downtown Savannah. It had been a while since she'd eaten any seafood and the idea of fresh oysters and beer sounded really good after a week of scrounging in the school breakroom and way too much pizza. No matter how good Italian food tasted, after eating it two or three days in a row, it got old. She promised to check it out.

"You want me to go with you?" Misty offered. "I love Tybee Island."

"Thanks, but no. I'm going on my bike to save on gas. Besides you are pregnant, you can't be tramping all over Tybee Island this late in your pregnancy. Marco would skin me alive. All you would need was to go into labor hundreds of miles from the hospital… and him. I'm not planning on staying any longer than necessary. Once the funeral is over, I'm coming straight back home. I can't afford to miss more than one or two days of work."

She let out a tiny huff but didn't really seem that disappointed by her response. "It was worth a shot. At least I won't have to work with Caesar for more than two nights. Something about the boy gets on my last nerve.

But he does follow orders, at least as long as he keeps his phone out of his hands. I threatened to stomp the damn thing yesterday…well, I gave him the choice between me stomping him or the phone. At the time I didn't particularly care which he chose, I just knew one had to go."

"Think it will help?" Andrea knew Misty was too kindhearted to actually carry out the threat, but the thought of her kicking the arrogant young Latino brought a grin to her face. She'd thought about doing it a time or two herself.

"Haven't seen it in his hands today."

Andrea wasn't sure whether to laugh or worry. With Ceasar, it could go either way. She was certain he only worked the job at the restaurant to cover up his less than legal activities. There was no way he could afford the new things that constantly appeared while working for minimum wage as a dishwasher two days a week. Not that he had ever attempted to involve the pizzeria in his outside income. Marco considered all his employee's as family, and hurting family was something the hot-blooded Mexican would never do. She could hear the rumble of his deep voice as he sang along with the latest chart-topper accompanied by an occasional impromptu drum solo on whatever pot he was currently cleaning. Family!

***

Andi had planned to leave out around six am the next morning. With the idea of getting away before Misty's overworked mind remembered that they could take her car and split the gas, she rushed to get her things together and take off. She shoved a couple of changes of clothes in her saddlebag, along with her kit and a swimsuit. She pondered whether she should pack a dress, then realized it would be hypocritical for her to wear one. Her grandmother had been one of her biggest supporters when she had come out during high school. Nana had never questioned her choice of clothing while she was alive, she doubted it would be an issue now. If it offended her aunts, no big deal. Their nose was usually so high up in the air, it was a miracle they didn't drown when it rained.

Tipper announced his need to go out, so she grabbed a leash and made a quick run for the grassy area out behind the apartment building. No one usually played in the small clearing, it was too close to a briar patch and snakes had been seen occasionally. This made it a perfect bathroom for Tipper, no risk anyone would accidentally step in one of his piles. This was great since she was not required to clean up behind him. Minutes later she was back in the apartment searching through the small stock of canned food for sliced beef. Serving him his favorite helped ease the twinge of guilt she felt about leaving him alone or a few days.

Well, not exactly alone, Cooper would be in and out, but there was no guarantee he would remember Tipper needed attention. She quickly typed out a quick text to remind Cooper to take Tipper out for a bathroom break before he took off for the day and to make sure he had plenty of water. Cooper had bought an automatic dry food dispenser last Christmas after forgetting to feed him one morning. Guilt was one of Tippers' favorite motivators, he knew exactly how to play up the tiniest imagined slight by either of his humans. She was sure to be sub-jected to some type of emotional repercussion for daring to leave him alone when she got back from Savannah. He sometimes pouted more than Cooper.

An hour later than she initially planned she got on her bike and hi-tailed it out of town.

***

The city of Savannah was as beautiful as Misty remembered but Andrea's mind was overwhelmed by the funeral tomorrow. A quick stop by the funeral home showed her there was no way she could spend hours shaking hands and reminiscing over memories of her Nana with complete strangers. Instead, she had slipped away at the earliest opportunity. Her mother would make her pay for it later, but it was much easier to ask forgiveness than disrupt the solemn surroundings by vocalizing the thoughts running through her head. As she pulled her bike into traffic, she debated what she should do. The idea of sitting alone in her motel room wasn't very appealing. The motel was close to the college; the school was out for the semester and the rooms were discounted. Visitors always wanted to be downtown in the historic district, near the airport or out by the beach. It was

Thursday, and there would be nothing on television. She decided to head to Tybee and check out the oyster bar had Misty mentioned.

***

The salt weathered boards on the outside of Salty's Real-deal Oyster Bar didn't hint at anything special inside. Like many of the seaside buildings, it was a simple rectangle set of pylons. Whoever built it had like the natural look, and over time the rough-cut cedar had faded to a soft grayish blue color. Going by the number of vehicles in the parking lot, it seemed pretty busy for a weekday. She was surprised and happy to see a roped off area specified as Bike Only Parking. Pleased by the curtesy, she pulled into a space next too three well-used Harleys, noticing the club emblem painted on two of the tanks. Her dressed out Triumph was often misidentified by less knowledgeable as one of the more popular Harley Davidsons, but Trumpet lovers would never confuse the two. Lately owning a motorcycle had become less of a social stigma and more a status thing as weekend warriors bought expensive bikes and took the road. It wasn't as easy to spot them in the summer. During cool weather, they stood out in their shining new leather; vest, chaps, and jacket all perfectly matched. Often, she wondered how many cows had been sacrificed to the God of Vanity to provide all the fancy new biker outfits. She had shopped second-hand stores to find her own beloved bomber jacket; an aviator style that was easily forty years old. The leather was soft as butter and the stain had faded to a soft greyish brown over the years. She had thought about having it stained black because that was considered the norm but decided she had never been one to follow meekly behind the next person in the line. Her jacket was as unique as its owner.

Unfazed by the advertisements posted everywhere for tourists in town, she had passed by the more famous sites like The Lady and Son without a second thought as she'd searched for the smaller local favorite. No one inside would pay her much attention. She was wearing her favorite blue jeans; the ones with both knees blown out, a baby blue Tee shirt claiming *Divers Go Down* and her heavy leather riding boots. After being carded a few times at the college bar back home until the doorman got to know her, she had learned to carry her I.D. Misty had warned her not to carry much money and leave her wallet and credit cards locked in the motel safe since there were people who preyed on unwary tourists. She didn't project tourist, but she knew from experience the locals could spot a stranger in seconds. Better safe than sorry.

She pulled open the heavy door and stepped inside, stopping by the entrance long enough for her eyes to adjust to the difference in light.

Inside was the typical seaside décor you would expect to see in a seaside restaurant and saloon. A long bar made of the same weathered lumber as the building ran the length of the room. There were 5 are 6 tables, all set up to seat four, painted an odd shade of eggshell blue and white. Grey wood walls were left bare of paint or stain. Someone thought it was cute to dress several taxidermized fish in crazy outfits as if they were tourists fishing for humans. It reminded her of that steakhouse down in Atlanta she loved.

It was happy hour and the bar was packed with

regulars enjoying the two for one special on Corona and tequila. She had never developed a taste for either, her tastes ran more to a wine cooler or Budweiser. When no hostess appeared to seat her, she pulled the chair out at a small table near the back, stretched out her legs and waited until everyone stopped looking at her and went back to their normal activities. She felt right at home and completely safe.

After a couple of minutes, a middle-aged Barbie sauntered in her direction. Andrea was surprised she didn't fall forward she could have made a fortune at Hooters. Like the famous doll, she had a waist so tiny a man could reach around it with both hands and touch fingers, and a bubble butt you could set your beer on. Someone had spent a lot of money crafting that body. Too bad they hadn't followed through with the rest, her face was cute but far from perfect and that blonde hair had come out of a bottle. Between the daisy dukes that barely covered the cheeks of her ass and the barely-there tank top, her waitress left very little to her imagination. Andi had a vivid imagination.

Apparently, the restaurant had a very lax employee protocol. The waitress plopped down in the chair across from her and asked her what wanted. Andi's first impulse was to ask her to show her those tits, but she figured that could go two ways, and one left her without dinner. Instead, she ordered a dozen oysters and a Heineken to start; figuring she would decide after she sampled the shellfish. The waitress made a comment or two about her tattoos; light, casual flirting any waitress would do to increase her tip, and then she wandered off to place her order. The attention was nice, but she didn't read anything into it. Andi had learned the signs and could easily spot another lesbian. Barbie might be bi, but she wasn't gay.

A tall skinny man at the bar called out for Sara as she returned with the oysters. He didn't appear very happy to see the pert and sassy waitress standing by her table.

"Hang on, Bradley, I'll be right there," she called over her shoulder.

The casual banter as Andi slurped down the first chunk of raw meat made it pretty clear she wasn't inter-ested in more than her seafood order. But Barbie-- make that Sara was curious about something.

"Your stocking up on oysters huh? Got a busy night planned?" she winked as she swapped out a full saltshaker for an almost empty one.

"No more than any other night. It never hurts to be prepared." She noticed that Sara was leaning forward as she talked, making sure she got a good glimpse of her breasts and of the hot pink bikini or bra she was wearing under it. If she noticed Andi checking her out, she didn't offer any outward sign. Instead, she smiled and passed her a menu.

"I'll check back in a few in case you want anything else." After a quick smile, she moved off toward the bar.

Andi noticed she looked just as good leaving as she did walking toward the table. After a while she started undressing Sara with her imagination, peeling back the layers until she could visualize the taut, curvaceous body underneath. The tall blonde wasn't her type, but it was fun to flirt even if she knew it wasn't going anywhere.

Bradley was giving her dirty looks by now, so she grinned, deciding she might as well give him something to glare about. She held up her empty bottle and nodded

when Sara looked her way. The waitress would be back

with her second beer in just a few minutes. Most of the

people at the tables around her were already eating and

the ones that were not eating were watching the wides-

creen TV over the bar.

Andrea couldn't tell from the catcalls and laughter if

it was a Wrestling match or a baseball game, but it must

have been a good one. Locals, they all seemed to know

each other. Flirting with Sara could get her in one hell of

a fight, but she had this sadomasochistic streak in her that

could not overlook a challenge.

"Hey Sara," she called out. "Come mere."

Sara waved a couple of fingers, signally she'd be right

over, then finished delivering her order to a table on the

other side of the bar. "You want something?

"What's there to do for fun in this town?"

"It depends, you gonna be in town long," she asked.

"That depends on how much fun I'm having. You

got something on your mind."

"Just wondering if you needed a guide to show you

around." Then she burst my bubble. "My kid sister thinks you're hot. She's too shy to walk over and introduce herself, so I figured I would do it for her." She waved her hand and a skinnier, younger, dark-haired version, got up from the far side of the bar and joined us. Andrea felt a tiny bit of disappointment, but let it go almost immediately. She was only in town one day, and any company was better than no company at all.

"This is my sister Maggie. Maggie, this is…" she stopped talking, realizing she had no idea what my name was.

"Andrea. Nice to meet you, Maggie. Join me?" She felt a tiny bit of guilt after it crossed her mind that the name fit her well. She was soft and brown, with the inquisitive eyes of the curious birds. Like a magpie, she looked everywhere as she talked. Everywhere except at Andi.

Maggie flopped down eagerly into the chair beside her. She already had a drink, so Andrea offered her an oyster.

"No thanks, I can't stand them raw. I like my fish

fried."

"But you hang around a raw bar?"

"Not a whole lot of options around here." She pushed her hair back away from her face and tucked it behind her ears. Andrea had to admit she wasn't bad looking once she removed the frizzy barrier and overlooked the braces. She had baby blue eyes and a great smile. After she got past the frightened lamb phase and opened up a bit, the evening might not turn out to be a total disaster after all.

"So, what is there to do around here?" Andrea knew it was a Thursday, not a great day to go out anywhere. But Savannah was a college town and there had to be something to do after dark. Not everyone went home between semesters.

"Most come for the beaches, but it's still a little cool for swimming. There's always fishing. A couple of the bars have bands on the weekends, but no one goes out on a school night."

"School?" Her heart plummeted when she thought about the possibility the girl was underage.

"Yeah. I go to the technical college in town. What about you?"

Andi relaxed. She was over 18 at least. "I'm here for my grandmother's funeral tomorrow. I live north of Atlanta, a little town called Subligna. Well, more like a crossroads with a couple of stores and a gas station. Most everyone works in Rome. I go to school there myself."

A brief hint of disappointment flashed in her eyes, but they quickly went back to the soft sparkle Andi thought was so attractive.

"So, you don't really know your way around. Would you like a guide?"

"Possibly," she replied. "You ever been on a motor-cycle?"

"Nope, you ever been on a sailboat?"

A sailboat? Now that sounded like fun. Sailing was something she wanted to try but had never got around to doing. It was something she could check off her rapidly growing bucket list.

"Nope," she replied and added a heartfelt grin. "But I'm willing to give it a try."

"Well," she said, "I guess tonight's gonna be a first time for both of us. It won't take long to show you the sights around town. Afterward, I really could use some company on my boat. It's hard to sail one by yourself."

"Sounds good to me. I'll finish up my oysters and take a walk down the pier while you clear it with your sister. My Triumph is parked right outside."

She smiled. "See you in a few."

***

Maggie was right, it didn't take long to ride through the tourist areas of Savannah. The city streets were set up in squares around large public parks. Some of the old houses were probably beautiful in the sunlight but simply looked like any other Victorian or Georgian style mansion. Georgia was full of them, as long as you stayed away from the path of destruction left by Sherman. There were one or two clubs open but neither interested her. Too many drunk men and not enough women always ended up in some type of brawl, and she needed to stay out of jail for the funeral.

Maggie spotted a 24-hour convenience store and

motioned for her to pull the bike over.

"I need to stop and pick up some fuel," she shouted so Andrea could hear her over the sound of the motor.

"Fuel? I thought you said we are going sailing."

"We are; the fuel is for us."

Since Andrea needed to hit the bathroom anyway, her request couldn't have come at a better time. Between the bike's vibration, the feel of Maggie's plump breasts against her back and the accidental placement of her hand in her lap, it was making it difficult to keep her mind entirely on driving. At least emptying her bladder would take away one distraction.

The stop didn't take long at all, and it relieved her of one minor nagging issue. Since Maggie had purchased a twelve-pack of brews, she was either old enough to buy it, or she had an ID that stated she was. Either way worked for Andi.

Maggie managed to balance the fuel and herself without any problem, and they reached the marina shortly after their pit-stop.

"Pull into that lot. I will get George to keep an eye

on the bike while we are out."

Andi stood waiting on the dock of salt-worn planks and studied the area where near where she had parked her bike as Maggie talked to a wizened sailor with a distinctive limp and arms covered by faded tattoos. There was a small attendant's building close by, and the old man on duty promised Maggie he would keep an eye on it until they returned. He was on duty until daybreak. Other than the sweeps he was required to make of the parking lot and the pier, he would be sitting less than twenty feet away from it all night. That satisfied her initial worries about leaving her bike in an unknown area. The old man reeked of retired military or cop. Either worked.

Maggie had borrowed the attendant's building to change out of her work clothes into something more appropriate for sailing. She had shed the oversized sweater and was now wearing nothing but cutoffs and a blue bikini top. With her hair pulled back into a ponytail and without the baggy clothes, she was definitely the source of many a schoolgirl's fantasies. Andrea only tool a minute to strip off her jeans and was now wearing a pair of athletic shorts and tennis shoes, locking the rest of her clothes and boots in her saddlebags.

"Well," Maggie said. "This is my baby." She pointed to a twenty-foot sloop crafted from aged teak and mahogany. Someone had spent a lot of money when they bought this boat. Andrea had expected to see a smaller cat with a single sail, like some of the private school kids sailed on the lake back home, not the beautifully crafted boat with the small cabin before her.

It must have taken hundreds, if not thousands, of hours of hard work to make the wood of the pristine sailboat shine as it did. No amount of liquid gold would get this kind of gleam, it took sweat equity, paste wax and scraped knuckle hand polishing over a long period of time. Longer than Maggie had been living. Now she was wondering who Maggie was?

"I bet this thing set you back a wad of cash."

"Not really. I spent almost as much on my car. Well, maybe half as much. Luckily for me, my parents like to spoil me. Can you untie that rope by your hand without falling in?"

Andrea realized that the question wasn't as crazy as it initially sounded. The boat was moving in the swell and she had to time it correctly or she would end up in the water. Finally, she gave up trying to reach it from the boat, jumped back onshore and untied it, leaving it wrapped once around the cleat hitch, so she could hold the boat securely while she jumped back aboard. Once she was safely on the boat, she dropped the loose end and easily pulled the rope to the boat. It only took a few seconds to wind it up and stow it away.

Just watching Maggie move around the boat getting everything ready to sail, was making it hard to pay attention to her instructions. Her body language was throwing off intriguing hints, and the idea of the two scantily dressed women adrift on the ocean was sounding sweet in her ears.

Maggie offered her a rakish grin and reached into the cooler for a bottle of fuel. She had bought a twelve-pack of Heineken; so, she either planned on staying out a while or getting wasted. Either option sounded like fun to Andrea

"Careful," she said as Andi moved to sit in the bow of the boat. Maggie watched as she carefully maneuvered around a small square opening just beyond a small cabin.

"Should I close this door?" she asked as she slid by it.

"Hatch," she replied, "and why?"

"As much as I love holes, this is not the kind I enjoy falling into."

She laughed. "Do you like swimming?

"Yeah."

"Good. You're gonna be my grinder.'

"I've been told that before."

She laughed and cranked a small trolling motor and then began steering us through the maze of boats in the marina.

"Just stand by the boom and help me until we get out of the harbor."

"Boom, whys it called a boom?"

"Because that's the sound it makes when it knocks you off the boat into the water."

"Damn. Thanks for the warning." She looked down.

"This seems solid, what is it called?

"A backstay tie off mount." She pointed to a long cable that went from the top of the mast to the mount. "That's the backstay."

"Great. It gives me something to grab onto when the pole thingy knocks me off the boat."

"There's life jackets under the seat if you need them."

"Thanks, I'll just sit here and enjoy the scenery." *Damn, she was hot. She knew it too.* She could tell by the way Maggie bent at the waist poking out her ass instead of squatting. She knew Andi's eyes were on her, too. She probably knew she was getting horny as hell watching her. She really hoped Maggie wasn't just a tease. That had happened to her once, and the result had not been pretty.

Once Maggie had guided the sloop into open water, she cut the trolling motor and raised the sail. Andrea sat back and enjoyed the way the boat skimmed across the water, as it almost danced across the waves. It reminded her a lot about how she felt riding her motorcycle in the wind. She hadn't this good since the time she'd rode the

Dragon's tail. Now that was an experience she'd never forget. With luck, this would be too.

It wasn't long before they were over a mile from shore, without another boat in sight. Maggie ran parallel to the shoreline, keeping the distant lights in sight at all times. After a while, Andi got her sea legs and moved to stand close behind her, hands on her hips as she guided the boat. She could feel each movement of the muscles of Maggie's ass through the thin cotton of her swimsuit and it was really beginning to turn her on. Her body responded to the implicit invitation even though no actual words had been exchanged. Andi could feel her muscles trembling and her breathing quickened. Her own blood was racing. Despite the chemistry between them, she felt a bit of guilt knowing she would be leaving as soon as the funeral was over. It was the same thing she'd been giving Cooper hell for doing. Sara had been very accepting of Maggie's interest in Andrea. Obviously, it was no secret Maggie was gay. *What the hell, just go with it.*

She brushed the hair off her neck, letting her lips brush across the nape and travel up to her ear. Maggie shivered as a new wave of pleasure shot down her spine. Andi could feel the heat from each breath she made on the skin of her suddenly sensitive arm. Her mind kept warning her this might now be a good idea, but the growing intensity of desire was quickly driving out all reasonable restraints.

Maggie leaned back against her chest and she took the hint, allowing her hands to slide upward across her torso until she could hold a firm breast in each hand. She responded to the gentle squeeze of her nipples with a slight moan, pushing harder against her fingers gentle fondling as she silently urged her on.

Andi felt her own nipples tightening, her breasts forming taut peaks beneath her tee. Feeling a bit more confident, she reached between their bodies with one hand and unsnapped the clasp on her swimsuit top. Maggie didn't complain, instead, her buttocks began a slow gyration against her hips in response to the sensation. Andi was beginning to feel quite a few peasant sensations of her own as her body signaled its arousal by quickly intensifying the heat growing in her loins. She took a deep breath. Very slowly she shifted her weight; unconsciously molding her body to Maggie's.

The combination of Andi's lips on her neck and her hand on her breast must have been getting to her because one of her hands drifted back to Andrea's ass to begin a slow up and down caress. She allowed Maggie to continue her strokes for a few moments, then decided she wanted more. "Can you park this thing somehow," she asked, her voice ragged and tight.

"Yes…help me to drop the sail."

Andrea really hated to leave those fantastic orbs, but she was long past ready for more than Maggie's hand on her ass. Luckily, it only took a few seconds to drop the sail and toss out the anchor. There was a brief moment of awkwardness as they both stood wondering who should move first, so Andrea solved the impasse by pulling Maggie into her arms as her mouth claimed her lips. As their lips met and fused, the passion that had been smoldering deep within her, flared into a blazing inferno. Her eyes darkened, reflecting the sensual pleasure brought on by the erotic stimulation. Her body shuddered as Andi trailed kisses along her neck and shoulder, before claiming her lips one again.

Maggie groaned, stretching her neck upward and arching back to allow her greater access.

As Andi's hands began exploring Maggie's body, she could feel her heart hammering in her chest. Her breath came in gasping shallow pants, while bursts of red hot desire made her tremble with longing for the other woman's touch. She lifted Maggie's hands to her own breasts before returning to her own exploration, trailing kisses down her neck and across her breasts while her hands stroked and caressed her body. Once she found the sweet spot, her hands kneaded the cheeks of her ass while her thumbs stroked down the inside of her thighs. Maggie closed her eyes enjoying the waves of pleasure coursing through her body.

As usual, Andrea's body reacted to this being their first time together with a few urgent requests of its own, and she decided they needed to change position. Sliding her hands to Maggie's ass, with her hands beneath each cheek, she lifted her and stepped forward, sitting her atop the low cabin. She immediately moved forward between her extended knees, pulling Andrea back into another deep kiss before pushing her back flat against the top of the small cabin. Maggie's fervent cries grew strong and quick.

Andrea sighed. She tasted amazing, so warm and sweet, so right...

Chapter 7

Two days after her crazy misadventure in Savannah Andi was still enjoying the aftereffects of her hookup. Despite her best intentions, she had done exactly what she had promised herself she would not do, taken advantage of a lonely girl, and possibly damaged her in the process. She could still see the pain in Maggie's eyes as she had loaded up her bike to leave the next morning. It wasn't as if she could have stayed. She had to go to her grandmother's funeral. But there was no real reason why she had immediately begun the long ride home as soon as the service was over. Other than her own doubts and fears.

Cooper texted her saying she was 'lucky no one wanted to pursue a permanent relationship with her since she was such a ho.' Not that he had never been guilty of a hit and run hookup. But she should 'never forget that he would always be there to pick up the pieces of her broken heart.'

She replied, "You suck," and ignored him for the rest for the day. Despite his smartass attitude, she knew Cooper was right. The only interesting woman that she'd met since the breakup with Katie lived three hundred miles away. For now, she would have to be satisfied with an occasional hookup with someone she met in a club or online.

That evening, following a brief period of sulking and several shots of Jack Daniels with Cooper she was ready to go out and begin enjoying her three-day weekend.

The prospect of online dating again depressed her, but when a cute nurse name Elizabeth suggested they meet for a drink at Excess later that night, Andrea had hesitantly agreed.

"You go, girl. I'm extremely impressed." Cooper flopped down on the bed next to her, kicked his shoes off and began flipping through channels on the television. Nothing seemed to catch his attention, but he kept cycling through them in hopes he had missed something he would like to see.

"You don't think I was being a little hypocritical hooking up with a stranger I knew I would never see again?"

"Oh totally. You are a first-class slut. But damn, it sounded like you had a blast. Maybe we should think about making Savannah a stop on our vacation trip to Daytona?"

"I don't know. Maggie was great, but face it, she was just a quick smash and dash. I'm not moving to Savannah and there is no way she is leaving a life like that. It makes a great memory. I'd really like to keep it that way. I mean, why take the risk of running into her again, when we can head straight south to sunny Florida?"

"Sounds good to me. When do we take off?"

"That depends on your sister. It's her first baby and they have been known to be cantankerous, especially when it comes to when they decide to be born. I don't think we should chance it until after the baby gets here."

"So at least six weeks. Should we make reservations or just drive until we find a vacancy?"

"Let's risk it and go without reservations. That way we can check out more than one area. I want to go to Orlando anyway."

" All right, Disney World!"

"But of course. You're the only man I know with a Disney fetish."

Cooper pretended to be offended. "You mean everyone doesn't have Minnie Mouse tattooed on their ass?"

Andrea broke out laughing. Cooper joined in and soon it had turned into a pillow fight. After they both gave up and collapsed back onto the bed Andrea asked Cooper what he wanted to do that night. This was the first Saturday night they had off in months. Usually, the restaurant was so busy Misty couldn't spare them, but the city was working on the street by the pizzeria and the road was closed until Monday. Business was practically non-existent, so they had an unexpected but badly needed night off. It was already after seven. The bars would be open by nine and packed by ten. The question was should they go early and grab a table or go late and make an entrance?

"I say early, Excess is usually busy on a Saturday

night. I am not going to wait in some stupid line to get in."

"What about that new place that just opened?"

"I think that is more a concert hall than a dance club. I really want to go to Buckhead and make the circuit. We haven't done that in a while."

"True. It might be fun to see some of the old gang. That is if any of them are still around. Last time I checked, everyone was married, in jail or dead." She grabbed her phone off the table and texted a few old friends from high school, asking if anyone was going to be out. Most said no, but enough said they would be at Excess that it seemed like the dance club downtown was going to be their destination for the night.

Cooper was lucky to find parking in a covered lot about a block from their destination. With this being the final week of the semester at most of the local colleges, she had expected it to be busier but apparently, a lot of the students had finished their requirements and headed home for the summer. There were the usual tourist crowds from out of town but most of them parked at their hotels and walked around the city.

Excess was a retro club harkening back to the disco craziness of the seventies and eighties. From the outside, it looked like any other brick storefront on Peachtree Street. Inside, was entirely different. The owners had painted all the walls and ceilings black. They had hired a muralist to paint a galaxy scene on the ceiling using neon paint. All the walls were decorated in crazy meme takeoffs in bright colors that glowed in the dark under the black-lights scattered around the room. The dance floor was raised and surrounded by a narrow railing with a flat top that allowed the dancers to set their drinks down while they danced. Sometimes they were still there at the end of the song. The owner had even managed to locate a vintage disco ball that now hung in a place of prominence directly over the dance floor.

The only real difference in Excess and a vintage club was the addition of two misting stations to cool down the dancers if they got too hot. Andrea knew they were really to help prevent overheating caused by the Ecstasy sold in every club in the area. The local police did their best to prevent the sales, but they knew they were fighting a war they could never win. Within five minutes of their arrival, they had been approached by three different people offering their choice of three different party drugs.

Andrea felt like she might be a little underdressed for the bar but figured after a couple of drinks no one would notice. Most of the women were wearing short sexy dresses and most of the men looked like they were going to church. Her jeans and black tank top were just edgy enough to stand out without seeming too basic. As usual, Cooper was in all black. Lately, that was about all he wore. With his pale skin and silvery blonde hair, he had the pensive emo look down pat. At least it was better than his pastel period.

"Well, grabbing a table is out. There isn't an empty one in the place."

"Then let's get a drink and make a lap. We might get lucky and spot someone we know with an empty chair."

"Sounds good. First rounds on me." He turned and headed across the crowded room to the long mahogany bar on the far wall. "Whatcha want?"

"Jack and coke. On the rocks."

"Sounds good to me. Make that two," he told the busy bartender. He nodded to two girls making out a couple of stools down the bar. Andrea smiled at the sight of the public girl on girl action. Usually, she had to go to a gay bar to see anything even closely resembling a public display of affection. "I guess things are loosening up."

Andrea let her eyes travel to a tiny black girl with pale blonde hair down to her hips. She wondered if it was her hair or a weave. Nowadays if you had enough money, you could buy anything and look like anyone. She had never considered any of the enhancements herself. Not that she needed it. While not exactly beautiful in the traditional sense, she was a tall, slender brunette whose Latin blood gave her a certain exotic edge that made the traditionally beautiful girls seem bland and unexciting in comparison. Her colorful tattoos hinted at a raw sense of danger that made her irresistible to both men and women. She had pulled her hair back into a tight high ponytail that only seemed to accent her high cheekbones and sparkling eyes. Somehow, without trying she had achieved the just stepped off the cover of Vogue magazine look every other woman in the bar sought to achieve.

She was unconsciously moving her feet to the beat coming from the two oversized speakers to either side of the DJ's booth. Her drink was almost gone and now the throbbing rhythm enticed her to join the crowd on the floor.

But where was Cooper?

***

From her perch on the barstool, she surveyed the room, her classically beautiful face relaxing into what was almost a smile. A smile that did not come easy for her. She sighed. It was the same old crowd. Nothing new, nothing worth…*wait. Who is that? It couldn't be!* She couldn't keep her eyes off her. Tall, slim, sexy as hell, with long dark hair and golden bronze skin that would cost her a fortune at the tanning salon. Maybe Cherokee? Except for the baby blue eyes. She had to get closer. *Act confident. Like you have your shit together.* She set her drink on the bar and began to make her way across the crowded room.

***

Andi was tired of waiting by the time he reappeared.

" I appreciate the heads up before you disappeared."

"Oops. Sorry. Saw Mikki and wanted to catch her before she vanished. Unfortunately, I wasn't fast enough."

"She will show up soon enough once word gets out that you are here. Come on. Let's go dance."

"Soon." Cooper glanced around the room, looking for more familiar faces. Spotting a group from school about halfway down the wall, he tapped Andrea on the shoulder and pointed in their direction.

Great, she thought. *Of all the people to run into.* She plastered a fake smile on her face and followed Cooper as he weaved his way across the room to the table. Most of the people at the table were old friends, one, however, had never come close to being in the friend category. Taylor had developed an attitude toward her in middle school and had let it grow throughout high school. It had started over a girl they both liked, and it had developed into a headbutting contest from that point forward. It had been two years since she'd last seen the bitch, but it was evident she had not let the pissing contest go. Cooper, on the other hand, she absolutely adored. At least Shae and Gina were there, the two girls swung both ways, so there would be someone to dance with. She really wanted to get wasted and dance the night away. Her grandmother's death had taken more out of her then she liked to admit. Not to mention picking up a total stranger in a bar without any backup. It had been so out of character it had shaken her to the core.

If Andrea had one weakness, it was alcohol. She didn't know why she drank. She had seen what excessive alcohol could do to her family. Knowing it was a weakness of hers, she had made it a point to limit it to the rare social occasions she went out, partly because she hated wasting her money on something that disappeared in a few hours and partly because the only time she got into trouble was when she was wasted. She truth was really enjoyed the high; the feeling of invincibility she got whenever she drank. Back in high school, she drank because all her friends were doing it. Same with smoking, except where alcohol made her wild, pot always calmed her down. Her friends thought it made her cool and she did nothing to disillusion them. Like now, she had taken a Xanax and after three drinks she was feeling no pain.

Cooper had hooked up with some friends he knew from another club. He grabbed her hand and all three of them made their way to the illuminated dance floor. Two more girls joined the crowd, gyrating all over Andrea and rubbing against each other's body. Gina was dancing with her ass to Andrea's when she felt someone new slide in to face her. Once her buzzed mind realized who it was, Andrea was too shocked to say or do anything. It was the blonde bombshell from school. The one perfect match she had not given a chance. Her dream girl. For a brief second, the thought she must have tripped and hit her head. Maybe she was unconscious. But just in case it was really happening, she considered walking away and sitting the song out. Logic lost out to lust and she began moving again.

Dancing a few feet away, Cooper noticed the new arrival in their midst and gave her two thumbs up.

Gina didn't especially like anyone interfering with Andrea's attention but figured what the hell, it was just a dance. She placed her hands onto Andrea's hips and slid in as close behind her as possible, hoping the other girl would get the message and move on.

If she noticed Gina staking her claim, she didn't seem to care. If anything, her sultry movements became even more suggestive, as though she was trying to seduce Andi without words.

Andrea wasn't sure what was going on. She looked around and didn't see Kim. Nor did anyone seem to be paying them any attention. When the song ended, and the slow romantic ballad began, she turned to walk back toward the table when her arm was caught.

"I think this is our song."

Shrugging, Andrea turned back, pulling the girl into her arms. She was a surprisingly good dancer, and their bodies quickly fell into a natural rhythm as they floated across the dance floor. She was a perfect fit, her shoulder reaching just under her arm so that her head fell perfectly against her shoulder. She moved as if in a romantic fantasy, swaying with the music. When the song ended, Andi didn't want to let her go without at least trying to understand what her intentions were.

She walked with her back to her table. A couple and two other girls were already sitting when they arrived, none of whom were familiar to Andrea. All four appeared curious about who she was, but no one asked.

They invited her to sit down with them, so she did, figuring someone would let her know if she was stepping on someone's toes real soon. She was right. The interrogation began almost as soon as she sat down.

"Dawn; are you going to introduce us to your friend?" one, openly hostile woman asked. Dressed in faded jeans and a tee-shirt from a well-known Mall chain, she was in her early thirties, a few years older than the rest of them. Evidently, she was also the more aggressive of the group.

"I would introduce you, but I don't know her name," she replied.

"Andrea." Andi made a mental note of her name, Dawn, since it was the first time she had heard it.

"Well, I'm David, Dawns' brother. This is my girl-friend Tabitha, her sister Pam and Pam's friend Sherry."

Andrea nodded her greetings, unsure exactly what she supposed to say. Dawn surprised her by answering for her.

"Andrea's the girl I told you about. The one I made the perfect match with. I've been looking for an excuse to talk to her for a couple of months. Of course, this is not the best place to talk, so we are going to go outside. Don't freak on me, her group is already giving me the evil eye and I don't think I can handle you doing it too."

Andrea felt herself blushing. She was usually the outspoken one, so it was funny to hear someone else giving orders and making plans. Especially someone so tiny and cute.

"Give me a sec and let me text Cooper where I'm at so he does not worry." She sent a quick, I'm outside talking to Dawn message and then she followed the girl out onto the terrace. They found a table near the wall and sat down. Despite the other people sitting or standing nearby, it was strangely romantic. The late-night sky was full of fluffy clouds. As if understanding what so many couples wanted, the full moon shone down between them, adding just enough light to the terrace to make it comfortable while still leaving it dark enough to feel secluded. The club had installed bushy evergreen trees throughout the terrace garden, adding another layer of implied privacy.

"I was wondering what I would have to do to get your attention," Dawn said as she sat down on the flat stone topping the short pillars surrounding the terrace.

"Trust me, you had my attention from the first moment I saw you. I just don't believe in hitting on someone's girlfriend."

"Kim is not my girlfriend. Not that she wouldn't like to be. I've had my eye on someone else for a while now. This crazy girl that works at a pizza parlor. But I can't seem to get her attention." Dawn stepped closer, looking up directly into her eyes. Their faces were so close, she could feel her breath against her skin. Her eyes swept her face, searching for something. Light a flame fed fresh wood she felt a warm rush of heat throughout her core. She could feel her limbs tremble. But it still surprised her when she leaned closer and pressed her lips lightly against her own.

Her touch went to her head faster than the Jack and Coke as her kiss sent her senses reeling. Without giving her to step away, she leaned forward and pressed her lips against her mouth, claiming her mouth, tempting, seducing a deeper response. Felling her lips relax and separate, her tongue eased them apart, exploring and teasing, sending ripples of heat down her body. Dawn unabashedly kissed her back, biting, sucking and taunting her tongue with her own. When they finally broke apart Andrea's head was spinning. But not so much that she wasn't surprised at Dawn's next words.

"We are going to have to continue this when we can have a bit more privacy. What are you doing on Wednesday?"

"Did you just ask me out?" Andi wasn't sure what to say. She was usually the aggressive one in a relationship. It disturbed her that such a tiny woman could be so assertive. She took a deep breath, steadying herself, regaining some control over her turbulent emotions.

"Duh? I gave up waiting for you to make a move. I was beginning to wonder if there was something wrong with me." Her lips trembled as she fought back a smirk before she gave up and laughed playfully at Andrea's perplexed expression. "Next time you want to ask me out, don't take so long to do it."

"That's not going to be a problem," Andrea replied." But maybe we should go back inside before someone comes looking for us. I don't know about you, but I need a drink."

"I think it might be too late for that," she said.

Andi looked around and spotted Cooper heading her way, a serious look upon his face.

"Hate to interrupt but do you know what time it is? The look he gave her was meant to convey there was an important reason he was asking that question. One glance at her cellphone brought it all back. *Ten o'clock. Shit! She'd forgotten all about the nurse!*

"Uh, Dawn. Much as I'm enjoying this, we are going to have to leave it for another time. I kind of…have a previous engagement." She braced herself for the expected shitstorm.

Dawn seemed to understand what was going on

without an explanation. She gave Andrea a quick hug, said "Oh…no problem. We can take it up another time. Call me tomorrow and we can make plans," and then with a casual "See ya" to Cooper, she disappeared back into the crowded bar.

Just as she passed through the door it clicked. She had forgotten to get her number, Andi rushed toward the door, but Dawn was nowhere in sight.

Cooper shook his head. "No wonder you never seem to be able to handle a relationship. You can't even hand the basics. We best get back to my table. I left Ronnie guarding our seats."

Andi didn't argue. Ronnie was a total airhead. All it would take was some cute guy to flash a smile her way and she would be gone. Like most aging Queens she was over the top, wildly flamboyant, with a heart almost as big as her personality. Cooper adored her and swore he would be just like her when he grew up. Since he was twenty -two now and showed no sign of growing up, she didn't expect changes in his behavior anytime soon. While Cooper loved sparkle and flash, he had never been attracted to women's clothing or thought of himself as she. He simply loved men.

Still, she was really happy to see her sitting at the table when they went back inside. It was almost impossible to find an empty one after nine o'clock on a weekend. She gave the section waitress her order and sat down to wait. Thank goodness the drinks arrived in minutes.

Andi sipped hers as her eyes scanned the room, looking for Dawn without success. Evidently, she had left the club.

Spotting a tall, gorgeous woman standing on the steps who was also scanning the room, Andrea's stomach gave a brief lurch. Elizabeth was just as beautiful as her dating profile had promised, with her brown hair and deep blue eyes. Obviously, she had recognized her from her profile picture and was now coming to join them. Andrea wasn't sure how to handle what had just happened. Nor was she now in the mood for a blind date.

As Elizabeth drew near, she gave Andrea a tiny wave of acknowledgment before stopping a waitress long enough to order a drink delivered to their table. As she approached, Andrea stood and lightly bumped her lips against her cheek before introducing her to everyone not dancing.

"Glad you could make it! Can I get you a drink?" Andi asked, feeling self-conscious because she had been making out with another woman minutes before she arrived.

Elizabeth smiled. "Thanks, but I already ordered one. That's probably what the waitress is bringing now. I'm sorry I am late. Hope you aren't aggravated about having to sit here alone."

Cooper tried to stifle the laugh he started and somehow managed to snort the swig of Jack he'd just taken through his nose. He started coughing and Ronnie slapped him on his back which only made him laugh more.

"Oh, did I miss something? she asked, glancing around. Silence settled over their table. Andrea wondered what were you supposed to say to online dates when they asked a question like that anyway? Cooper and Ronnie were not making this any easier. Luckily one of their favorite songs came on and they both headed to the dance floor leaving Andrea and Elizabeth to talk.

"Have you been using Meet Me for long?'

"Actually, you're my first real on-line date,' Andrea answered, sounding rather proud of herself. "I've tried *Its just Lunch* but that's all it was …lunch. How about you?"

"Oh, you know, once or twice… nothing to write to my parents about." Her rosy lips parted showing perfect white teeth and the tiniest tip of her tongue.

"I can't get the hand of this online dating thing," Andrea said. The woman was gorgeous. Why was she still looking around the club?

"Recently separated? You seem nervous."

"Yes, is it that obvious?" Damn, she meant from Katie, not Dawn.

"Yeah, but it's okay…How long were you with her?"

"About eight months, how about you?" Andrea replied, pleased to find some common ground.

"We were engaged but…" she hesitated as if she wasn't sure what to say to Andi, especially since they were both so recently single. Then it all came pouring out.

Does she ever stop and breathe? By the time she finally escaped, the barrage Andrea knew everything there was to know about Elizabeth's recent painful separation and had definitely made the decision to avoid online dating from that point on. One thing was evident, Elizabeth was not her perfect match. In fact, Andi tried everything short of ordering her away from the table, but the woman couldn't seem to take a hint.

Cooper finally saved her from what might have become a disastrous public demonstration of her temper by claiming he was feeling sick and needed to go home. She had never been so excited by the prospect of leaving a beautiful woman before.

By the time Andrea finally crawled into bed, her head was really killing her, she had decided to stay single the rest of her life and was seriously considering becoming a nun.

***

Loud raucous laughter finally woke her up. The digital clock on her bedtable said it was past noon in giant red letters. Moaning softly and cursing all men under her breath, she stumbled into the bathroom. The mirror over the sink showed just enough for her to realize she looked almost as bad as she felt. It wasn't exactly a handover, more a general feeling of blah. The aroma of freshly perked coffee tugged at her. That's what she needed!

Cooper was sprawled out on the sofa, laughing hysterically at a cartoon. He didn't look up as she passed by on her way to the kitchen, but he somehow managed to notice she had her pajamas on inside out. As she poured out a large mug of the heavenly brew and took her first sip, a soft purr of satisfaction slipped out. Cooper had even thought to pick up fresh donuts, though she had no idea when he had found the time to go to the donut shop. It could have been a week ago. There were only two left, but that was enough to settle her roiling stomach. Her thoughts about Cooper were distracted by the calendar on the wall above the bar. Yesterday's date was circled with red and ten o'clock was underlined three times. Her blind date; the waste of a perfectly good Saturday night. She could not believe she had passed over a possible hook up with Dawn because she got lonely and agreed to meet a total stranger at the club.

An hour later, just as the latest episode of *American Dad* was finishing, Cooper remembered the donuts.

"Sorry. Ya snooze, ya lose. If it's any consolation, the ones from Krispy Kreme are much better."

"Pig." He was complaining about the lack of edible food in the refrigerator as she passed him on the way to the couch. He refused to consider Rahman noodles a viable candidate for breakfast and insisted they head to the local Waffle House before he starved.

When he offered to pay, she grabbed her keys.

***

Dawn often found herself wishing she was alone. People were always curious about what events of the past few years could have pushed her into a decadent slide from being a lively energetic teenager to a cold-hearted, narcissistic, twenty-three-year-old tease. She often asked herself the same question. *"What happened? What tore out your soul and left you so damaged?"*

She already knew the answer but thinking about it helped. *People like you rarely ever get a second chance at happiness.*

You gave up. You stopped holding onto an ideal after she destroyed the illusion. Thanks, Melissa.

Once she had believed even after everything that happened between them, that things were going to be okay, that she was going to be okay. Not any longer. Now she wished Melissa pain, hoped that she would die cruelly... No, death was too merciful. She died every time she pictured her quirky smile. When she closed her eyes and imagined the feel of her hands and her lips. She hated to dream, they all turned into nightmares.

For a long time, Dawn had fought to come to terms with reality, but no, she couldn't…a part of herself was lost. And she knew she would never get it back again. She built her wall so high no one could ever hurt her again. Then she began hunting.

It was quite brilliant, her plan, she would find someone similar to her ex-girlfriend. Not necessarily in appearance, but in other ways, personality, outlook on life, intelligence, even popularity. Then she would destroy them. It was difficult initially. Several times she would find herself enjoying the women's company. Once or twice, she even began to wonder if there was a possibility that she was wrong. Then memories of Melissa would come into her head and she would break down again.

She was so lost in thought she didn't realize her phone had buzzed twice. It was from Kim again. Dawn wasn't interested in talking to her. Not today, not since meeting Andi. Not since kissing Andi.

Memories of that Kiss washed over her. She felt something she hadn't felt in a long time. Hope.

She cut her phone off on the third attempt. The traffic cleared up, and she headed toward the bank to make a deposit. It was hard to believe it had been seven years now. Seven years since Melissa had destroyed her heart. Maybe she was ready for a change.

She turned on her phone, composed her short text, and sent it. It was time.

Chapter 8

Andrea picked up her phone and scrolled through her messages once again. Nothing. Not even a wink or a wave.

Copper saw her expression change and decided enough was enough. "Just let it go, Andi. If she doesn't have the sense to realize what she's passing up, she ain't worth you sweating over."

"I know," she replied. "But there's something about her that intrigues me "

"It's only been a couple of days. And it was just a few dances in a bar," Cooper said, trying to keep his voice noncommittal. "She was probably too drunk to remember you."

" Nobody is that drunk," she replied. "I'm one of a kind."

"Pshhhttt…let your head get much bigger and

your gonna need to wear a neck brace to carry that ego around."

The clusterfuck Saturday had unexpectantly strengthened Andi's resolve against not pursuing permanent relationships. It was easy to forget how nice it had been to have someone around all the time, especially when it meant not having to go on first dates. After the Meet Me fiasco at the club last night, the idea of never having to face sitting through an hour of brokenhearted drivel sounded wonderful. The only good thing that had happened was running into Dawn. That kiss had shown her she wasn't totally dead inside. It wasn't much, but it was enough to increase her optimism. Maybe her heart was finally healing. Perhaps Dawn would be the one to make her whole again, at least the algorithm was in her favor.

Unfortunately, during the crazy conversation on the terrace and Dawns slipping away during the hubbub, she had not gotten her phone number. She had no idea how to reach her.

Hoping to at least have a contact point, Andi immediately logged into the Meet Me application looking for

Dawn's profile, but it was gone. Nor did a search across three other dating platforms produce anything. Since she did not know Dawn's last name, she could not google her either. She browsed through a few of the pages of other kids from school, hoping to spot a mention of Dawn or even Kim, with no luck. That class was over for the next two weeks. She thought about asking Thumper to talk to his mother, but he was not online. Cooper was working so neither of them was any help. Finally, in frustration, she closed the search thread and started aimlessly browsing through ransom social media posts but that got boring pretty quickly.

What was it about Dawn that pulled at her so? She was beautiful, with a sculptured face so perfect, it didn't seem real. Maybe her face was too perfect? She had fantastic eyes, yet, there was a sadness hidden in the hauntingly beautiful depths that brought out her instinctive urge to protect her. But honestly, there had been a few times when something in her expression made her feel like Dawn was not being totally truthful about something. Not that whatever she was hiding was going to stop her from asking her out; if she could find a way to contact her. Hell, she had said something about Wednesday, but Cooper's unexpected interruption had kept her from finding out what she meant. Unlike the vast majority of the women she met, she had been attracted to Dawn from the moment she first laid eyes on her. Now she couldn't get the girl off her mind. She was still sitting in the same spot thinking about the entire situation while Cooper got ready for their weekly shopping trip.

There was nothing better to unwind after a hectic week than a Sunday afternoon trip to the mall. Most of the time they didn't even buy anything. Window shopping, for clothes and dates, was enough. Today would be a little different since she had to find a birthday gift for Thumper. It gave her an excuse to wander through stores she normally wouldn't care about visiting. And the Mall was packed.

After sifting through way too many cd's, trying out at least ten different colognes and laughing at Cooper's modeling of several outfits that he wouldn't be caught dead wearing out in public, she gave up and bought

Thumper the three-book fantasy series he'd been talking about in class a couple of days earlier. She knew his mother would never think to buy him books. She didn't wonder what Cooper had bought. His version of the perfect present was a gift card.

They were sitting in the coffee shop of the local B&N when the bitch from class walked in, a tall, lithe, redhead wearing faded jeans and a black lace camisole. Surprisingly, she was alone. Andi couldn't recall ever seeing her without a pack of fawning minions trailing behind her. She wondered if she was being fair, judging her entirely on how she acted in school toward her. Maybe underneath that frigid exterior was a real human...Nah. Bitch is, as bitch does.

They watched as Kim strolled past the racks of magazines and new releases from established authors heading directly to the aisle holding romances.

"Do you see what I see? Probably as close as she gets to real emotion."

"Don't let it fool you. She's probably trolling for lonely women desperate for some kind of romance in their life."

"You have to use bait for that. Have you taken a good look at her? I'm still trying to figure out what Dawn see's in her."

"Maybe she's got a tongue like a snake."

"Cooper, you are not right."

Kim browsed through a few books, looking for something to pique her interest while moving slowly toward the coffee shop. If she looked up, there would be no way she could miss her. Sure enough, less than a moment later she raised her face toward them, meeting Andi's gaze directly, a challenge evident in her sparkling green eyes. Now she was standing in the aisle scowling at the two friends.

"You think she knows you ran into Dawn at the club last night?" Cooper had the audacity to smile sweetly at Kim, and then wink.

Andi kicked him in the shin and then laid her forehead down on the tabletop, bouncing it up and down a few times to simulate beating her head on something. After a few seconds, she raised back up and answered him. "Hell no. If she knew I was playing tonsil hockey with Dawn, more than her hair would be red. She doesn't like me, and frankly, I could care less about her. Besides, Dawn claims she is not her girlfriend."

"I wonder if she knows that," he said when Kim cut her eyes his way and frowned. "I wonder if she realizes she going to wrinkle if she keeps screwing her face up that way. Since you are not eating it," Cooper reached over and snatched part of Andi's brownie.

"Bitch! I wasn't finished with that. I'm not concerned about her at all. That's Kim and Dawn's problem, not mine."

"Either way, she's gone now. You ready to check out a few more stores?"

"Yeah, let's go. I could use a new pair of sunglasses. Mine flew off on the way home last night and I was not about to tramp through the brush looking for them. I hate riding without them."

"You hate paying the ticket you mean. You ain't fooling me. I saw a picture of you in South Carolina. No helmet, no sunglasses. The Hut was only a few stores down from the food court. They spent at least a half-hour trying on the various styles of sunglasses before Andi bought a pair identical to the pair, she'd lost the night before. They were still laughing about her lack of taste when Cooper suddenly grew quiet.

"Uhhh, Andi?" He pointed toward the door; his mouth twisted into what she called his snippy bitch face.

Standing in front of the store was Kim, staring at her with eyes brimming with suspicious condemnation. *Damn, but the bitch was annoying.* "Just ignore her." She picked up her bag and the two walked out the door. Andi's eyes met Kim's head-on, and their gazes locked for a few seconds before the other woman walked away.

Cooper snickered, and Andi popped him on the arm, but her mouth twisted into a self-satisfied smirk. Kim may not matter in the greater scheme of things but getting one up on her felt amazing. She had never had any problem relating to another woman, yet Kim had hated her from the first day of school. She had thought she'd left all the petty bullshit back in high school. Boy was she wrong. It had only gotten worse.

"Which way?" Cooper asked after they finally started moving again.

She was tempted to trail along behind Kim but realized that would accomplish nothing and it could cause complications she really didn't need. "I need to go over to Academy. They are having a sale on Athletic wear and I could use some swim trunks."

Since Academy was one of their favorite stores Cooper was happy to go browse through the sales racks for an hour or so. There were always a lot of good-looking guys inside the sporting goods store and occasionally he got lucky and collected a number or two. It was after one now, he figured an hour of shopping, then back home to get ready for work at five. It was going to be a long week.

***

Two days later and no contact from Dawn left Andi ready to write Saturday night off as another of life's disappointing learning experiences. She didn't have time to dwell on 'what ifs''.

The pizzeria was packed, which was extremely rare for a Tuesday night. The players and families of the local little league baseball teams were there as the coaches passed out trophies. Everyone was pigging out on the unlimited pizza buffets. Misty had called in all employees. Now they were busy filling glasses, clearing tables and occasionally offering a helping hand in the kitchen. The kids were eating the pizza as fast as they set them out. Andi was reminded of a plague of voracious locusts devouring everything in sight. Next year, if Misty asked should they host the little league again, she would do her best to discourage her. The restaurant was still open to the public, but she prayed to whoever might be listening that no one would be crazy enough to come before they closed.

At least until the bell above the door opened and Dawn walked in.

She fought to keep a shut eating grin off her face as the petite whirlwind whizzed towards her, snubbing a chubby preteen boy who was frantically trying to get her attention. Andi quickly refilled his soda before heading over to the only empty table in the building, the small two-seater right by the front door that was usually reserved for customers waiting on take-out orders.

"Hi. Welcome to the madhouse. Will you be eating in or is this takeout?"

Dawn looked around at the frantic craziness and grinned. "Well, I had thought to order a pizza and ask you out for dinner tomorrow but now I'm not so sure that's a good idea."

"It's not? Dinner tomorrow sounds really good. But it will have to be an early dinner, I have to be at work by six." She was amazed by how good she felt upon seeing the object of her obsession walk into the Pizzeria.

Dawn smiled.

Andi felt like the sun had just broken through all the storm clouds plaguing her lately. Visions of tiny bluebirds and butterflies fluttering around a field of yellow daisy's, while white lambs frolicked in the warm sunshine filled her mind. She grinned, not caring if everyone thought she was going crazy.

"It's been a tough night huh?"

"It passed tough about two hours ago." Andi picked up a menu and held it out for Dawn to look at.

She leaned forward taking the menu from her hand.

Andi felt tiny goosebumps form on her skin and the hair on her arms stood on end as Dawn's slender fingers brushed against hers. She let them linger there for a few extra seconds, her face blank, her green eyes unreadable. Andi couldn't help contrasting them, her skin rough and darkly tanned, Dawn's soft and much lighter. She was suddenly very happy the girl had come to sit in her booth. Talking at the club was not enough for her to get a good read. She leaned forward over the table, placing a napkin and silverware in front of her.

"So, have you decided what you want," Andi started, the realized what she had just said. She offered a coy smile and waited; her eyes locked on her mouth as several different expressions crossed the startled girls' face. She waited, practically holding her breath, to see what her reaction would be.

When it came, it took her totally by surprise. Before she could react, Dawn had sprung from his seat and planted her lips on hers in a brief but wonderful kiss. She stood there on stunned silence as Dawn gathered her things.

"Forget about tomorrow night," she said. "What time do you get off tonight?"

"I—what? Off?" She startled guiltily, wondering if Dawn had any idea, she had been picturing her naked in her bed, while she did her best to get her off.

Dawn took a step forward, coming so close to her face that their noses were practically touching. "I don't think I want to wait any longer. Let's do something when you get off." Her bright green eyes and silky voice sent another shiver down her spine.

"I still have almost an hour. I get off at ten." She looked around to see if Misty or Cooper had noticed the unexpected kiss. Everyone was distracted, invested in their conversations; so, they either did not notice or if they noticed, didn't care enough to pay any attention.

"Good. I really didn't want pizza and I bet you're getting sick of eating it, too. We can grab a bite together. Do you like Chinese?"

"Ah, okay?" She was having trouble answering, which was strange since she was usually the more aggressive partner on a date. She couldn't remember the last time a

girl had asked her out…if one ever had. She had definitely never been asked out by a miniature tornado.

Dawn pulled out a business card and scribbled the
name and address of the Chinese Restaurant on the back.
"I know the owner. She won't mind serving us after ten.
In fact, she will probably insist on staying open as late as
we like. She stays open later, until eleven, anyway."

"Okay, I should be there by ten-fifteen."

"Don't keep me waiting." She walked out of the restaurant before Andi could say anything else.

Andi stood in the exact same spot and watched until
she was out of sight before collapsing onto the chair she
had just vacated.

"Was that who I think it was?" Cooper asked as he
and Misty came over to see what was going on. The baseball crowd was thinning out as the teams finished eating
and left the restaurant. Everyone who wasn't busy was
looking for a private spot to take a break.

"Yes. It was Dawn." She picked up a napkin holder
and filled it from a bundle that had been stored beneath
the register before moving on to the next table.

Misty shook her head and muttered something about Peyton Place before heading for the kitchen, satisfied the confrontation was nothing of concern.

"Well, what did she want? You're grinning like you just won the lottery, so I can assume it was good news."

"She wants me to meet her after work for dinner."

"Are you sure that's smart?" Cooper was torn. He wanted to see Andi happy, but there was something about the woman that made his skin prickle. Nothing scary-- just odd.

"Not really. But I'm going anyway." She passed Cooper the card with the restaurant info on the back.

He raised an eyebrow and looked at Andi, a question evident in his eyes. "Davidson Automotive? Funny place to have dinner." He knew the info was on the back of the card, but he was enjoying making Andi sweat.

"Duh, smart ass. I guess it was convenient. Or maybe she works there. Who knows? I just want to finish my side work." She paused. "Do I look okay?"

Cooper stepped back and took a good look. Her thick brown ponytail was loose and sloped down toward one shoulder instead of being centered in the middle of her back. She didn't wear a lot of makeup, but what little she had on was on its last legs. It would take more than a wet finger to remove the mascara smudges around her eyes. But she had a sparkle in her eyes that Cooper hadn't seen in a long time, so he wasn't about to ruin her evening.

"Beautiful as ever. Your pony is a little wonky and you might want to touch up your mascara, but other than that, you look perfect."

"I look like a raccoon again, don't I?"

"Yeah…but a sexy one."

"I don't deserve you." She put one arm around his shoulder and pulled him close in a sisterly hug.

"No," he said, "you don't. Better treasure me while you can. A tall, dark stranger may sweep me up onto his horse and carry me away to live in his harem in the desert. Who would come to your rescue then?"

"1-800- I-need-a-superhero?"

Cooper made a non-committal grunting noise and muttered something about *fool me once,* and she just grinned. If she hurried with her sides, she could possibly clock out a few minutes early and make it to the restaurant by ten. Whistling under her breath she reached for another napkin dispenser.

Chapter 9

Instead of heading for the popular all you can eat Chinese buffet near the movie theater, Dawn had sent directions to meet her at a small, extremely secluded restaurant in the Boho section of Rome, the next city over the ridge cut. The hostess led her to a private booth along the back wall where Dawn was waiting. Unlike most Americanized Asian restaurants, this one was decorated in a traditional Asian style. She could see two couples sitting at small ornate tables not much larger than a typical coffee table. Scattered around the table were brightly colored pillows to lounge on instead of chairs. She followed the hostess to an alcove along the back wall. The ornately carved teak booth was swathed in heavy brocade curtains that could be drawn close for intimate dining. Once she slid into the booth, the hostess pulled the curtains closed and left them alone.

Andi had to admit, the atmosphere was killer. There was a small candle on the table set in the neck of a small wine bottle. Two small sconces mounted on the wall behind both seats offered just enough light to prevent an accident without making the enclosed booth feel too bright or too dark. It was probably one of the most romantic settings for dinner she could remember.

She looked around, noticing there were no menus. Dawn must have noticed her confusion because she immediately mentioned that the restaurant offered a full dinner for two and she had already ordered it.

Almost on cue, the waiter appeared with bowls of soup and a flaming appetizer platter.

"If the rest of the food is as good as this it's all right by me," Andi said, spearing a stray mushroom from the soup bowl and popping it into her mouth. She had never had this particular soup, but it was fantastic, full of chicken and shrimp and all kinds of Chinese vegetables. Even the friend wonton strips were fresh.

Dawn snatched the spoon from my hand, using it to drizzle some of the cherry sauce over an eggroll. When she was finished, she used her fork to break it in two and passed half of it to Andrea. They sat together in silence for a few minutes while enjoying the taste and texture. The chef had mixed chopped pork, chicken and shrimp into the fresh cabbage roll, giving it an unusual flavor combination. Andi realized she could easily make a meal on just the soup and appetizers, but now she was wondering what further surprises would come out of the kitchen.

"This is great. How did you find this place?"

Dawn smiled. "I googled impress your date. It was this or rent a carriage."

Andi broke out laughing at the self-satisfied smirk on Dawn's face. They both began speaking at the same time, stopping again, and again to avoid talking over each other. By the time the main course arrived they were talking to each other like they had been friends for years.

Andi was surprised by how much she was enjoying herself. The food was possibly the best Chinese style food she had ever eaten, and the amazing company simply made the meal even better. She realized she knew almost nothing about the mysterious and elusive woman, yet she was already more interesting to her than any woman she had recently met. With that thought in mind, she decided it might be a good time to ask her for her phone number…and maybe her last name.

"I hate to bring this up, but I have no way to contact you. I don't even know your last name. Don't get me wrong, it was an amazingly original way to deliver your invitation, but what would you have done if I had not shown up?"

"I would have called Kim," she replied.

"Just like that huh?"

"Exactly like that. Kim would have been here in ten minutes, fifteen tops."

"What if she had other plans?"

"She would have broken them. She would never leave me waiting in a restaurant alone."

Andrea smiled but something about the way Dawn talked about Kim made her uncomfortable. Still, as the meal wound down, Andrea realized she didn't want the night to end. "Would you like to take a walk along the boardwalk by the river? I haven't seen all the new improvements made since the Music Festival last year."

Dawn readily agreed. She reached for her wallet and pulled out a business card, passing it to Andi with a smile.

Andi slipped into her pocket without looking, not wanting to appear too curious. To be honest, she had been expecting the waitress to arrive with a check, when Dawn had pulled out her wallet. But she simply said the check had already been taken care of. Apparently, she had also taken care of the tip. Shrugging, Andi pulled on her windbreaker, and they left the restaurant. She didn't protest when she took her hand as they strolled along, acting like two high school kids on their first date.

It was a full moon and the park was busy, full of couples wandering along in the moonlight. Andi had been telling the truth when she said it had been a while. The old path along the river had been upgraded and there were benches scatted randomly along its length. She opened her mouth to ask if Dawn would like to sit and talk some more, and was surprised when Dawn shook her head no.

Instead, she grabbed her hand and pulled her body

up against her, using her hands to pull her head down in a deep kiss that sent her senses reeling. When they both came up for air, Andi smiled and lowered her head to meet Dawns in another kiss. She stepped back, allowing her racing pulse to slow and her breathing to go back to normal. Kissing Dawn was unlike kissing any other girl before. It was almost like she had taken a drug; all she could think about was pulling her back into her arms again. It was as of her body recognized something it had been missing and wanted to claim it before it disappeared. Dazed and shaking, she had to take a few deep breaths to get her roiling senses back under control.

She'd kissed other girls on first dates. She'd done a lot more than a kiss on first dates—now she didn't want to rush things and mess up the burgeoning romance. Normally, she would have stopped it right after the first kiss, wanting to establish boundaries from the start. But this was different. She should have anticipated something like this happening. Maybe not this exactly, but something since it had been her idea to take the walk. She'd picked up enough one-night stands to know she was edging close to breaking one of her own rules of conduct. Never mix raw emotion with sex.

Oh, fuck it, she thought, *if it feels right, it is right.*

Her hands gripped Dawn firmly around her waist while Dawn's arms pulled her closer until they were chest to chest. She could feel her tongue battling her own, eagerly circling and sucking until her senses swam, it was all she could do to resist the urge to slip her hands underneath her top so that she could caress her skin, but she resisted. Despite wanting to continue, she gently pushed Dawn back and broke away.

Dawn's baby blue eyes flashed with excitement. Andi had no doubt that she saw something similar, in her own turbulent gaze.

"I think it might be time to call this a date", she said.

"If that's what you want," Dawn replied. "It's awfully early."

"I have class in the morning and then I have to work tomorrow. So, for me, it's not early." It was an excuse and we both knew it. Dawn knew she'd give in sometime soon. It was only ever a question of when and where it happened.

"Fine, but you owe me. And I intend to collect." She gave her a wistful little half-smile and began walking back toward the restaurant.

Andi had come on her bike and it was still parked in front of the restaurant. She ducked her chin to conceal the grin that extended from ear to ear. She was struggling to come up with a decent way to say goodbye when the fingers gripping her shoulders tightened and she was pulled forwards. Our lips met and for a few seconds, nothing else mattered. It was not sexual. It was not playful. It lasted about as much time as it took for her brain to catch up and realize what was happening. Three or four seconds of absolute bliss that she would end up wasting hours over-analysing once she got home.

"I'll call you later," she said.

Andi just nodded. She had no idea how Dawn had got there, whether she had driven, or come by Uber, or even walked. She could live in the apartments on the corner or on the other side of the county. Dawn surprised her by getting into a black MG spitfire that was parked a couple of spaces down from her bike. It took all of her willpower to wait until the car disappeared from sight before she groaned. Throwing her leg across the bike's saddle, she kicked the vintage Triumph over, grinning when it started it on the first try. It had been one hell of an interesting night. She gunned the motorcycle and pulled out into traffic, deciding to take the bypass instead of the slower surface streets. It cut about ten minutes off her trip home. She made her usual turn off the bypass onto the road that skirted the base of Ghost Mountain, not paying much attention to the black truck that turned in behind her.

***

"Damn, damn, damn!"

Andi lifted her bike back onto two wheels and groaned. The fender that had hit the pole was bent upward. There was no way she could straighten it out. Silently cursing the driver into the fiery depths of whatever hell he believed in, she put the kickstand up and began to dig through the tools in her emergency kit. There was nothing inside to bend the metal, so she had to be satisfied with removing the entire front fender. At least it was the front, and she didn't have to take off anything except the center nuts. The tire was holding air, but she had no idea how long that was going to last. The bearings were shot too; the wheel would roll but it was no longer stable. It could spit the bearings anytime. It took her almost an hour to make a drive that usually took her ten minutes. The tire was wobbling so badly she was scared to drive faster than a crawl.

Cooper was watching for her to pull up.

"What happened? Why didn't you answer my call?"

"I lost my phone when I hit the ground. I will go back tomorrow and look for it."

That's when Cooper realized she was limping, her clothes were wet and muddy, and she had blood on her right cheek.

"What do you mean, hit the ground? Did you have a wreck?"

"Something like that."

By the time Cooper reached her side, his anger was

forgotten. As his hand stroked her bruised cheek, tears began to ease out, first a single tear that slid down her cheek, then a flood as all her barriers fell.

"It's going to be alright. It's just a bent fender. You are okay and that's all that matters," he whispered, in an attempt to make Andi feel better about her black-streaked eyes. Cooper stepped closer, pulling her against his shoulder. She burrowed her face against his chest, so her crying was muffled.

"Talk. Tell me what the hell happened?"

"It's kind of blurry. I remember thinking the truck behind me needed to dim their high beams. The light kept reflecting back into my eyes. Then it suddenly sped up, passing me on a blind curve. I jerked the wheel to keep from sideswiping it and must have hit an icy spot because the bike began to slide. I slid sideways and clipped a telephone pole. My knee is killing me, but I don't think anything's broken."

"That was no accident. There is no way they could have not seen you go into the pole. Somebody wanted you to wreck."

Andi wanted to argue but in the back of her mind,
she wondered if Cooper was right.

Chapter 10

Instead of going back to the apartment, Andi found herself perched atop a barstool at the pizza parlor, debating between having a beer or something stronger as she watched Misty finish the nightly close down chores. The last couple of customers were leaving as she reached the door, so she knew everyone would still be there. Closing down on a Friday night usually took several hours. Her husband was in the kitchen with Jose and Paul cleaning the equipment and doing the nightly prep work for tomorrow.

"Is the grill still hot," she asked? That was the problem with Chinese food, it tasted great, but she was always hungry an hour after she finished eating.

"Yeah, if it's something simple." The oven is already broken down for cleaning, but Paul usually leaves the grill until last.

"How about a steak sandwich?" Misty nodded and then she headed for the kitchen to tell Paul. She was back in seconds, joining Andi who had begun rolling silverware while she was gone. Misty was happy for the help, eager to get the monotonous job finished for the night.

"You want something to drink with that?" It wouldn't take Paul long to grill the thinly sliced beef and he still had some home fry's leftover from the buffet.

"Yeah, a coke." She waited until Misty was behind the bar and then asked her to add a shot of Black Jack to the coke.

Misty hesitated. She clearly had something on her mind. She hoped she was willing to talk about it. That's one of the things Andi about that drove her crazy, one minute she would be closed off and private, the next you could not get her to stop talking. You never knew which one you were getting.

"Whiskey on a weekday?" she asked as she grabbed the bottle of Jack Daniels off the top shelf. She poured the shot and passed it and the coke to her, then leaned against the bar, waiting.

Andi downed it, chasing it with the coke. The Kentucky bourbon burnt her throat making her wince. "Another."

Misty's right eyebrow raised just a smidgen, but she still didn't ask. However, the look she gave Andi as she slid it across the bar said it all.

"Don't give me another even if I ask. I still have to get home." Andi slumped down on her stool, placed her elbows on the bar and offered her a weak smile.

"Okay. Give," Misty said. "Or I will call Cooper and you know how he gets when his dates are interrupted."

For the millionth time since leaving the restaurant, Andi thought about what had been said, what hadn't been said but insinuated and what she should have said. Then she started talking about her date.

When she had told her about Dawn's behavior and her unexpected, but wonderful kiss goodnight, Misty poured her another shot of jack, then thought about it and poured it back in the bottle.

"Well, I could say she's being a bitch, but then again, you said you kissed her twice by the river," she said.

"Then the goodbye kiss was nothing like the other kisses. Something changed. Talk about mixed signals. Didn't you say she has a girlfriend."

"Well, Kim is always with her, but I can't swear they are together. It's more like Kim wants her and wants to make sure no one else gets close enough to interfere."

"Well, you have two choices. Ignore it and act like it never happened. Or kiss her again and see what happens next." She looked up as Paul rang a bell to let her know she was needed in the kitchen. " Be right back."

Misty was back in a matter of seconds with the order. She sat a fresh coke, minus the whiskey, and the sandwich on the bar, along with a bottle of catsup and a saltshaker for the fries.

Andi took a bite and sighed, enjoying the taste of the hot juicy steak, grilled onions and peppers, provolone cheese, and fresh lettuce and tomato. Good solid American comfort food was always great for the soul. She wasn't sure if it was the food, the company or the whiskey, but she felt herself relaxing for the first time since she got off work. Misty always had that effect on her, she knew when to be a friend and when to be a sister. She was going to be a great mother. "It might just be better to forget about it." She took a long sip of the coke before reaching for her sandwich again.

"You could always forgive Katie. How many times has she texted you today?"

"Seriously. Do you really think she'd miraculously changed her personality and decided to become a faithful girlfriend? Nope. I'm going to wait a few years until I'm in my thirties. By then there should be a flood of recent divorcees available, all looking for someone like me to ease the pain."

Truthfully, there were things she missed about having Katie around. Her party girl nature made it easy for Andi to slip from alpha jock into her more feminine persona. That was always good for her self-esteem. Sometimes her ego really needed the attention, even when it came from men. Unlike some of her friends, Andi had not always been certain she was not Bi-sexual. Back in high school, she'd tried a few random hookups, with an especially at-tractive man or two, not that she had ever been tempted to walk away from her lesbian lifestyle. It had been more of a reassurance that she was right in her choices, and her mother was wrong. However, once that decision had been made, she had not wavered.

The problem was Katie. When it came to sex, Katie could, and often did, swing both ways. Sometimes she would get in a crazy mood and join her; laughing and cracking jokes; dancing wildly around a bar while drunk men brought them drinks hoping to get lucky. Often, she would end up hitting on strange girls in the bathrooms. The only problem was while she had considered it a game, Katie was really into it. So, when the oversized redneck with the shaved head had tapped her on the shoulder on her way back from the bathroom one night in the Romper Room and accused her of sleeping with his ol lady, she knew he thought she was Katie. She had tried to explain he had the wrong woman, but that didn't sink into his alcohol rattled brain. She wasn't drunk, but that didn't help her when he swung. It had taken three stitches to close up the cut and a weekend in bed before her concussion headache eased off. Katie had taken off to Biloxi with the unfaithful wife and she hadn't been seen since. But she did continue to text her daily.

Andi refused to become her fallback girl again.

"Well," she said, "I think I'm going to head home now." She handed Misty a twenty to cover the food and alcohol she'd drunk.

"You want me to take you home?"

"I've got my bike."

"You can leave the bike here, you know that." Her eyes went to the clock on the wall, ten till one. Mike would be making his rounds soon.

"I'm not drunk—"

"You are awfully close to the limit and we both know it. Just, please? For me? I'd hate to have to find a new waitress. Good help is impossible to find around here." Mike was a good guy but if he thought she was driving under the influence he would not give her a pass.

Andi's face softened. "It's only a couple of miles. I'll ride carefully and take the back route. That way I will have to go slower. You know I won't do anything crazy."

"Okay, but I'm following you until you turn on

Pine. It's only a couple of blocks out of my way, so don't argue."

***

Her first instinct when she parked her bike was to run inside and text Cooper. Instead, she texted Misty letting her know she was safe and heading to bed. The truth was, she wasn't even sure what the kiss meant if anything. It wasn't the kind of goodbye kiss she usually received after a date. It was something more. Like an entire life of promises all rolled up in a kiss. She wasn't sure she was ready for that kind of commitment, but she was certain she wanted Dawn to kiss her again. Maybe Cooper would come home instead of crashing with whoever he was out with, so they could talk?

She sent him a text saying call me A.S.A.P. and sat back to wait on his reply. Falling back upon the arm of the sofa, she looked around the room, thinking seriously about cleaning up the mess. Instead, she grabbed a handful of chocolate chip cookies and began surfing the television, finally deciding to watch the latest version of her favorite television comedy. Unfortunately, she couldn't keep her mind on the television.

What did she think about Dawn? There was no questioning that she was sexually attracted to her. She had dreamed about her the last few nights, vivid sexually packed dreams that left her flushed and covered in sweat despite the AC running wide open. She could close her eyes and picture her now, sprawled out on her bed, naked body trembling as she ran her hands along her sides up to her perfectly shaped breasts. She could almost feel the warm flesh of her peach-colored orbs on her tongue or hear the soft gasps and moans as she rolled the taut nipples between her lips. No, whatever was causing her doubts, it had nothing to do with physical attraction. That's why she needed to talk to Cooper. He was a totally unbiased ear; one of the only people she knew that would not judge her for being tempted. Instead, he would listen to her talk, ask a question or three, and then offer an opinion based entirely on what she had said, keeping his own opinion to himself unless she asked.

When two AM arrived, and she still hadn't received a reply to her text, she gave up on him responding, shook her head, rubbed the sleep from her eyes and then decided it was better to call it a night.

She slouched off all her shoes, leaving a trail of assorted clothing across the bedroom on her way to the bathroom. Still hoping for an answer, she left her phone on the counter while she ran a hot shower, glad to let the water relax her after what had turned into a stressful night. The double head shower was as close as she ever got to a sauna. Refusing to dwell any further on what might be; she let her mind drift to beach vacations and sexy masseuses as she enjoyed the warm cascade. Every so often, she caught herself glancing toward the silent phone as if her thinking about it would cause it to announce an incoming text.

Finally, the water started to cool. She gave up and turned off the shower. Aggravated by runnels of cool water dribbling down her face, she used her fingers to push her wet hair out of her eyes and then sloughed off the excess liquid, before toweling off and brushing her teeth. Realizing she had forgotten to grab any clean clothes, she walked naked into the bedroom, debated digging through

her underwear drawer for a few seconds, then decided
fuck it and crawled into bed.

***

The intermittent sounds of two men's laughter and
the television woke her sometime the next morning.
The deep red reflection of the digital alarm clocks time
readout on her ceiling said it was almost noon. Sometime
during the morning, she must have turned off the alarm,
since the clock was sitting on its side, with its face pointing upwards. Nor was it beeping. Still naked, she headed
for the bathroom, using the time to get her head together.
She would be in for a question and answer session and
now that the initial haze of bliss had worn off, she was
dreading facing the inquisition. Knowing they were both
waiting, was a nightmare. Five minutes later, dressed in
bright yellow pajama pants and a white tank top she stiff-
ened her backbone and walked into the living room.

Cooper and Thumper were perched on the sofa
cradling mugs of desperately needed caffeine. Her mouth
watered at the aroma of the strong, nutty roast coming
from the mug Coop was holding. Fresh hot coffee was

a small comfort, but one she adored. Dinner with Dawn the day before was still in the forefront of her mind as she flopped down on the sofa between them. Thumper gently patted her back as he passed her the cup of coffee Cooper had been sipping on. She cautiously lifted her heavy head from where it was buried in her arms to take a drink of the nectar of the gods. *Heaven!*

A soft growl from her stomach reminded her that she was hungry…again. She had been blessed with a fast metabolism which let her eat as much as she liked without gaining weight. The downside was she burned the food off so fast, she was always hungry.

"A wolf never changes his ways. Especially a lone wolf," he muttered.

Before she could comment and then overcompensate by mentioning the numerous texts and voice mails she'd left on both of their phones, Cooper mentioned food and headed toward the kitchen.

Oh shit. He was cooking. That meant he was upset, and she was in for it.

Andi could hear multiple pots rattle as he prepared breakfast. He added butter to the small frying pan, then stirred in a couple of eggs, scrambling them well done as she preferred. The big cast iron skillet spattered and crackled on the other side of the stove, bacon he'd set to cooking earlier browning on low heat. Andi was really glad Cooper liked to cook because all she ever seemed able to force her body to do for breakfast since childhood was to pour milk over cold cereal. Sometimes even the milk was too much effort.

Cooper popped two slices of bread in the toaster, grabbed a plate for the bacon and eggs, then waited for the toast to pop up. Eggs plated, and hot coffee poured, he carried the tray into the living room.

Andi ate in silence, needing hot food more than conversation. The boys had their mind on the cartoon they were watching, so after she finished, she waited for it to finish, cradling her own mug of coffee with both hands. The idea of being double teamed by the two polar opposites should have made her smile, but she knew that whenever they decided it was time to give her hell, they would not hold back.

"I know you both have something to say, so go ahead and say it," she said as Thumper changed the channel to a daytime talk show neither one of them really liked.

Cooper sat across her, face blank and unreadable.

She had slept, been fed and watered like a horse after a long run. She had no excuses remaining since they both knew she didn't have to go to work until six.

Thumper offered her a sideways grin that meant he could sympathize but… Dressed as usual in emo black on black, he had added a leather jacket, his dark textured hair ruffled in such a way it meant he'd ridden his bike here. That was another wonderful thing about Thumper, he also had a motorcycle, a Harley. If he had been a woman, she could happily settle down with her and live the rest of her life in blissful oblivion.

That's the great thing about her circle. It wasn't large, but everyone in it was solid. They clapped loudly when she had good news, held her when she cried, and backed her up whenever she was threatened. That's what she wanted in a relationship. Someone that would stand beside her, even when she didn't have much to offer except her presence.

She could tell Thumper was worried. Even Cooper had a tight-lipped expression on his face, one that Andi had learned to associate with him being forced to do something he really didn't want to do. It was clear that she was the reason for their concern. She had an idea it had something to do with Dawn but not why. It had only been dinner, and a kiss. Regardless of her own reasons, she knew that she did not ever want to be the cause of her closest friends worry.

Neither of her friends would look directly into her eyes. Thumper stared at the television and Cooper was texting, so she simply started talking. "Come on guys, it's not like I smashed her or anything close to it. We just sat and talked. Well, we kissed a couple of times but that's it. It was fun going out with a girl that could hold a conver-sation. You know, one that wouldn't bore me to sleep." She picked up a piece of toast and took a small bite. "I…I think I like her. Like…I want to see where it goes," she continued while still trying to chew.

Thumper raised an eyebrow and Cooper sipped his own coffee, neither willing to respond.

"That's great. Cool. Both of you pouting. It's not like either of you know her." She choked on her last bite of toast started coughing.

Cooper slapped her on the back and Thumper let his mouth morph from a thin line into a quirky grin. It wasn't much—but she could feel the atmosphere in the room lighten. Before she could open her mouth to say anything else, Cooper stood up, placing his empty mug on the tray.

"I'm gonna be late for work if don't take off, not everyone gets to come in at six. I'll see you later," he said quickly.

Before she could reply he was out the door.

"Don't take it to heart," Thumper said as he helped stack the dishes in the dishwasher. "He's really worried about you. He says Dawn is really pretty, and if he liked girls, he would probably hit on her himself. There's just something about her that gets his hackles up."

"I know. That's why he took off. He promised he would never lie to me, and he knew he would have to say a few things to me I didn't want to hear. That's why I love him."

"Yeah. He knows that too. Well, I'm going to take off myself. I have dialysis at three. They say my liver isn't cleaning my blood the way it should be."

Andi immediately pulled him into a heartfelt hug. She didn't say anything, but she knew Thumper understood by the words he'd said. None of us liked to talk about his condition. He was on a waiting list for a new liver but with AIDS, the chance of him ever meeting the require-ments necessary for a transplant was little to none. The sad part is he had done nothing to deserve it. He hadn't had unprotected sex, hell, he'd only been sixteen when he was diagnosed. The doctors suspected he'd been exposed by a tattoo needle. That had been seven years ago, and his body had continued to deteriorate. But he refused to go down without a fight.

After Thumper left, she picked up the rest of the dirty dishes around the apartment and put them in the dishwasher. She was out of soap again. Mentally making a note to buy some on the way home and get the dishes done, she set the pots to soak in the sink with the last of her laundry powder. She hated to do that since they always tasted of soap unless she ran them through the dishwasher after soaking. She used a paper towel to clean the cast iron skillet, regreased it and set it back in the oven. It was her baby, and she never let a drop of water touch its surface. The antique frying pan had belonged to her great grandmother and made the best cornbread and pineapple upside-down cake. Nothing modern could ever get that brown sugar crust the way the old cast iron pan did.

Maybe Cooper was right. She was rebounding after a really bad relationship and she wasn't thinking clearly. Still, that didn't change how different she felt when she was with Dawn. The fact that no one really knew a lot about her didn't matter. She was already growing anxious to hear from her, so much so that she couldn't concentrate. Was she falling in love? The possibility sent a shock through her system. Maybe it would be better to find out a bit more about her. But what would she do if she found out something she didn't really like? Would she be willing to walk away? Could she walk away?

She didn't know the answer and it scared the hell out of her.

Chapter 11

Dawn watched as a hungry crow snatched a late-season meal from the Azalea bush outside her window. The busy honeybees working among the colorful flowers tried to avoid the intruder, continuing on their drive to gather nectar. Nothing would interrupt the need to provide nourishment for the hive throughout the coming winter.

Dawn wished she had their determination. After five hours of restless tossing and turning without ever falling asleep her head was about to explode. She'd finally given up as the sun was peeking through her blinds. That was two hours ago.

It was a perfect day to sit outside and do nothing. The hammock was calling her name. She gathered her sunglasses, a large glass of tea and a fluffy pillow and headed that way. Just before she reached the hammock, her phone started ringing. She glanced at the caller ID and frowned. *Damn. How does she do it? She's in New York with her parents, how can she know I'm awake?*

She snatched the phone off the table, pushed the button and announced, "Hello Red, what's up? No, I'm at home. Yes. No, I haven't stopped thinking about what you said

"I hope your thoughts were half as entertaining as mine has been. I had to take a cold shower just to go to sleep. We got in late last night."

At least you got some sleep. She was suddenly glad Kim couldn't see how embarrassed she was. As she sat back on the hammock, she tried to figure out how she was going to get her off the phone. That problem was solved when she heard Kim's next words.

"Throw on something nice. I'll be there to pick up shortly."

Dawn groaned. "You're taking a lot for granted. What if I don't have time to go running off with you."

"Make time. We can argue about it when I get there. I'm about to turn onto your road." Kim laughed, making her feel as if her feelings on the subject didn't matter. They probably didn't. She would show up regardless.

"Better hurry, unless you want me to catch you in your undies. On second thought, take your time." The abrupt click and sharp dial tone as she hung up put an end to any further conversation.

Dawn sighed in frustration. Instead of arguing with Kim it was easier to do as she said. She turned to her closet, looking for something to wear. It would have been nice if she'd mentioned where they were going. Her eyes fell on a chocolate brown jumpsuit she had bought on impulse just a week earlier. The designer cut followed the curves of her body, but not in a seductive or cheap manner. The dark brown color was perfect against her pale skin. Luckily, she had just washed her hair. She just needed to brush it out. At the knock at the door, she had just enough time to slide her feet into sandals before opening it.

Relief flooded her system as Kim stepped inside. She wasn't overdressed.

Kim had pulled her curly red hair back into a loose bun and secured it with a turquoise and silver clip that matched the color of her silk blouse. She had on slacks, but they were cut in a dressier style than the ones she usu-ally wore. Wherever they were going, it wasn't blue jean casual.

"Make yourself comfortable. Give me a few minutes to do my makeup and I'll be ready." She headed for the bathroom.

As she walked away, Kim admired the way her cute little butt twitched back and forth. "Take your time. There's no specific time frame."

She didn't say exactly what had no specific time, but her comment still caught Dawn's attention.

Kim sat down in her favorite recliner and brushed white hairs off her blouse. Dawn and taken in a stray a few weeks earlier and the damn cat must have decided the recliner belonged to him. He was standing in the kitchen doorway, glaring at her. After that first intense scrutiny, he ignored her completely, deciding it was more important to stretch out on the windowsill in the sun. One day she hoped to have a home like this one with Dawn, but a cat was not part of her fantasy. She decided to have Jimmy get rid of it. He could scoop it up one day while Dawn was at school and make sure he dumped it far enough away that it could never come back. She might pout for a few days, but she'd soon find something else to fawn over. That was the problem with Dawn, she was always looking for something to mother. Perhaps she could buy her a puppy. Something purebred, maybe a Weimaraner or a Beauceron. None of those mutts she is so fond of.

"Do I look okay?" Dawn asked as she settled back into the old leather recliner.

"Beautiful", she said, admiring the natural way her light blonde hair framed her perfectly made-up face. She hated it when a woman wore too much makeup. Dawn always seemed to know exactly the right amount to wear. Just like her outfit. She hadn't told her where they were going, but the outfit she had picked out could be worn in a variety of settings. Dawn was classy, she knew she would never have a reason to be ashamed to be seen with her.

"You were not exactly clear on the phone," Dawn asked as they walked out the door. "Where are we going?"

"It's a surprise." She reached out and opened the passenger door on her Land Rover, motioning for Dawn to slide into the buttercream leather seat.

Dawn hesitated. Kim was like that, one minute she could be such a bitch, then, without warning, she would do some little thing, that was so out of character, it threw her off. Like opening the car door for her. She decided it wasn't worth the fight and sat back, enjoying the way the seat molded to her body. The Rover was new, but that didn't surprise her. Kim's parents were always buying her something. Dropping a couple of hundred thousand on a car was no big deal. And her jumpsuit didn't clash with the interior. Once she had worn a lime green outfit that looked cheap and garish against the smoke grey interior of one of her cars. Kim had insisted she change before going out. Now she always picked neutrals.

She was surprised when they turned toward down-town Atlanta. She assumed they were heading somewhere in the neighborhood, maybe the country club for a late lunch. So, what was Kim up to? Suddenly, nervous she took out her favorite perfume and spritzed her neck and wrists. The scent always gave her a tiny boost of confidence.

She was surprised when they pulled up in from of her parent's favorite restaurant.

"I thought this place didn't open until five?" It was normally closed at this time of the day. However, the parking lot was full of cars, most of them luxury models. Since the restaurant had a large open room that was often rented for private events, she figured that was why it was so busy. It bothered her that she had no idea what was going on. "Should we have brought a gift?"

Kim didn't reply so she let it ride.

We walked in together but did not hold hands. Kim had always frowned on public displays of affection, especially during social events. And this was obviously some type of event, even though she had not been aware of anything upcoming when she'd checked her calendar last week.

The enormous room was packed with people of all ages, holding lively conversations that echoed around the room. Soft classical music was playing in the background. Most of the men were gathered together into separate groups, laughing and joking together. They all looked our way when we entered. One looked her up and down, and then made some comment that made the others laugh. Even without hearing it, she was certain it was about her…and it probably wasn't flattering.

The women present were talking together in small clusters around the room. A few had settled into the conversation pit and were quietly talking amongst themselves. Two little boys sat at their feet, playing with miniature cars. None of the looks they gave her made her feel comfortable.

"Kim!" An excited voice came from the direction of the restaurant kitchen, followed by an extremely pretty, petite young woman. She obviously didn't follow the *No public display of affection* rule. After enveloping Kim in a hug, she kissed her soundly on his cheek. Noticing Dawn for the first time, she raised an eyebrow in silent inquiry.

Kim laughed. "Dawn, this is Tereasa, my favorite cousin. Tereasa this is Dawn. No other information will be forthcoming. So, don't bother asking."

Tereasa giggled. "Yeah, in your dreams." She nodded

toward a familiar face, Kim's mother. "Just try that line on your mom. Let me get a seat nearby first, I want to watch the fireworks." She winked. "It's going to be loads of fun."

After their introduction, Kim muttered something about keeping her mouth shut as Tereasa disappeared, leaving her alone with Dawn.

Dawn was instantly overcome with a nervous fluttering sensation in the region of her stomach. She looked around, seeing no place to sit except in the corner with the three women with children.

Tereasa must have seen the confusion on her face; she came to her rescue. "Come on, I'll introduce you around. I think everyone is in shock. Kim never brings a guest, and I think we were all prepared for an entirely different type of escort. You are a pleasant surprise." She led her over to the other women and introduced her around.

Dawn was pleased to see the hateful expressions had vanished. Except for one. A puzzled look came over her features and she looked her up and down, studying her, sizing her up. The look she gave her when she finished could have frozen fire. Somehow, she made an enemy, but she had no idea why. The woman was too old to be interested in Kim, so it couldn't be jealousy. She made a mental note to ask her about it later.

The women's conversation turned to normal things, the children, family life, their husbands, and jobs, the normal conversations women had whenever they got together.

Dawn was the only unmarried woman present. This was the family get together, and no one was sure exactly what to expect. She noticed a photographer wandering around the room and asked if anyone knew who it was.

"Society Page. They always send a reporter to this type of event. They take lots of photos, so be ready when they start on yours."

Dawn wasn't sure why they would be taking her photo, but she didn't make a comment.

Kim was standing next to her father talking to an offensive linebacker from Atlanta's major league football team. They were obviously all good friends. One of the men must have said something about her, because Kim looked her way, threw her head back, and laughed out loud. She wondered what she found so funny.

She saw the two men shake hands, then he walked over to join the group of women. They all turned toward Kim and her father. She noticed the clock over the mantle said it was five o'clock, they had been there for over two hours. Kim was waving for her to join them, so Dawn excused herself from the sofa and headed in that direction. Then she noticed her mother and father were approaching with Kim's mother. She had not even known they were there. As she moved to stand next to Kim, she could hear Kim's father begin to speak. His words made her stomach drop.

"Thank you all for joining us here today. This is an important day for our family, a day of new beginnings. There's someone I want you to meet. She's a bit shy, but I don't think it won't be a problem. Kim, won't you make the introductions."

Kim stepped forward, pulling Dawn with her. She had her fingers entwined tightly as if she was afraid Dawn might bolt like a frightened deer. "Smile," she whispered before saying, " I'd like to introduce you all to Dawn Dixon; my fiancé.

Flashes began to go off.

***

As soon as the car door shut behind her she turned to Kim and screamed, "What the fuck were you thinking, making an announcement like that without warning me. Do you know how that made me feel? I had no idea what to say. That reporter must think I'm mentally deficient. It was a…a… a clusterfuck!" The word was perfect. It was simple, and it perfectly summed up the events of the past few days

Kim's face fell and her eyes welled up with unshed tears. "I'm sorry. I was trying to surprise you. I thought it would make you happy."

She gave her that puppy dog gaze again, and Dawn's heart melted. "You're an ass, but I forgive you". But she really didn't. She had held on to the idea of a relationship with Kim for so long because Kim was the first person to ever say they loved her. Even her parents avoided the words, turning it into a question instead of a statement by saying, "You know we love you, don't you?" Even after everything Kim had done, she always held out the hope that things were going to be okay between them. That she was going to be okay with her. The only problem was the entire time Kim was speaking, all she could imagine was the look on Andrea's face if she sees the article. Her only hope was that Andi doesn't read the society pages

Chapter 12

The doorbell kept ringing over and over again. Now the dog was barking too. It was obvious that whoever was doing their best to bring out the hidden demon had no intention of going away until it confronted them at the door. Waking Tipper was their first mistake. Forcing her to get out of her warm bed was the second. People rarely got a chance for a third.

Andi grabbed her robe and headed that way, hoping she could make the noise stop before it woke up everyone in the house. She shuffled to the door, peeking through the eyehole to see which one of her friends had lost their key this time. Most of the time it was Cooper. Except she knew there was no way Cooper would be coming in at this time of the morning. By now he was either curled up next to Mr. Rightnow in a king-size bed somewhere; or sound asleep in his own boudoir. Maybe it was Thumper.

She made a mental note to hit the hardware store for a new batch of spares. Lately, it seemed like she'd been passing out replacements every week. She'd be willing to bet she could go and clean Cooper's room and find at least ten.

It wasn't Cooper or Thumper.

Finding Dawn standing on her doorstep was the last thing she expected at six am in the morning. She froze, unsure what she should do next. *How did she find out where she lived?*

***

The bell buzzed again. It seemed like Dawn had no intention of giving up, so she took a deep breath and opened the door.

"Hi. I wasn't expecting to see you…today…at my door…at this time in the morning."

"I like to keep people guessing," she replied. She glanced in the door, taking in my entire living room and kitchenette in seconds. "Well, are you going to invite me in?"

Andi hesitated, wondering if she could stall long enough to come up with a reasonable excuse to avoid that very thing. With no imminent emergency that might pull her away from the apartment, she resigned herself to the upcoming personal mortification and stepped to the side so that Dawn could enter. With no advance warning about her imminent arrival, the apartment looked like a tornado had passed through earlier that morning. If she had known Dawn tended to casually drop by, she could have cleaned all day and at least given the impression that she had her shit together. Not that Dawn wouldn't easily see through the lipstick on the pig. It was a bit of a pigpen.

While watching the movie, Cooper and Thumper had pigged put last night. Then they had both passed out on the floor, leaving her with a mess and no help to clear it away. There were two empty pizza boxes on the table by her couch, accompanied by a six-pack of empty wine coolers. The sink in her glorified kitchenette was full of dishes soaking in cold water because she'd forgotten to turn on the dishwasher when she'd crawled into bed the night before and it was too full to hold any more. Her textbooks were scattered along the back of the couch, and on the floor nearby. And there was a basket of her dirty laundry standing in the corner next to the stackable unit because she had forgotten to buy laundry detergent…again.

"Welcome to my humble abode. You have to excuse the mess; the maid took the day off. Good help is so hard to find nowadays."

"Hi, hope it not too much of an inconvenience, I thought you might want to grab some breakfast before heading to class."

"No. No problem. I'm just surprised to see you. And half asleep. Do you want to come in?"

She stepped to the side, holding the door with one hand.

Dawn stepped forward, stopping when the sound of a door shutting caught her attention.

"I thought you were gonna take a quick shower," she heard from the direction of the bedroom. " If you're not coming back to bed, I'm going to grab the shower first. We've got time for breakfast before I take off. I can make you pancakes to make up for falling asleep on you last night."

Dawn's head jerked in the direction of the female voice, her lips parting in surprise, "You're not alone?"

Shit. Andi had completely forgotten all about Misty crashing there the night before. "That's Misty. She's—»

Dawn's hand covered her mouth. "I'm sorry. If I would've known I was interrupting, you and your...your...I wouldn't have..."

Andi sighed. "Misty crashed her last night. We were about to—»

"You don't have to explain. Really." She walked toward the apartment door.

"Andi, what's taking so long? You need to get ready." The female voice called from a room in the back. "I'm out of the shower, almost ready to go."

Andi groaned. Misty had the worst timing. Andrea was right on Dawn's heels as she scurried towards the exit, confused by her reaction. "Wait a second." She caught the uncomfortable woman by the arm of her jacket, and she stopped.

"God, this is so awkward," Dawn said, avoiding her gaze. "I thought it was just you here. Now it makes sense."

"What makes sense?"

"Nothing," she answered. "Just forget I came by. I should have called first."

Andi stared at her, trying to figure out why she was suddenly flustered and in such a hurry to leave. Something about Dawn wanting to leave so abruptly made her…annoyed. Why? She had no idea Misty being there would make her so jumpy. Then it clicked. Dawn didn't know who Misty was.

"We can drop Misty off at her apartment on the way to grab breakfast. Normally Cooper takes her when she stays over, but he must have forgotten his sister was coming last night. She's pregnant and her husband is out of town."

"His sister?" Andi grinned, relaxing a little.

"Yes. We fell asleep watching movies. Hang tight,

okay? I'll be right back. Let me throw on some clothes."

She started to turn, but Dawn tugged on her arm. "Wait..." She stammered for a moment. "I'm so embarrassed. I thought..."

"I think it's kind of cute. Give me two minutes. I'll be right back. Okay?"

"No, you don't have to do that. I'll just go, we can do this another time." She continued to inch toward the door. "Just hang on, I'll take a quick shower and be right with you." She turned and headed toward the bedroom to let Misty know what was going on.

Dawn could hear the two women talking but she couldn't make out what they were saying. Then it dawned on her that the apartment had two bedrooms, both with private baths. *Why was Misty using Andi's bathroom if she had a perfectly good one in Cooper's room? An even better question was why was she sleeping in Andi's bed?*

When Andi returned from her quick shower, Misty was in the kitchen searching through the refrigerator and the living room was empty, Dawn was gone.

To top off the morning, Jose showed up to drive her

to the restaurant leaving her wide awake with nothing to do until classes that afternoon.

Damn. What is it about that woman that gets her so riled up.

First, she shows up without bothering to call ahead. What if she had been with another woman, it's not as if they had made a date. Common courtesy would have been to wait until she was invited, that way she could have straightened up the place. Anyone that knew her knew housekeeping was way down on her priority list. There was always a basket of dirty laundry on the floor of her closet. And of course, the sink was full of dishes. She loathed doing dishes ever since her parents had declared it was her chore back in middle school. It had never seemed fair that her brother got to ride a lawnmower around the yard, and she got to scrub toilets. Just because he had a hunk of flesh hanging outside his body

She grabbed the clothes basket and headed for the oversized closet off her kitchen that held her washer and dryer. Most of the time she carefully sorted them, but to-day she did not bother. She threw everything in together and tossed some detergent on top of them. For a second she debated adding bleach, then placed the bottle back on the shelf, shut the washer lid and went toward the kitchen. Five minutes later the dishwasher was loaded, and all the counters were wiped down. She didn't feel any better, but the apartment was reasonably passable.

Not that it mattered, the crazy blonde had vanished as quickly as she'd appeared. She dug out the last of the chocolate ice-cream and collapsed on the sofa.

I wonder if I'm too damaged to become a nun.

***

Dawn wasn't in class that day. Kim was in her usual chair, and she was just as nasty as usual. She had moved to a table near the front of the class, working with another girl whose lab partner was also absent that day. Ms. Anderson was in a particularly buoyant mood as she passed out the assignment: differentiating and identifying several microbiological pathogens on a multi-slide. Some of them were easily identifiable, like Staphylococcus Aureus, or Giardia Lamblia, others could only be identified after several tests ruled out different groupings.

"I got Alpha Streptococcus Pyogenes, Group A, how about you?" Thumper was excited about finishing the slide.

"Maybe we should run each other's slides. I got Beta Strep Pneumoniae, group D." They swapped slides and repeated the tests. Her initial instinct was that it was group D, a more virulent variety but that would have been wrong, as this sample was definitely from group A. She turned to tell Thumper. "You're right. Its group A.

Thumper started laughing. "I was about to tell you the same thing; this one is Beta. Do we have to differentiate between faecalis and faecium? Now I know why she's in such a good mood. Mom likes to throw a curveball every now and then, just to see anyone is paying attention. Putting both varieties on the agar is exactly how her wicked sense of humor works."

The strep was the last of the eleven varieties included, and they had almost missed the fact that she had A and B variety of Strep on the slide. Andi wondered how many would identify one and count the ten as complete without finding the eleventh? Thank heavens they had not taken serology yet. There were over 90 variations of strep. She looked around and noticed that everyone else in the class had turned in their results and left for the day. Oh well, either way, they had eleven on their slides, and they had double-checked. Hopefully, they were all the right pathogens. She gathered her books and followed Thumper to the front of the class.

His mother glanced at their results, not making any comment either way. " I'm going to the Mall on the way home. Do you need me to pick up anything for you?"

"No. I can't think of anything. We are going to meet Cooper for lunch. Andi has to work so Coop and I intend to play video games and veg out the rest of the day."

"Don't you have to go to the clinic today?"

"Nope. Went yesterday. I wasn't feeling great, so I moved up my schedule." He gave his mother a big grin, now that she had flipped from teacher to mom. It was amazing they had made it through ten of the twelve weeks without anyone in the class finding out she was his mother.

"Take it easy on the spicy foods. You've been eating

a lot of pizza lately. Please try to get him to eat a salad or some vegetables, Andrea. Cooper thinks that French Fries and Pizza toppings are everything you need to be happy, but my son could use a few more of the fresh uncooked variety."

"I'll do my best, but I'm in the same boat as Cooper. My idea of eating vegetables is to order a deep dish supreme with extra olives, bell peppers, and mushrooms on it."

Seemingly frustrated, Ms. Anderson shook her head, but she didn't press the subject. She added their test papers to the stack in her briefcase and followed them out of the classroom. They went one way down the hall, and she headed the opposite, going to the teacher's break room to eat lunch.

Thumper had to go by the business office on the way out, so she decided to take a short cut through the body shop. Cutting through the work area was frowned upon because there were so many possible ways to be injured. Around noon the place emptied out and she could usually pass through without anyone noticing her. Today was no different. Most of the bays were empty and the two students she passed were not paying any attention to her as she slipped out the door. She made it through the door and was feeling relief when she felt a hand clamp down on her shoulder.

Damn.

***

When Andi felt the hand clamp down on her shoulder, she knew she was in deep shit. There were stories of students getting expelled for cutting through the auto shop. Others mentioned being barred from using certain halls and parking areas. Either way, she was going to catch hell. She took a deep breath and turned around to face the music.

Instead of an irate instructor or overworked security guard, she found herself facing Dawn. She vaguely remembered holding the door pull ready to pull it open but instead, Dawn closed it abruptly.

" Fancy meeting you here. I didn't know you were taking auto shop."

"I'm not. I was taking a short cut. What brings you

here? I noticed you were not in class."

"I was already too late and knew I would have to do a makeup test anyway. So, I decided to get a tune-up. My motor isn't running right."

"Seemed like it was purring along fine the other night." Andi couldn't help but grin as Dawns' face flushed. She lowered her eyes, her long lashes shielding the fiery emotions hiding inside her aloof facade. There was no one was in sight, and all the doors to the shop were closed. There was no one hanging around smoking since the class had already started. This might be her only chance. Andi's mind was racing. Before she could think of another reason why she should not do it, she reached out and caught Dawn's wrist ensuring she could not run away. Dawn pulled back against her grip, but it was evident she wasn't really trying to get away.

Clamping her lips to hide the confident smile fighting to break through, Andi leaned back against the door as she gently pulled her towards her. Her head fit perfectly below her chin. She could feel her body tremble. A whiff of jasmine and honeysuckle, that bright, clean scent you get right after a spring rain, made her breathe deeply. It was crazy how such a simple thing could make her forget everything that had gone wrong lately.

Fuck it. It will be worth it. Andi mustered up her courage and turned her mouth down to hers. As her mouth claimed Dawn's pillowed lips, her arms tensed, pressing her back against the shop door, one hand touching her hip and the other hand wrapped around the back of her neck. The kiss held all the passion and desire that had been building up since Andi first saw her in the breakroom.

Dawn met the urgency and force Andi's lips produced with a matching heat of her own. Her long slender fingers gripped her shoulder-length hair, attempting to pull her closer. The kiss lasted for quite a long time, the pressure gradually becoming slower and softer. But every so often as they came up for air, Andi could feel her fingers tangle in her hair once more, drawing her back into her arms once more.

Eyes tightly shut, Dawn pressed her into the side of her car, sucking her face like she was trying to steal a piece of her soul for herself. Andi pressed her hipbones against hers, enjoying the way Dawn squirmed against her. She kissed her like she hadn't kissed anyone in a long time. After a few minutes, Dawn's soft hand slips under the edge of her shirt and the unexpected flash of heat caused her to bite down on her own lip. Tricks she hadn't pulled out in months had her deep into the moment, so deep she didn't sense Dawn flicking anxious glances at the heavyset man standing behind her. It was only her sudden disentanglement that alerted her to the idea that they were not alone. However, when she turned to look at whatever had made Dawn uncomfortable, no one was there. She decided it was her imagination.

"I didn't expect to run into you here. But it is a pleasant surprise." Andi didn't care how she ended up making out with Dawn in the parking lot behind the automotive shop like a pair of oversexed teenagersAndi. She was happy it happened. However, Dawn didn't appear to be quite as happy. She was chewing on her bottom lip, a nervous habit Andi had noticed during dinner. Something had her in edge, and it had something to do with the automotive department.

"Jerry should be through changing the sparkplugs in my car by now. Where are you headed?"

"Lunch. Cooper is waiting. Hell, by now Blacky is waiting too. I hate to run but…"

"No, I understand. Text me later?" Dawn shifted her weight uncomfortably and cut her eyes toward the garage. It was obvious she wanted to go back inside.

"Sure. Maybe we can catch a movie or something? Or maybe go for a ride on the bike."

She nodded yes and opened the door without saying a word.

Andi watched until she vanished back into the garage, then turned and jogged toward the main parking lot. Cooper was waiting by the car, a cheesy grin on his face. He was still wearing the outfit he'd been wearing when he left work the night before. Apparently, he had come straight from wherever he'd spent the night instead of going home and changing. Blacky was sitting on the trunk, texting someone. He nodded as she joined them.

"Interesting look. Since when did you start wearing

hot pink lipstick?" He nodded toward the car mirror.

"What? Oh, shit…" Andi wiped at her mouth with the tail of her lab coat. She needed to bleach it anyway. Andi noted that Coopers' clothes were clean, and he was freshly showered. So, whoever he'd crashed with, they were not a new hookup, he felt comfortable enough to do laundry there. That made her feel a little better, but not enough to cut him any slack. He was up to something she was certain she would be better off not knowing.

"I want to ask you where you were, but I get the feeling I'm not going to like your explanation."

"You won't; because I was with Donovan."

Fuck. He was back in town. Why is life being such a bitch?

Coop looked guilty. That was never a good thing when it referred to her best friend. It took a lot to make him feel the slightest bit of remorse for his actions. Spending the night with the one person who had almost destroyed his life before was easily the worst thing he could have done in her opinion. "I can't believe your weak ass went right back to him after everything he put you through in New York. You know he a self-centered prick.

He's only using you. The first new face that catches his attention, he will be gone again." She gritted her teeth to avoid saying everything she was thinking out loud. Donovan Lewis was nothing but bad news. She understood the attraction. He was the epitome of the stereotypical ideal gay man; great complexion, perfect teeth, a really pretty yet chiseled face. He spent at least an hour every day working out at the gym to keep that fitness model perfect body His hair was worn shoulder length and styled by one of the best stylists in town.

Like a lot of egomaniacs, he never worked a job, figuring to ride his looks as long as possible. He always seemed to have money, courtesy of several older, and still closeted, sugar daddies he kept on the string. When one finally caught on to the charade, he would simply cruise the bathhouses in Atlanta until he found a new one to milk. He was all alpha male, despite his metrosexual appeal. Totally toxic.

And he was Coopers' Achilles heel.

They had known each other since middle school, not that they were ever friends. While Cooper had been openly gay all through school, Donovan had played the game, dating women, playing football, anything to keep his parents from finding out. In his senior year, his parents had been involved in a major traffic accident, his father was killed, and his mother ended up in a nursing home. Donovan had taken early graduation and moved to Dekalb County to be near the Nursing home she was in. Living on Briarcliff Road had been something of an eyeopener for him. He'd gotten a job at a twenty-four-hour donut shop on Cheshire Ridge Road, working the late-night shift. He'd met and become friends with several of the drag queens working at a nearby burlesque club. Within six months he had changed completely, leaving Donavan behind and adopting the Donna persona as part of the show ensemble. He learned to cover up his alpha male leanings, adopting many of the simpering gesticulations and feminine attributes used on stage into his everyday life. Unfortunately, like so many find out, the glitter was usually as a disguise to cover up the darkness hidden just below the surface. Donna's search to achieve the slender waif life body considered so attractive on stage led her to experiment with weight loss medications. Over the counter diet pills led to prescription pills. When the doctor refused to renew the prescription the third time, she turned to the street. Crystal meth was cheap and easily found in the bars. Within a few months, she had stopped snorting the crystal and turned to a needle for a quick fix. Cooper had found her turning tricks in the parking at one of the bars by the park downtown. It was questionable which man had been the most surprised.

Andi remembered that time period well. The two had hooked up, and then they took off, going clear across the country to California. Once all those bridges in Cali were burned, they tried New York for a while. Eventually, Cooper realized he wasn't very happy with Donna's favorite method for making money, and he definitely wasn't happy with his life.

He came back to Georgia and got his life back together. He had been doing so well, working at his sisters' restaurant, and taking dance classes. He had even enrolled for college with her, even though he couldn't start that semester. Now every goal he'd worked for was in danger.

Thumper was puzzled by Andi's attitude. He had heard her mention Donna or Donovan a few times but hadn't really paid that much attention to the conversation. Though he always thought two women together was kinda sexy, before meeting Cooper he tended to avoid gay men, feeling at the back of his mind that gayness might be contagious. Now that he had gotten to know him, he realized just how stupid that fear had been. Part of his mindset came from his father, who had been a redneck homophobe who had spent most of his early life railing against men in skirts. Thumper wondered how much of that hatred had been tied into his stint in jail, and how much was because of his own father's paranoid attitude. Looking back, he was certain many of his own phobias were related to the HIV Thumper had been exposed to. Even though he said he believed the doctors' statement that the virus had come from a tattoo needle, Thumper was sure at the back of his mind he wondered if his son was secretly gay.

Now that he had full-blown AIDS, Thumper had learned a lot more about the autoimmune disorder that was destroying his liver and shortening his lifespan. His disease may have started with a dirty tattoo needle, but the virus that caused it had been spread through promiscuous sex, predominantly during the 1970s and 80s before it became common knowledge.

His dad had disappeared years ago before they could ever discuss it. He'd run off with some waitress he had been sleeping with behind his mother's back. It had been eight years, with no contact, so he could be dead for all he knew.

He grinned. If anyone had told him one day, he would be competing with a woman for a phone number, he would have thought they were crazy. Now he didn't think anything about debating a hot body and a beautiful face with Andi. He had even conceded that a guy's six-pack looked hot, even though he had no urge to run his tongue down it and see if it made music as Cooper suggested. This guy Donovan, however, sounded like TROUBLE." How many times have you been through this cycle with this guy?"

Cooper got quiet. "Too many. It's always the same

thing. He shows up, I get emotionally attached. He disappears without even saying goodbye. I don't know why I do it."

Andi turned to look him in the eye. " I do. You a ho!"

Everyone broke out laughing.

"Speaking of ho's, who was the blonde on our doorstep at six am this morning?" Cooper jiggled the arch of his eyebrows in a suggestive manner. Then he leaned forward to hear her answer.

"Dawn. But she didn't stay. I think she was uncomfortable about your sister falling asleep in my bed last night."

"My eight-month pregnant sister? The one whose husband is away on his National Guard week of service? You're kidding me."

"Nope. She didn't wait around long enough to meet her; she just ran for her car while I was taking a shower."

"Well, that sucks. Get my sister home okay?"

"No. She had the baby. We didn't know how to reach you."

"That's good. Wha--?" Cooper finally sat forward, then slumped back as Thumper and Andrea laughed.

"Your gonna pay for that one. Just wait."

They all started laughing again.

Chapter 13

Friday finally came and Andi couldn't believe how eager she was for their date. Dawn had not been in class the day before and she was half worried the girl would not be at home when she arrived. It was crazy. She hadn't been this nervous about a date since her sophomore year in school. There was a note on the apartment door when she arrived, and she expected to discover an excuse for her absence, instead, it said: ANDI, IM IN THE SHOWER. COME IN-MAKE YOURSELF AT HOME. BE RIGHT OUT.

Andi grinned, imaging how Dawn looked in the shower, all soaped up, water streaming down her naked body over her taut nipples and across her stomach. Her first impulse was to strip down and join her but that might not be taken the right way since it was only their second date. She thought about pouring herself a glass of wine from the bottle she had brought but decided to drink a coke and watch television instead. Twenty minutes later she heard the blow dryer cut off and the door to the bathroom open. Ten minutes after that Dawn finally came out of her bedroom.

She was worth the wait. The black silk sheath hugged her body, playing up every curve without looking cheap or trashy, something she hadn't seen a lot of lately. It was a welcome change from the women she tended to pick up in the bars.

Her ex was a clothes horse, she could never have enough outfits hanging in her closet. After years of buying her expensive Christmas and birthday presents, she had a good idea what a dress of that quality cost. Dawn didn't strike her as the second-hand store type, it was evident she was in the habit of spending good money on designer clothing. She made a mental checkmark on the positive side of the tally sheet.

As Dawn entered the room Andi's face lit up, at first with her eyes, the darkest doe brown eyes lightly flecked with hints of green and yellow that lightened and darkened with her mood, and then in that impossibly sexy way that made her knees go weak. Her level of concentration was unnerving, she seemed to look deep into her soul. Dawn wondered what she saw when she looked at her that way? There were a lot of skeletons in her closet and it was impossible to believe she hadn't been darkened by some of her previous interactions. One shower suddenly didn't seem like enough.

Andi must have been reading her mind because she smiled. "I'm suddenly not hungry for steak. We could stay here on the couch and send out for pizza if you'd rather not go out. Just relax and watch TV, unless you got a better idea?"

Her disappointment made her laugh. Since she had obviously been inside her fridge to put the wine on ice, she knew there was nothing worth eating inside it. It was obvious she wasn't thinking about food. Dawn was glad her back was turned so she could not see how red her face had just become. "Nope. You promised me a steak dinner, and I expect to eat."

"That can be easily arranged." Andi winked, reaching

for the snap on her jeans.

Dawn overlooked her tempting insinuation, moving past her out the door in the direction of the parking lot.

Andi arched an eyebrow, questioning her decision but didn't comment. Until she saw her standing in the space staring at the motorcycle. Andi laughed, she hadn't even thought about Dawn in the short black silk dress and heels riding on the back of her bike. To make matters worse, a roll of thunder in the distance pointed at the distinct possibility of rain in the near future.

"Perhaps I should follow you to the Pizza parlor. You can leave your bike there and we can go in my car." Her eyes were silently pleading, an expression that Andi understood clearly after years of dealing with Cooper.

"That sounds good to me." *Damn, she's beautiful when she smiles.* She put the bike into gear and pulled away.

***

Dawn's car was just as she'd expected, low and sleek, pearl grey, with chrome accents and the lingering aroma of musk oil and fresh leather. It was beautiful. It was expensive. Andi was suddenly overwhelmed by self-doubts.

She must have sensed my hesitation as she opened the door. "Better fasten the belt tightly, you know what they say about women drivers."

Andi was starting to enjoy herself. She'd only known her for a few days, but she was already beginning to relax, as though she'd known her for years. She reminded her of Libby, her youngest sister. Libby liked to play the clown, but when times got serious, she was always the first in line to help. The thought of taking Dawn to meet her large, extremely diversified family brought a smile to her face. They would love her. She was still smiling when the puzzled woman started the car.

The steakhouse Dawn chose was part of a chain, but it was one of the better chains. We were shown to a candlelit booth in a quiet alcove, perfect for a romantic rendezvous.

Dawn appeared to know the maître de, as we were seated as soon as we came in, without having to wait in line for a table.

Andi decided it was time she set some boundaries. After checking to see if Dawn had any preferences, Andi ordered for both, choosing firecracker shrimp as an appetizer and the loaded baked potato and salad.

She couldn't help comparing her to her ex Katie. When Katie had taken her out, she always turned the dinner into a contest of wills, forcing her to accept her choices even if she had expressed interest in another dish. That had caused more problems than she'd planned for because she enjoyed experimenting and Katie refused to try anything new. She knew exactly what she wanted, and nothing would make her expand her culinary horizon. "Next time, you can choose."

"Sounds fair, I did order all the Chinese food without asking you if you had any favorites."

"True. It was great. I really enjoyed trying something new."

Dawn had a glass of wine with her dinner and Andi sipped on a Singapore Sling, a drink she'd never tried before, but one the waitress had suggested she might like. She had been right. The fruity sour drink was good, really good.

Andi's choices came out and they were perfect. The

Ribeye steaks were thick and juicy, cooked to perfection with just the right amount of seasoning, the potato was covered in cheese and bacon, and there were two cups of salad dressing for her salad. She was even eating the fresh whole grain bread, one of her peeves. There was something about fresh bread, still hot from the oven that made her feel happy.

As Dawn dug into her food, Andi grinned. Her dates tended to peck at their food when out with her and she enjoyed seeing one with a hearty appetite for a change. She signaled the waitress, requesting another round of drinks. Andi had no idea what was in them and after two she didn't care; she wasn't driving anyway. By the third one, she was feeling no pain.

She thought they talked on the ride back, but she couldn't remember much of the conversation. She did remember Dawn had to help her out of the car. She was glad her bike was at the restaurant; she wouldn't be tempted to try and ride it home. "I don't know why I'm having so much trouble walking. I only had 3 drinks."

She wanted to dance but her feet refused to listen to her head. Dawn caught her as she tripped over a flowerpot and started falling. It felt amazing to be in her arms. She tried putting her arms around her neck, but Dawn turned her around and ordered her to start walking towards the door of her apartment. As she began wobbling in the general direction of the front porch, Dawn followed behind her just in case she lost her balance. The sidewalk was uneven in places and it was hard enough to walk on when you are stone-cold sober. It must feel like walking on a ship at sea to anyone who was not used to it.

"You have no idea what you've been drinking. A sling has all the white liquors in it, vodka, gin, tequila, and rum. Then it's topped with cherry brandy. It's like drinking two and a half drinks at once. You, young lady, are wasted."

"I am not wasted. Watch." Andi laughed, trying to twirl around and losing her balance again.

Dawn managed to catch her before she fell. This time she pushed her toward the door of her apartment. Somehow, she managed to get the door open without letting Andi go, maneuvered her inside before depositing her on the sofa.

Andi wrapped her arms a bit tighter around her neck as she lowered her to the couch and dropped down beside her.

"I expect a lot of women have fallen at your feet." She was feeling wonderful. And Dawn looked so cuddly, she couldn't resist laying her head in her lap.

***

Dawn shifted her weight, trying to move into a more comfortable position. She wasn't sure what to do when Andi snuggled down into her lap. To say there were sparks between them was an understatement. The attraction was mutual and growing stronger. The idea of finding out what buttons to push to make her scream out her name was extremely seductive.

It wouldn't be the first time she'd taken advantage of a drunk woman, but right now that was the last thing on her mind. Well, maybe not the last thing, Andi was sexy as hell and if she didn't get her head out of her lap, drunk or not, she may not be able to stop herself. "You are going to have to move, my full bladder is bitching about the weight. I better go."

"Well, I guess if I have too, I don't want you blaming me for ruining that dress." She reluctantly raised herself back to a sitting position.

Dawn was back in minutes. She settled back down, leaning against Andi's shoulder as she flipped through channels looking for an interesting movie.

"What about it? Are there throngs of women constantly proclaiming your beauty to the world" Andi asked, as Dawn snuggled into her shoulder.

"Not exactly." Most of the women I've dated were more concerned with my bank account. Carla was the one that never mentioned money, and she fooled me completely. She was the most mercenary of the bunch. It turned out she was wanted for theft in California. She's serving time now."

"What about Kim?"

"Kim wants a fantasy. She refuses to understand I am not her girlfriend."

"Well, I can't blame her. You are…beautiful." She locked her eyes on Dawns, looking for some hint of what the other woman might be thinking.

Dawn fought down a blush. "You're not too bad yourself, even if you are a bit of a puzzle."

"Flattery will get you anywhere, but I guessed you already figured that out." Her grim was devilish and full of insinuation. "I've been called a lot of things by a lot of women. A bitch, a slut, and once a cheap tart, but I think this is the first time anyone has ever called me a puzzle."

"Yet you claim you are not very adept at the art of flirtation," she replied, squirming her way upward into her arms.

"At heart, I'm just a big kid. I'm supposed to be good at games. Flirting is just a game of words and innuendo." Andi used her weight to push Dawn back against the sofa, immobilizing her by pressing her body against hers, both wrists clasped tightly. Dawn was unable to move her hands or her body. They were pressed so closely together, she could feel every inch of her body, some parts more than others. Her knee had slipped between her legs, forcing her to press against her mound. Her body's response was immediate, a warm flush swept over her as her senses awakened in anticipation. She could feel her muscles trembling as Andi's released one wrist, allowing her hand to travel along her side casually tracing the outline of her curves.

"Once a player always a player, isn't that what you told Cooper," she whispered. Her face was so close she could feel her warm breath on her skin.

Suddenly nervous, Dawn wet her lips, using the tip of her tongue to trace the outline.

Andi noticed, she noticed everything. For a fleeting second, their gazes locked, and time stood still. She was finding it hard to breathe. Gently she pulled her closer, cupping her face between her hands. She curved into her body, letting a tiny moan escape as her loins tightened once again. She was so hot…and willing, so why was she hesitating?

For a second, Dawn thought Andi would not kiss her, and she *really* wanted her to kiss her. She desired it, even craved it, with raw desperation that threatened to overcome her body and soul. Andi knew it. And still, she made her wait.

Finally, when Dawn was certain Andi was just playing

games, her lips came down.

*****

Andi wasn't sure if it was the alcohol and moonlight, or garden variety curiosity, but she openly responded to Dawns' kisses. She was gazing down into her face, her intent perusal moving gradually downward as she studied her eyes, her mouth, the soft pulse at the v of her neck. She was suddenly overcome by the need to taste her lips. Gently at first, she brushed them, tasting the sweetness of the rich red wine mixed in with her own natural flavors. It wasn't enough. Eagerly she sought her mouth, her tongue probing, her teeth nibbling, she couldn't seem to get enough of her. Her lips trailed kisses down her neck and across the curves of her breasts causing her nipples to tighten and distend. Her hands slid downward, cupping her ass as she pulled her close against her. The alcohol loosened her inhibitions, releasing her from the usual restraints she put on herself. Gone was every intention of taking her time, getting to know her before moving into a physical relationship. She felt like they were meant to be together. So why wait?

***

Dawn could feel Andi's erect nipples through both layers of clothing, and she had to fight the temptation to reach under with her hands. Then the other woman's teeth bit gently on her own nipple, sending a wave of raw desire over her, flooding her body with a hunger she had never felt before. Her heart was beating much too fast. She needed to get her mind off the sensations flooding her system before she lost all control. In spite of her inner turmoil, she wanted to feel Andi's naked skin against hers. She wanted her, all of her. But…it was too soon. The other woman was too drunk. Feeling like a victim had happened to her often enough that she knew she never wanted to put another person in that position. As much as she wanted to continue, she would rather wait until Andi knew exactly what she was getting into.

She pushed her away and sat up, visibly trembling from restrained desires. " This is not going to happen."

"Why? You were ready to tear my clothes off thirty seconds ago! What kind of crazy bitch are you? What do you do, sit around and think of things to do that will piss me off?" Her brown eyes darkened becoming almost black as waves anger and frustration flooded her senses.

Dawn recognized the savage in Andi's expression, and she was afraid she might have pushed her too far. She slowly got to her feet.

Then she took a deep breath and stepped away from the trembling woman who had just been in her arms. The look she gave her had been dark and skeptical before. Now she rolled her eyes in an obvious challenge.

***

Andi knew she needed to get control of her emotions before she said something she would regret. Damn…she wanted this woman. She could not remember ever wanting to make love to someone so much in his life. She wanted to throw her on the bed and explore every curve, every crevice, every little dip, and dimple. But it wasn't going to happen tonight.

She wasn't sure what she'd done wrong but somehow, she had unintentionally struck a nerve. There wasn't a snowball's chance in hell things would change, but she had to give it a try. "Why are you so upset? I bet a lot of women try to make love to you. I want you, and you want me, too."

"Correction. A lot of women try and smash me. There's a big difference." Dawn was used to men hitting on her in random places while the women ogled her like she was an exotic species to be worshipped from afar. Normally this wouldn't bother her, but Andi was different. She hadn't acted unsure or afraid, nor had she hesitated about going after what she wanted. Even with the alcohol, Dawn should have anticipated something like this might happen. Maybe not this exactly, but something along the same lines. She finally met a girl she could really get into and now she had to walk away before the kind of damage was done that could not be repaired.

Finally, Andi relaxed. "Damn. I never dreamed I'd ever say this, but I'm not looking for a hit and run romance. Or even a one-night stand. No matter how great the idea of carrying you into the bedroom and showing you how good that could be, feels right now. Look, Dawn, I'd much rather rip your clothes off and lick you until you scream. Several times. But if that's the way you want to play it, okay."

"Andi, you're drunk and I'm only human. We both need to step back and think about what we are getting into."

"I thought getting my tongue into you was what this conversation was all about."

"I'm not going to try and talk to while you're in this condition. I should have made you stick to wine. I fucked up. So, I am going to leave while I still have the willpower to do it. And you are going to bed. Alone. And when I get home, after I take a cold shower, I'm going to get very, very drunk."

"Go?" That wasn't the answer Andi wanted. "Fine. Leave. Get out of my house. Don't bother me again." *She might be drunk, but Dawn was an arrogant bitch. Probably sucks in bed. I'd be better off with a vibrator.*

"But---" Andi's alcohol addled brain was slowing beginning to realize Dawn was leaving. " What did I do?"

"Fuck woman! You're drunk. And I'm horny as hell. I think it's time for me to go."

"Damn woman. Make up your fucking mind. Stay, stay, stay, go. You don't make a bit of sense."

Your right. I'm being pulled two ways. This is not a good feeling. No, don't argue… I'm leaving. You're too drunk to talk to."

Just like that, the bond that had been growing between them for the last few hours was gone

"Fuck you." Andi stood up abruptly and stomped over to the door. She held it open as she announced, "Don't let me keep you." She slammed the door behind her as she passed through it. The bitch was crazy. Getting her all worked up and then Red Light. She couldn't believe what had just happened. Dawn was supposed to proclaim her love and then she could sweep her off her feet, carry her to the bed and ravage her like in the movies. She needed to salvage something from this night, or it could be over before it even began.

Andi wheeled and stalked across the room, stopping long enough to grab her jacket, then followed her out the door, only to realize her bike wasn't in the lot. It was still at the Pizza Parlor. And Dawn was already in her car, backing out of the parking space, *Fuck!*

***

Andrea was still cussing when she walked back into her apartment. What in the hell was wrong with her? She'd never let a woman get under her skin this way, especially one that she'd just met. Maybe she was just horny. It had been a few weeks since she'd had sex but the brief bout with celibacy was usually not enough to affect her emotions. How had things gone so fucking wrong so fast? She wanted Dawn, despite every internal alarm screaming run, run fast! And Dawn was more than willing, even though she was pretending she didn't want her. She could tell that from her kiss. So why was she sleeping alone tonight? She might be wasted but that was a bullshit excuse and they both knew it.

She glanced at the clock, noticing it was almost one A.M. Something about that time was nagging at her. Then she recalled it had been about the same time Dawn had taken off the other night. A little after midnight. It was all she could do to fight the silly impulse to walk outside and look around for a single glass slipper or a couple of very confused white mice.

There was something about Dawn that pulled at her, a feeling she had not experienced since the breakup with Katie. She knew it was only a matter of time until they passed the breaking point and base instincts took over. When she was with Dawn, all her good intentions vanished. She didn't even have to touch her; one look into those sea-green eyes and she was drowning. Hell, just thinking about her got her juices flowing.

She needed to find a way to release the pressure, and she needed it soon. She decided to head over to Tits &Tails and check out the newest dancers. It had been a few weeks since she'd frequented the club. Usually, she avoided looking at naked bodies with no hope of release, but there had to be a few unattached dancers. She grinned, most people had no idea the vast majority of dancers were, if not gay, at the very least bi-sexual. With any luck at all, she could fix two problems at one time. Her bike was at the pizza parlor, so she could swing by and pick it up. She dialed the local cab company and ordered a ride.

Tits & Tails wasn't fancy. It was the kind of place where everyday people could set at the long mahogany bar and enjoy a couple of ice-cold beers without feeling like they needed to go home and get dressed up first. Most of the customers were regulars who knew each other, if not by name, at least by sight. The interior was like a thousand other strip bars, painted cement block walls, a bunch of cheap pressed wood tables and dime store chairs scattered around a large rectangular room. Everything was centered on a short runway with a lighted circular dance pad at the end. Two small floating dance pads, complete with the mandatory gold-painted dance poles, graced either side. Every available flat surface was mirrored.

A bleach blonde in a nurse's uniform was gyrating on the stage when she entered. She offered her a co-quettish smile, then with the proud dramatic movement of a seasoned burlesque dancer, she began to unzip and discard the practical white uniform, exposing a bright red corset. A matching garter belt held up dark silk stockings. Twin shelves of black lace and wire cupped perfect cone-shaped breasts, allowing just enough flesh to show to pique the customer's interest.

Patsy gave her a brief come closer wink, then moved into the familiar breast shake that many of the old-timers sitting by the stage adored. Teasingly she unsnapped the corset, link, by link, by link, in syncopated gestures timed to the beats of the rhythmic song. Then she turned her back to the audience, opening the corset wide, before dropping it to the stage floor. Almost casually, she removed a long clasp pin that was holding her hair upon her head. A quick forward shake and it tumbled around her shoulder, falling in a shimmering wave almost to her buttocks. When she turned back around, the hair hid most of her breasts, her tresses offering only a brief glimpse of the perfect orbs to the watching crowd.

Realizing they would not get to see much more without a prompt, several of the customers tossed money onto the stage; mostly ones and fives, but one man added a twenty-dollar bill. But that was enough to achieve the desired results. She turned and flipped her hair behind her, gyrating lower as she thrust her peach-colored breasts forward for their approval. Her skin was pale and firm, still supple with the elasticity of fading youth. One of her breasts was slightly bigger than the other, but the rose-pink nipples were symmetrical, and standing taunt and tall. A scattering of darker hair escaped the edges of the g string she wore under the garter belt, mute proof that she had not been born a blonde. All in all, Patsy was a tantalizing vision of female sexuality

She was also an ex-girlfriend. Not that it made a bit of difference to Andi. She was there to drink, check out the new dancers and hopefully, pick up someone new. But hell, the night was still young, and Patsy was hot. Who knows, it could be a way to rekindle some of the old flames.

Chapter 14

The Zoo was in a transitional neighborhood that had once been the epitome of old money. During the sixties, the Five Points area had become an alternative art center, home to Hare Krishna popup temples, burgeoning neo-pagan Wiccan outcasts, a few strip clubs and a mecca for free love acolytes and underage runaways. Now it was home to college students, a smattering of musicians and dancers and most of the local LGBT population. Located in the basement of a pre-World War II high rise that had been converted to a combination mini-mall and apartment complex the Zoo dance club had become a popular destination for both gay men and women and straight adults looking for a safe location to dance and have a few drinks.

It was also Cooper's favorite place to meet new men.

Tonight, was no different. The fall semester had begun, and thousands of new students were searching for new spots to dance away their freshman fears. There were several intriguing possibilities sitting at the bar when they walked in.

Andi immediately began looking to set him up. She scanned the club, hoping to spot someone who would light the fading spark interest in her pessimistic best friend. Then the door to the club opened and he walked into the room.

" Damn! Who's he? Is he new?"

Cooper looked to see who Andi was mooning over. He was certain he didn't know him, there was no way any of the group would have overlooked someone that hot. Not with that face and that body. Handsome enough to have stepped off the latest Latin Telemundo---last to the party, and cocky as hell; such an attractive combination. To make it even harder to resist him, he had a smile that could weaken the sturdiest of knees. His were visibly trembling. Cooper was certain if someone had taken a picture it would show his mouth was gaping open and drooling.

As he walked down the stairs to the main floor of the club, Cooper noticed he wasn't especially tall, he was probably only a couple of inches taller than his own five-seven. He was definitely in great shape; he could see his muscles move under his skin-tight tee as he moved. He was dressed in jeans and a faded t-shirt saying *I heard you were looking for Mr. Right. Will Mr. Right Now, do?* The logo made him grin. An intricate tribal tattoo that snaked down his neck and across his shoulder then continued down both heavily muscled arms to his wrist; making him wonder what was hiding under that tee. He didn't blame Andi for noticing; the man oozed sex appeal. He was just about as close to his image of the ideal top to his bottom as a party-boy could imagine. *Wonder if he goes for blondes?*

Andi grinned at Cooper, egging him into going out to the dance floor. Cooper was dressed for attention. He had tipped the ends of his pale blonde curls with cobalt blue, highlighting the way they framed his face. Then he'd used the same color liner to outline his eyes before adding just a hint of mascara. After adding a pair of black skinny jeans and a strategically slashed turquoise tee shirt that exposed sun-kissed skin, courtesy of the tanning bed they had visited earlier, he looked like he had just stepped off a surfboard in Malibu.

Andi noticed a slight frown curving Cooper's glossy pink lips and turned back to see what had upset him. Payton, one of the club's dancers was all over him, grinding his ass into the new guys' groin. He didn't look particularly interested in the dancers' actions, but he wasn't walking away either. She was surprised to see that Jermaine, the club's head bouncer, wasn't all over him about leaving the pedestal on a weekend. During the week, when the club was slow, it was not unusual to see one of the dancers shaking his ass for the older drunks in the viewing circle, but no one looked too closely. Jermaine liked to tell stories about the old queers he'd caught rubbing one out beneath the table. She always thought it was more that Jermaine was pushing forty and could imagine himself being one of the old men in the future; than he didn't have the heart to bust them. He must be in the back or outside on the lot.

Payton was having a blast. That changed as soon as the song ended.

Jermaine's deep voice came over the sound system. "Hey, Payton. You forgot what day of the week it is? Get your ass back on the block." Everyone in the bar broke out laughing and the DJ went right into one of the club's favorite songs.

"My drinks are gone. Anybody else needs a refill?" Thumper said, lifting his empty mug high.

"Can't have that." Cooper bounced to the bar and ordered a round for the table before heading toward the back of the club, hoping to find an empty stall before the song ended and everyone headed for the bathroom during the break. For once his luck held, and he was able to go right in, closing the door firmly behind them.

He grinned, remembering how Andi had teased him about the sexy black jockstrap he'd squeezed into. "It's not like I'm looking for a new man but think about how hot my ass will look if I get the chance to show it off."

"You are always looking, and you know it." She loved teasing him.

"I could wear blue lace; it matches my eyes. But that might be too matchy-matchy." He held the cornflower blue silk strap against his face, looked in the mirror and shook his head no before she could even respond to his comments.

Andi didn't take it personally; she knew he had already decided on the black leather and was just going through the motions anyway.

Cooper was only single because he wasn't ready to risk having his heart shattered again. His last relationship had ended badly after he came home from school early and found his boyfriend in bed with the man who ran the dry-cleaning business on the corner. He had not even considered the old bear a threat. Since then his tastes in men tended to change daily. Last week he had been into musicians. The week before that it was firemen. He strongly anticipated finding another man tonight, and while he probably wouldn't be leaving with Mr. Right, he had learned to be satisfied with Mr. Right Now.

"I got lucky with Dawn. Maybe tonight will be your night." She batted her eyes at him in a suggestive manner.

Cooper rolled his eyes and Andi laughed. She knew that Cooper wasn't jealous of *her and Dawn*, just their relationship. He wanted someone special in his life too but refused to admit it. At least he was no longer flirting with Thumper. That ship had sunk.

The door opened to the bathroom just as Cooper was finishing up. Despite his intention to keep his eyes on the wall, he allowed himself a quick glance, noticing it was the new Latino guy, standing at the urinal beside him. Quickly adjusting the rapidly increasing erection into a position that didn't threaten to pierce through the stitching on the black leather thong, he slowly slipped the zipper over the bulge and turned to wash his hands. He was certain the man had noticed his uncomfortable adjustments because he had a big grin on his face when he turned toward the sink beside him.

Cooper winked and headed for the door, making sure there was an extra sway in his hips as he picked his way across the room to the table. His eyes skimmed over the sea of faces, searching for the handsome stranger. He needed to get his mind out of the gutter. There had to be someone he could dance with. Someone like…Patrick. Perfect!

Pat was standing near the edge of the dance floor, watching two college kids undress each other on the dance floor. A few minutes more and Jermaine would be carrying them toward the door, but in the meanwhile, Pat was enjoying the impromptu floor show. Cooper could see him debating his choices, stay and watch the two guys dance or return to the bar for another beer. Pat was always hitting on him. It was too bad he wasn't drawn to him; he was really cute if you were into the hairy bear types. He would make a perfect foil.

Cooper detoured by the bar long enough to grab a longneck, and slice of lime, then he walked directly up to Pat. He took a long swig of the beer, sucked on the lime and passed the bottle to Pat. Patrick grinned. He swigged down the rest of the bottle, used his teeth to take the slice of lime from Cooper's teeth, squeezed the last bit of juice out and announced, "Let's go dance."

Cooper did his best to hide his smirk. Pat was so predictable. He loved to dance and would take any opportunity to get onto the dancefloor. Seconds after they reached the dance floor, his eyes were locked on the pair making out nearby, and he was edging closer.

Cooper had his mind on another quarry.

He always enjoyed a challenge. By the end of his song, Cooper knew he would have everyone's on him, not the oversexed college boys. As the first notes of Drake's latest filtered through the sound system, Andi and Dawn joined them on the dance floor. Even Thumper got up and danced when one of the regulars asked. It was common knowledge he was straight, but they could not resist trying. Once Thumper got over his initial phobias, he became a favorite dance partner, since he could care less about their weight or appearance.

Cooper closed his eyes and let his body lose itself in the dance. The music filled his blood, and he could almost hear his heart beating in time to the drums in the song. Naturally graceful, his body floated across the floor. When the song ended and he finally opened his eyes, Pat was gone, and he was dancing with the enigmatic stranger.

Chapter 15

"Al? I thought we could go to dinner, maybe catch a movie?"

"Sorry, hun. I have a previous engagement," Alejandro nodded in the direction of a chunky man sitting alone near the door. He had a towel wrapped around his hair and was wearing sunglasses in the steam-room as if that might prevent anyone from recognizing him. The idea was hilarious as his face appeared at least five times a day on the television during the advertisement for his furniture store. The towel might hide the black hair with its distinctive style but did nothing to cover that highly recognizable beard with the silver streak up his chin. Or that Roman nose. Big Money, of course.

He sidled up against the old man's side and whispered something in his ear. The old man blushed. Then he smacked Alejandro right on his bare ass cheeks.

Cooper couldn't help but follow the arc of his hand as it moved toward Al's perfectly rounded buttocks. They were one of his favorite memories.

Alejandro ignored the crushed expression on Cooper's face as he walked arm in arm from the steam room with his latest friend. The elderly old coot had to be old enough to be his father. So, what if he had more money than common sense? And a wife that had no idea her husband was in the closet, although rumors abounded if she had cared enough to listen.

Cooper stepped forward to follow and felt someone's hand fall on his shoulder.

"Let him go. He's not worth it. Such as shame you haven't learned to distinguish between crass and quality. Alejandro will always choose the man with the most money."

Cooper's blue eyes clouded and hardened with dislike at his words, mouth tightening in anger. "Let go of my arm." He wondered what his face must look like if the man had picked up on his distress so easily. What he needed to do was find a quiet place to sit quietly while he got his emotions back under control, but the stranger refused to leave him alone. Fine. He didn't care what the man thought of him nor did he care that he had jumped to his defense for some unknown reason. Ever since the night they'd spent together, he could not get him out of his mind. But Alejandro was not interested in a relationship. And he rarely showed up at Zoo.

Glen was surprised by the authority the melodious voice carried. His fingers loosened under its influence and he fought to override the unconscious compulsion to obey and step away. Instead, he gripped his arm tighter, pulling him closer in the steam-filled room, until his breath whispered against his face. "You don't need him. What you need is to have your ass whupped for thinking he was worth your time."

The stranger's eyes flashed dangerously, making Cooper groin tighten in response. Luckily, he was wearing a towel.

"You like that?" he asked coolly, but he did not step away.

Cooper thought it was strangely exciting, having

someone step in and take control like this. "Sometimes," he replied. "Depends on who's swinging the paddle

"Call me Glen. I'd like to get to know you. How about we grab a drink at the bar?"

His eyes were the color of spring grass, an almost jewel-like shade of pale green. Tiny gold flecks sparkled in them, lending a little welcome color to make the man more human. For some reason, Cooper couldn't tear his gaze away, even after the man released his arm. He wondered what he had in mind. Maybe he got off on saving pathetic losers? Cooper didn't think so, but there must have been some reason he was sticking around.

He took a second look, surprised by how attractive he was. Like most of the men in the gym, he was in good shape. Tall, well-muscled but not overly so, it was apparent he had gained his six-pack through hard work, not steroids. He looked to be in his early thirties, older than the men Cooper was usually attracted too. Short, straight hair shone like a raven's wing, highlighted by varying shades of red and brown, like the carved wood Maori mask hanging in the living room. His skin was slightly darker than his, possibly one of his parents had been African or Latino. The white towel he wore around his waist gave no indication of his occupation, but his nails were cut short and manicured, not worn and broken like many who did physical work. One interesting thing, he smelled of Old Spice, rich and earthy like his father used to wear. Then he shifted his weight and the tightly wrapped towel gaped open to reveal a hint of thickly veined muscle, quite a bit more than a brief glimpse usually provided.

Cooper's blood pounded feverishly, and he felt himself begin to sweat. He hated that this older man had noticed him, while the hot young stud he'd set his eyes on acted as if he didn't exist. That was the problem with coming to a bathhouse, a lot of the hot young things were working the crowd. He had never paid for sex and had no intention of starting today. Even for Alejandro.

He turned to the older man and smiled. "Let's have that drink."

***

Two days after the bathhouse experience, Glen was still a puzzle. He seldom said anything, as if a conversation was a rare commodity hoarded against some possible future shortage. When he did talk, his words were sparse, and to the point. Possibly this was due to his occupation, but it seemed ingrained; as if he had learned at an early age, to stop and listen before answering a question. He gave nothing away, not even a compliment. Nor did he seem fazed by Cooper's self-deprecating attitude.

Cooper was no closer to figuring out why he'd reacted that way in at the bathhouse than he'd been Friday afternoon. He lay in the darkness thinking about everything that had happened since then.

Drinks in the bar had led to dinner and dancing. Atlanta had an active alternative lifestyle population, and there were several clubs near the park that catered exclusively to the LGBTQIA crowd. The night had ended in a local Motel, not an especially expensive one, but not a cheap hourly flophouse either.

The sex was fantastic. They'd slept late, then went out for brunch at Brennan's, one of his favorite downtown restaurants. When they climbed into the cab afterward, he'd expected to head back to the bathhouse, and his car. Instead, Glen had directed the driver to an address in an exclusive Buckhead neighborhood. The rest of the time sped by in a blur, the vast majority of it spent in bed.

Cooper broke out in goosebumps as Glen turned to him in his sleep, wrapping his arms around his neck and pulling him close. He inhaled deeply. His scent was intoxicating, a mix of coconut oil, green apple shampoo, and old spice, a warm musky cologne. Glen had mentioned his father had hooked him on the scent, and he had never found anything else he liked.

Cooper swore inwardly, biting his inner lip, even as he sighed contentedly. It had been one hell of a weekend. He propped himself up on one hand and studied the face of the man sharing the bed. Though darker complexioned than him, Glen's face was still flushed pink from the workout he'd recently completed. At some point, while Cooper was grabbing a shower, he must have fallen asleep. A stray hair tickled his nose and he sneezed, showering his lover with droplets of water from his still-damp hair. Several landed on Glen's forehead and his eyes opened. Like a flower uncurling, he stretched out from his fetal position, pulling Cooper down onto him, so that his face was only inches from his own. Coopers' hand came down upon his chest, and Glen's nipples hardened underneath it. His own groin tightened in anticipation. This idea was instantly driven from his mind by the shrill clamor of the cell phone on the nightstand next to the bed, a message reminding Glen that he needed to be in court in two hours.

Cooper acknowledged it as a silent reminder that his time was up. The clock had struck midnight and Cinderella had to go back to reality. His fantasy was over. He had no valid reason to stay—none he was prepared to share. Using the steel will he had honed after scores of one-night stands, Cooper shifted position until he had all of his weight on his arms. Walking away from someone he really wanted to spend more time with would be a challenge, but he had faced worse. Silently pleading for God to give him strength, he pushed himself upright, his trembling muscles the only outward sign of how difficult this was as he stood next to the bed.

He saw the puzzled look in Glen's eyes, and it

pleased him, but it didn't change things.

The room was still dark, but his eyes had adjusted enough that getting dressed was no problem. The only light was the glow of the alarm on the bedside table, but he could see the question in Glen's eyes as he rolled to his knees and held out a hand for Cooper to move closer.

Cooper perched on the edge of the bed, and let Glen pulled him into a final embrace.

Glen nuzzled into his neck, murmuring, "Stay..."

Frozen, Cooper's mind refused to direct his lips to say the word no. Why would he ask that? Everyone knew the unwritten rule about bathhouse hookups. No strings, no commitments. Just sex. His muscles trembled as he fought with himself, fought the impulse to pull him closer, to press his lips against those perfect pink ones, to feel the slight burn of his newly sprouted beard against his cheeks. He was surprised by how much he wanted to crawl back into the bed and pretend this moment had never happened.

"Mmmmm, you feel so good," Glen said, stretching his hand up so that his fingers tangled in his hair, pulling him closer.

Cooper could feel his tongue teasing his ear, his lips trailing across his neck, leaving shivers in their wake. His heart pounded so loudly, he feared it would break through his chest. Jaw clenched, he forced himself to move again, pushing his protesting body back away from his arms. When he felt his ankles bump against the bed frame, he carefully disentangled Glen's fingers from his hair, laying him back on top of the covers.

"You have court in a little over an hour. I have to get to school." He pulled a sheet over his slender form, then kissed him gently. For a moment he stood by the bed, trying to remember how to breathe. His hands were clenched to keep from touching him again, pulling him in his arms like he wanted to. Somehow, he managed to walk away. He could hear Andi already.

"Cooper?"

He paused. He was being ridiculous, he knew. It meant nothing that Glen said his name. He was probably reading too much into a simple question. Even if he did think he had feelings for him, they were not the kind of feelings a relationship was built on. Men like him would never be alone, one smile and they had the world ready to fall at their feet. It was a fantasy to expect more. In a few days, there would be someone new in his bed. If they met somewhere on the street or at a party, they both would pretend it had never happened. No one would believe what he was walking away from. While in the bathroom he'd googled him. An attorney with one of the biggest firms in Georgia, he was one of the most eligible bachelors in the state. The youngest son of a Texas oil baron, he had a ranch about half the size of England, a villa in France and a fancy yacht for when he got bored and needed to 'find himself.' He wore expensive custom silk suits, designed for comfort, not usefulness. His closet was full of Armani, Hugo Boss, Gucci, and Ralph Lauren, clothing that cost more than he made in a month.

He walked out of the room, closing the door behind him. Once the door closed behind him, he leaned against the door, letting his head fall back. He could pretend it wasn't anything except a hookup. If only he could erase the way he had felt. So good. So right. He knew he was torturing himself, but he couldn't help it. Closing his eyes, he reached one rough hand up to trail lightly across his neck caressing the place where his lips had been moments before. Glen might have no trouble forgetting him, but for him—the haven of oblivion would be a long time coming.

Chapter 16

Andi clicked the off button on the television controller and tossed it on the side table. Dawn had shown up at the apartment once again, with no warning, no call, no text nothing. Then she had the nerve to act as if she'd done nothing wrong leaving the way she had.

"You know, you really pissed me off. Are you bipolar or just rude?"

"Neither. Sometimes my mouth overloads my mind, and something it the other way around. My overactive imagination won, and I bolted."

"I left all the drama behind in high school. I was looking forward to breakfast with you. Instead, I found the room empty and Misty, who should have been resting, in the kitchen cooking."

"Yeah. I feel bad about that. How far along is she?"

"Pretty damn close. And her husband is in the

National Guard. He's doing his month of service now so he can be home for the baby's birth next month." She paused and opened a coke, took a drink and thought about what she was going to say. "You surprised me, taking off the way you did. And then you didn't show up at school. I was worried about you."

Dawn moved around so that she was standing behind where she was on the sofa. "I know I reacted badly, and I'm really sorry about that. I heard her voice coming from the bedroom and I couldn't help but be jealous. I admit it's crazy, especially knowing she is Cooper's sister, but my mind runs away with my imagination at times." She began massaging her neck and shoulders, then began moving her hands slowly down Andi's back, a move intended to relax, but somehow having the opposite effect.

Andi's nerves were on fire. Every touch of Dawn's hands made her body jerk. She needed to decide where this was going now before things got out of hand. Was she ready to get involved? Dawn did not strike her as the one-night stand type. She would expect a dedicated relationship. She went over it in her mind. Yes, she was attractive. In fact, despite the small amount of time in which she's been in the bathroom, she'd somehow become even more beautiful, if that was possible. There was no question about sexual attraction. It was a constant mental battle between her mind and her body now. All she thought about was getting her naked, in her bed, on the table, in the back of the lab, in the back seat of her car. She could care less about where it happened; as long as it was soon. Instead of being apprehensive about what was possibly going to happen, Andi was excited, feeling the tingle running down her spine before it settled into a growing throb between her legs. It was silly to delay the inevitable.

Before Dawn knew it was happening, Andi reached back and pulled her down across the back of the sofa into her lap.

Dawn relaxed into her embrace, allowing Andi's arms to circle her waist, with her back pressed against the back of the sofa. Her head fit nicely under her chin. The scent of Green apple shampoo wafted upward, Andi's favorite. It blended nicely with the light floral perfume she was wearing. For a moment or two, she sat listening to her heartbeat, feeling her soft intakes and exhales. It was strangely erotic. Finally, unable to resist any longer, Andi cupped her face the way she did when they first kissed outside of the club. Dawn's lips parted, just enough that she could see the pink tip of her tongue. Shifting her weight to one hip, she pulled her closer, hugging the smaller woman flat against her body as she leaned down and kissed her. The deep guttural moan that escaped Dawn's softly parted lips made her shiver. Her tongue traced her lips, before darting inside, meeting Dawn's tongue in a hesitant dance, a tentative encounter that left her unsure of whether she should plunge ahead, or surrender. Things had been intense between them, but this was taking it to a whole new level. She pulled back, giving her mind a chance to regain some amount to control over her body.

"Such great lips," she said as she ran her fingertips lightly across the silky skin. She forced Dawn's head back as she leaned in for another kiss.

Dawn sighed and melted into her embrace. That

one little moan had set her nerves on fire. The look in her eyes said Andi was feeling it too. She found herself drowning, unable to take a deep breath, yet unwilling to pull away.

Andi was fighting to remain in control. The warmth of Dawn's breath on her earlobe as she leaned down to kiss and nibble on her neck was sheer torture. Every breath upon her skin made her melt a little bit more. Andi realized she needed to slow down and think about what was happening. A few loose strands of hair fell across her face, aggravating her more than normal. Her temper flared long enough for her to reach up and pulled her thick brown hair into a ponytail, using an elastic band she'd noticed on the coffee table. It didn't help. She was still irritated and having trouble focusing.

She could smell the scent of desire rolling off Dawn's satiny skin. Sighing, she lay back along the sofa, pulling her down atop her, then pulled her into another kiss. As their tongues entwined, the kiss deepened, making the ache inside her grow until she was grinding her hips against Dawns, needing to feel her bare skin against her own.

Dawn must have been reading her mind; before she could give it more than a brief thought, she pulled her shirt over her head, letting it dangle, then drop from her fingertips onto the floor beside the couch. Her blue jeans followed until she was wearing nothing more than her red bra and panties.

Andi took that as permission that Dawn was more than ready to continue. Before she had a chance to reconsider, she had pulled her tee-shirt off, dropping it on the floor on top of Dawns. Her eyes went to the unchained door, then to the clock on the wall. Seven o'clock. They had at least three hours before Cooper got off work.

Dawn's breathing quickened as she caressed her neck and shoulders lightly before turning her attention to her breasts. With a quick twist of her wrist, Dawn's bra was unsnapped, the straps falling from her shoulders to leave her pert breasts on full display. Andi's breath hissed through clenched teeth as her eyes skimmed over the perfect teacup breasts, smiling as the cool air caressing her skin brought her nipples to a rosy peak. Eagerly she pulled one taut nipple into her mouth grazing it gently with her teeth before sucking. She rose to gently cup the other, gently squeezing her nipple before circling the tender nub with her thumb.

Dawn immediately returned the favor, raising both hands to her own breasts, giving equal attention to each one. But she wasn't happy with foreplay. Her soft hands drifted lower, cupping the cheeks of her ass, kneading and squeezing the tight flesh. By the time her hand reached the space between her thighs, Andi's body was on fire. Reaching down, her fingers skimmed the sensitive skin of Dawn's stomach making her gasp as she rubbed small circles on her stomach with her thumbs, leaving a trail of fire everywhere our skin touched. But she wanted more

It was almost a give and take as Dawn teased her a little while running her fingers along the edge of her basketball shorts smiling at the rush of wetness that moistened the soft cotton material. Andi's body trembled as her seeking fingers increased the pressure of their touch, rubbing the taut nub through the silk. She immediately rectified the issue, lying chest to chest in nothing but her boxer briefs. Her body flushed at the next warm rush of heat. Biting her lip to keep the cries under control, she tried to be patient, then gave up as her body reached its peak, then released the tension in waves of pleasure. She hadn't even got her briefs off and the girl had already pushed her over the edge.

The feel of her bare skin was intoxicating. Andi began to explore, using her fingers and her tongue to search out every sensitive nook and cranny. The heat between her thighs began to surge as Andi trailed kisses across her stomach, slowing moving lower until she could nip the swollen pink tip. Andi's tongue flicked out and Dawn's groans became louder. Her fingers teased the wet opening before she slid one, then the other deep inside. Dawn groaned and arched higher as she teased the velvet flesh, increasing the pace of each stroke as well as the depth until her fingers were past the knuckle each time. Dawn began to writhe beneath her touch, bucking her hips as Andi brought her closer to the peak. She pushed her thumb deep into Dawn's core, quickly pushing her over the edge. But she wasn't finished.

Swiftly kneeling between her legs, Andi slid her thighs apart and lowered her body to her stomach. The feeling of Andi's tongue against her already sensitive nerves made the blonde woman clench down tightly around her head, setting her competitive instincts into overdrive. Her flicks changed to circles as she sucked the nub deep inside her mouth, all the while keeping up the in and out strokes of her fingers. Dawn's head rolled as she tried to gasp for breath. Her orgasm was quick, building into a second as Andi continued her caresses over and over again. She clutched at Andi, only releasing her grasp once the spasms had subsided.

As Dawn reached her peak for the final time Andi shifted, pulling her up on top as she rolled flat on her back. They lay in a tangle, quietly enjoying just being together.

"Well…"

"Yeah…"

"Maybe we should move to the bedroom. Cooper will home soon. I don't think he's interested in joining in." Dawn grabbed her clothes and headed that way.

Andi gathered her things and followed the naked girl to her bedroom.

***

Andi's perfect dream was shattered when the phone in Dawn pocketbook beeped twice and began vibrating again. She woke up slowly. Sometime during the early hours of the morning, they must have fallen asleep. She had snuggled in next to Dawn's back, one arm draped her waist, and one leg was thrown possessively over hers. The shorter girl's head fit perfectly between her breasts, letting her snuggle without stretching her neck. They were both naked and the feel of her silky skin against hers had Andi wanting an immediate replay of last night's events. Just the thought of it made her core muscles clench and her breathing grow deeper. But nature called so she rolled over, taking one of the blankets with her as she headed into the bathroom. When she came back Dawn was already dressed and texting someone. Despite being curious about who she would be talking to at …she glanced at the clock…five-thirty in the morning, she didn't ask.

"I've got to take off," Dawn said, kissing her lightly before she grabbed her things and headed for the door. "See you in class." She bounced out before Andi could produce an argument.

Obviously, she had no intention of explaining the early morning call.

After Dawn's abrupt exit, she lay in the darkened room and thought about what had just happened. The sex was great, but she had expected to feel something more …some sense of togetherness. She was ready to fall in love, have a relationship, eventually a life commitment and a family. She didn't expect fireworks, just something. More than she was feeling. Maybe she was expecting too much too soon? The sex was great. Still, she couldn't help being slightly disappointed.

Chapter 17

Thumper surprised us all by showing up with a candy apple red Dodge Charger, claiming he had got an incredible deal on the car at the auction the night before. She had to admit it was a beauty. "Nice…could use a bath."

He grinned and reached into the back seat of the car. "And that's why I brought this with me. Grab a brush and lend a hand."

Cooper pulled the hose close to the car and filled the buckets Thumper had brought out with soapy water. We all picked a tire and scrubbed and brushed at the rims for the next few minutes, loosening the mud from the decorative spokes and removing the dirt from the white-walled tires.

Dawn took the hose from Andi and wet the body of the Charger down. With four washing it didn't take long to wash it. When the soap had been rinsed off and they had wiped the excess water from the car's body with old t-shirts everyone looked like drowned rats.

Thumper decided to keep the party going and dump the soap bucket, choosing Dawn as his main target but managing to douse Andi with the excess before running off. Then Dawn raised the hose and squirts it in his direction, soaking Cooper shirt and hair while enacting her revenge.

"I was just rinsing the soap off," she taunted as she ran back out of her reach.

Andi threw a smirk her way and snatched the hose from her with ease. Then she drenched her with the cold water.

Dawn refused to give up without a fight, laughing and squealing, she grabbed at the hose in order to put a kink in it, but Andi kept twisting it firmly out of her reach. Finally, refusing to accept defeat, she sprints to the side of the house and turns off the tap

Andi couldn't take her eyes off her. The water-soaked tee shirt molded itself to her body, drawing attention to her perfectly shaped breasts. She wasn't wearing a bra and the soft peach of her nipples showed through the thin white material.

Dawn casually combed back her wet hair with her fingers before tucking it behind her ears. Noticing Andi's interest, she licked the water from her lips, sending her pulse into overdrive.

Her eyes then blatantly wander to Andi's chest and she bites her lip, playing with the tiny silver ball on the side. When her eyes meet mine, she quickly averts her gaze, a blush creeping up her neck and across her cheeks. But they can't help but drift downwards again and she grinned as the pink on her cheeks deepens to a fiery red.

Thumper peeled off his shirt and walked over to Andi. When he reached her, he twisted the shirt over her head, sending soapy water down her face.

"Get a room, you guys," he called out as he ran for the apartment door.

Andi raised three fingers in a well-known salute but did not take her eyes off Dawn. Thumpers' suggestion sounded pretty good to her. Now all she had to do is convince Dawn…

***

"As much as you brag on your conquests, I expected you to finish the balloons hours ago."

"Even if they had photos of naked men it wouldn't help," Cooper replied from the living-room to Andi's comment. "I've been blowing up these ridiculous balloons for hours."

"It will teach you not to brag, Cooper," Dawn called from the dining room, "claiming to be better at blowing might not be exactly the kind of reputation you want to get around."

"Well, we could've rented a helium bottle for it. if someone wasn't so tight-fisted." Then Andi realized what she'd just said and started laughing. Cooper would claim that as a compliment, too.

"I did," Dawn said. "It's sitting over by the light switch. I wondered how many you would do before you began bitching." She was working in the kitchen. As Cooper stomped across the room to get the helium, she rolled her eyes and continued decorating the chocolate cupcakes with colorful flowers. The elaborate Baby shaped cake, which she had picked up at the bakery, had taken someone hours of hard work. It was the centerpiece of the table. Her cupcakes might not be as pretty, but they would taste just as good. Though, as she looked around her after she was finished with the icing, the topsy-turvy condition of the kitchen reminded her that her work wasn't complete. At least there was a dishwasher.

Andi's laughter echoed Dawns. She might prefer to wear dark colors, cover her body in tattoo's, act tough and keep her hair all spiky, but underneath she was as soft as the rest of them when it comes to a new baby. Besides, this was probably as close as she would ever get to having a baby shower. Misty was going to have to share with Auntie Andrea.

Cooper was scanning a new notification on his phone. "Hey, guess who's gonna be at the Omni Saturday? Troye Sevan! He's filling in for Vincent. Now I'm even happier we bought tickets."

"As long as Halsey hasn't canceled, I'm fine with whoever plays. Pass me the tape."

"Same here," Dawn said as she began chopping celery and carrot sticks. "How did you get Thumper to agree to go?"

"We promised to go to a Lynyrd Skynyrd concert with him." He tied the final balloon and collapsed on the sofa beside the box. "I just hope my sister can hang on until Marco gets home. He is missing out of so much of the baby hoopla."

Dawn laughed. "Have you ever considered that might be why he took his yearly service time now? He wants to be home when the baby arrives."

"Who cares, Pizza's here," Cooper said as he rushed to the door. He passed the driver a twenty through the door, then carried the two boxes to the kitchen. Half price pizza was one of the perks of working there. "Ummm. Still hot too. Want a plate?"

Cooper took a plate from Andi. And then slid two slices of the heavily loaded meat deluxe on; making sure he left room for the cup of extra marinara sauce.

Andi made a plate for herself and Dawn, grabbed two beers and headed back to the sofa. "Dawn. Food! Come eat."

Dawn was still examining her cupcakes and made no response.

"I don't think she wants pizza," Cooper remarked when she didn't acknowledge Andi or the food. *Just my best friend.* "What you watching?"

"I don't know, some sappy romance Dawn brought over. Love Actually, maybe."

"Seen it. Overrated. I think I'm going to go to my room and play a video game." He didn't wait for Andi to comment. Andi tended to zone out whenever Dawn was around. It would be silly to expect anything else. When she didn't respond he plopped down on the sofa and picked up an ornate hand mirror he'd left on the coffee table a few days earlier.

"So…, I need lip injections. I have no upper lip." Cooper laid down the mirror and picked up a slice of pizza.

Dawn finally decided to join them. Instead of responding to Cooper's remark, she picked up a slice. It was still too hot to bite, but she tried anyway, burning her lip.

"No," Andi said to him as she checked to see if Dawn's lip was hurt. It was pinker than normal, but the skin had not blistered. She would be fine.

"I'm serious." He laid down the mirror and Dawn picked it up. By twisting the mirror, she was able to get a look at the burn. It felt much worse than it looked.

"Still no." Andi took a drink of her beer and reached for the television controller. She was not in the mood for a romantic comedy. Maybe something interesting, like a good sci-fi or even an old fashioned western.

"But---"

"No fucking way. Period." She never knew when Cooper was serious. Last week it had been butt cheek implants after watching a music video.

"Love you, baby," Dawn said as she straddled her lap, blocking her view of the television with her body. She hated it when Andi paid attention to anyone else when she was around. So, she used the one thing he knew Andi couldn't resist, her body. Just as she expected, Andi forgot Cooper completely.

Cooper sighed. He might as well have gone to the bedroom. Andi was a ho. It was only ever a question of when not if she would forget all about him. Dawn's breasts were inches from her mouth. She couldn't resist. She was so fucking weak.

"Okay, Cooper, if you really want it. I'll grit my teeth and live with it." Andi said as she pulled Dawn's mouth down to meet hers. Dawn shivered as Andi's hands slipped under her bra, but she didn't pull away.

Cooper sighed. Her mind was on other things. As usual. "Naw. Forget I said anything. I just saw a photo and the girl looked like hell afterward." He flipped the channel, again and again, looking for something interesting.

"I need a beer," Dawn announced once she knew she had proven her dominance in the makeshift power ritual. She jumped up and headed for the kitchen, ignoring the puzzled look on Andi's face.

Cooper roared, a deep rumbling laugh that rolled across the room. "I give up. I'm gonna go play Halo." He started walking toward his bedroom as Andi threw the sofa pillow at him, missing him by inches.

Andi flipped through a few more channels, then realized Dawn had not come back. The kitchen was empty. Then she noticed a pair of red thongs hanging on the bedroom door. Suddenly she wasn't hungry for pizza. A wide grin split her face as she reached for the doorknob.

***

"Oh, man! It was great. The concert was worth every

penny of my hard-earned tips." It wasn't every day she had the opportunity to see two of her favorite singers together on the same stage. The night had started with dinner and drinks, and then the concert, Now, four hours later Andi was not ready for the night to end.

Dawn giggled and swung her around in a circle. Pride weekend was turning out great. The parade was a blast, even if they could not convince Thumper they should make costumes and join in. Then they had checked out the festival in the park until Thumper began to look pale and needed food before going to the show.

Cooper and Thumper looked at each other and then pretended they did not know the two silly drunks. They had given up on looking for potential dates' hours earlier. The city was packed with single men and women but after the tenth misunderstanding, they realized everyone thought they were a couple.

Cooper sighed. It was easier to go with it than try to explain. Not that he wouldn't have enjoyed spending some quality time in Thumper's arms. It just wasn't gonna happen, the man was so straight he would crack in a strong wind.

Then Dawn spotted a neon sign advertising one of the access stairways down to Underground. "Lets' go down and check out a couple of the clubs." She began tugging Andi toward the egress.

"Sounds good to me." It had been a while since she had braved the lower levels of the city with Cooper, instead choosing to hit up the clubs in Buckhead that were so much closer to their house. They were both anti-drink and drive, preferring to rent a motel room to crash nearby. If worse came to worse, and they were not able to find a room, Cooper had an aunt that lived within walking distance of their favorite hangouts. They knew they could always crash on her couch.

Tonight, was different.

Underground was on the southside of the city, in an area that at one time had been the mecca of entertainment. During the eighties and the nineties most of the big names, Billy Joel, the Eagles, Kansas, Black Crows, etc. had played at one of the numerous clubs built beneath the city in the old train tunnels. Now it was more of a shopping center with one or two bars. More for tourists than anything else. We cruised through the remaining clubs, drank another shot or three and decided we were going to walk back to the motel, too drunk to realize it was almost ten miles away, the temperature was in the eighties and we were going the wrong way.

We made it about two blocks before Thumper began to feel sick. "I need to stop for a minute. I think I'm going to barf."

He was pale and trembling. He had limited his drinking, only having one to every three the others drank, but his liver was not able to handle even the slightest amount of alcohol.

"When was the last time you went to dialysis?"

"Too long. I should have gone the day before yesterday." His color was a little better, so they began walking again.

Andi made a note of a glowing neon hospital sign atop a large building a couple of blocks away, just in case they needed to get him there in a hurry.

Cooper noticed that Thumper had one hand on his

side and winced with each step. It was obvious he was going to need to rest soon. He cut his eyes toward Andrea and she nodded.

Andi looked around, spotting the top of trees in the distance. "There's a park over there," she said, pointing toward the leafy boughs. "Let's head that way."

The mini-park had been built on a slice of public land located between three high rise buildings. Only about a block square, it was laid out like a sun, radiating outward from the centerpiece, a circular pool of water surrounding a large granite fountain. Cooper helped Thumper sit down on the narrow ledge skirting the pool, then sat down beside him.

"Stretch out on top the ledge and lay your head my lap. Take the weight off your side."

Thumper didn't say anything as he lay down and propped his head on Cooper's leg.

The mist off the water felt wonderful but Cooper didn't notice, his mind was filled with worry over his friend. His breathing had slowed, it no longer sounded like a busted steam engine. That was the problem of dealing with Thumper's illness, all you could do is be there for him. He knew he was dying. They all did. It was hard to accept the choices he had made as a teenager was stealing away his life bit by bit. He was easily the strongest of them all.

Instead of enduring daily dialysis and the life of an invalid, Thumper had chosen to continue his life as if he was not sick, doing the same things his friends did. The doctors had warned him his body could not handle it. He didn't care. If he only had one extra day, he wanted to live it as a normal man.

Cooper let his eyes drift to Andi and Dawn. They had slipped off their shoes and were wading in the fountain. Dawn saw him looking and splashed water in his direction, wetting both men.

Cooper grinned and returned the favor, slamming his hand down with enough force to send a wave of water over the giggling girl.

Andi broke out laughing at the look on her face. Dawn's mascara was running down her face like a clown and her hair was plastered to her head like a straggly wet mop. "You look like a stoned raccoon."

Dawn shoved her backward, laughing as she fell into the water. Andi came up sputtering, soaking wet and irritated as hell. She limped over to the edge of the fountain. "Give me a hand up, I think I may have twisted my ankle when I feel." She held her hand out.

Dawn reached to help her out and Andi took advantage of her trust, jerking her forward into the fountain with her. The two women went down into a tangled mess.

"Hey," Cooper said. "I wanna play too." He shifted Thumper's head to his rolled-up shirt and hopped up on the edge of the marble cowl, thought about it for a second and jumped back down. Once he'd slipped off his new shoes he leaped into the cool water.

Soon the three friends were having a great time horsing around in the marble pool. Passersby stopped to watch the fun, occasionally calling out suggestions to elude and warnings of impending dunks. Things got quiet when two mounted police officers rode up on their horses, but once they realized the officers were laughing along with them, they relaxed and resumed the banter.

This playful free-spirited fun continued for about fifteen minutes until the blaring sound of a siren and a man's voice from a loudspeaker broke up the entertaining spectacle.

"Get out of the fountain and down on your knees."

"Oh shit, that's Taggart! We are fucked now." Everyone knew the gung ho division commander. He spent a lot of time in the clubs in Buckhead. They must have assigned him to help out in the area during Pride week. Andi began trudging toward the edge of the fountain. By the time she reached the outer skirt, the other two had already climbed out and were down on their knees. The bystanders had faded into the shadows, many moving just far enough away to be able to film, others returning to the club. It would be all over Facebook in minutes.

Taggart was speaking to the two young officers on horse patrol and neither appeared happy to hear what he had to say. Both shifted their weight uncomfortably but were smart enough to keep their mouths shut. Taggart's voice rose in pitch and he gestured in their direction before speaking into his shoulder radio.

The men immediately moved to the kneeling trio, and bound their hands, using handcuffs on two and a zip tie on the third. Then they helped them to their feet and led them to the waiting squad car.

"Hey, man, grab my shoes, would you?" Cooper asked the officer leading him toward the waiting car.

He nodded. "Stand here until I get back. Don't move." Seconds later he was back with the shoes, but no socks. Cooper shrugged and slipped his feet into the loafers. At least he had something on his feet.

Taggart was enjoying himself. "…to an attorney, if you can't afford one, a public defender will be assigned your case. You are being charged with defacing public property and creating a nuisance. Do you have any questions?"

"Yeah? How do you sleep at night?" Dawn asked.

Taggart glared at her and shut the door.

At least they were still together. Chances are, once they arrived at the station, they would be separated, and Cooper would go into a holding cell with a bunch of men. This idea didn't appeal to any of them. Cooper was not muscular and definitely looked gay; if for no other

reason than the stereotypical hot pink skinny jeans and

paisley print pullover he was wearing. It would only take

one aggressive homophobe in the cell for him to end

up hurt. Luckily, the jail was packed and misdemeanor

charges like theirs were low on the priority list.

The desk Sargent pulled Taggart off to one side,

while we were escorted to a vacant bench and told to sit

down.

Cooper immediately rested the back of his head

against the wall behind us, arching his back as he took a

deep breath in and stretched his legs out, digging his heels

into the floor.

Andi slid her arm around Dawn, and she slumped

to lean her head against his shoulder. "I told you Taggart

fucking sucked."

"You were right," she said, his face softening. Dawn

untangled herself from her arm and hugged her over the

shoulders, pulling her into Cooper.

"What are we even doing here?" he asked. "It's not

against the law to play."

Her lips pulled themselves into an involuntary smile and she shrugged her shoulder.

Cooper cocked an expectant eyebrow, silent for a change. Misty couldn't afford to bail him out and he needed to be at the restaurant helping her open up. She would think he was with some guy, drunk and oblivious to anything but his own hedonistic needs. Until someone came in and mentioned the water fight, she would have no way of knowing what really happened.

He grinned as Dawn leaned even closer to Andi, their noses almost touching, He saw Andi catch her breath as whatever air remained in her lungs vanished. Dawn quickly kissed her.

" Hey! None of that shit. Sit on this bench and stay quiet," Taggart said. He crooked a finger at Cooper, then motioned it was his time to be printed and booked in.

Andi signed. It could have been worse, it was just past midnight, early Monday morning. At least it happened on a Sunday night. They would not have to stay in jail all weekend. It was going to be difficult enough to sit here for six hours. Not to mention, they all looked like drowned cats. She had no idea what her face looked like, but from the way the makeup had run down Cooper and Dawn's face, she imagined hers looked no better. *Wonder if my clothes will dry before court?*

Dawn let her head fall sideways, laying it on Andi's shoulder. She expected to hear someone call out for her to remove it but relaxed after a few minutes had passed. It was going to be a long night.

***

Andi woke with a start, unsure where she was when she first opened her eyes. The bench now held eight detainees. One, just to her left, smelled like she had bathed in stale beer, and then used bourbon as a cologne. She was snoring away on her side, curled up like a baby on the narrow wooden plank. Another, a barely legal teenage girl with a swollen face and blackened eye, reeked of marijuana smoke. She was crying silently.

Cooper was no longer in the cell.

She wondered what had happened to him and was about to ask when an officer approached and began waking everyone up.

"Up and at it, ladies, time for your closeup. The judge waits for no one."

She shrugged and helped Dawn to her feet. Dawn didn't say a word, she simply moved into the line in front of Andi and waited for instructions. Andi could tell nothing like this had ever happened to her before. Unfortunately, there was nothing she could say or do, that would make the situation better. They trudged toward the courtroom holding area, heads down, no one speaking, dejected and miserable.

The duty officer motioned for them to take seats in the front row on the right side near the entrance door. Most of the row was already taken up by male detainees. One or two were already wearing bright orange jumpsuits, visible proof that these were county inmates that were being brought up on additional charges or were un-bondable and forced to sit in jail until their court date. She wondered if either one had used their one call to phone their parents. They were well off, she knew that much about them, but nothing else. This was a simple misdemeanor, but the first time you are in court was always hard, even for something as simple as playing in a fountain.

She got her answer when Dawn blanched white as a fish belly and scrunched lower against the back of the bench. The tall, distinguished-looking man stopped at the bailiff and spoke for a moment before the two men approached the clerk of courts. The District Attorney was nodding, and two men were laughing about something together. A moment later they shook hands and the officer on duty made his way over to the bench, stopping in front of Dawn.

"Today's your lucky day. You're up first." He motioned for her to stand, and then unsnapped her cuffs.

When he didn't make her the same offer, she realized they would all be tried separately. Since it was common to try all members active in the same offense at the same time, this surprised her.

She stood as the judge entered the room and then sat as the bailiff called the court to order. Just as promised, Dawn's case was called first. It was a joke. After the bailiff called her name, she approached the bench. The District

Attorney said something to the judge, who smiled and nodded. Then he signed a paper and she was free to go.

She did not even look back at me.

Thirty-two cases and a lunch break later, we were the final case to be called before the bench. The district attorney read the charges and the judge asked a couple of questions, then we were sworn in. " You are charged with defamation of a public monument, how do you plead?"

"Not guilty, the same as our friend you heard earlier."

"Your friend is not on trial, you are. According to the report, you were fighting in a public fountain. Creating a nuisance and refusing to obey an officer."

"We were cooling off. Its ninety degrees outside. It was hot."

"So, you admit you were in the fountain?"

"Yes. Just like Dawn was. You already heard her case."

The judge raised an eyebrow and the clerk reminded him of his first case. He called the District Attorney and the Public Defender up to the bench and held a private conversation. Both men nodded and returned to their places.

"The Court finds you guilty. The sentence is six months in jail, however, due to mitigating circumstances, the DA has agreed to time served and a five hundred dollar fine. Please make arrangements to pay on your way out."

He slapped his mallet on a thick wooden rest. As he stood to leave, the bailiff announced that the court was recessed until Monday at 8:00 AM.

We stood there with our mouths open as everything was decided. Then we made arrangements to pay the fine.

Chapter 18

"All the Fried Rice gone?" Andi slid into the booth beside Cooper and reached for a fork.

Cooper nodded yes and passed her the bucket in his hand.

Andi examined the contents, decided it was close enough, and shoveled the Lo-Mein noodles into her mouth.

That was the one consistent thing he could always depend on when Andrea was around. She was always ready to eat. It was a miracle she didn't weigh two hundred pounds. It must be her metabolism. He noticed that despite the warm May weather, she was still wearing her leather jacket. She had probably been out joyriding since she got out of class. That explained why she missed the three o'clock business slowdown. Give her a choice between food and a beautiful afternoon for a change, the wind in her face won every time.

"Where have you been?" Cooper wasn't about to let her off the hook that easily.

"Getting off in one of the park bathrooms," she replied. 'you know I can't go long without sex. I have to find it somewhere, and there is always someone hanging out in the park, looking for a quickie."

Thumper let loose a short barking laugh that turned into a gurgling strangle noise and grabbed for a bottle of water. He had just taken a bite of the hot pizza and was struggling to force the sticky gob down his throat.

Cooper took one look at Thumper's bright red face before bursting into laughter. One of these days he would learn not to give Andi an opening like that, she was sure to take it.

"You can tell you're straight, any gay guy would know you have to blow then swallow," he remarked, patting him on the back to help.

Watching Thumper struggle to regain his composure reminded Andi of how much she treasured her two crazy friends. The sound of her name being called from the front of the restaurant drew her attention. Standing at the front of the room was the shy girl from English Lit, her chatterbox friend, and Kim, the red-haired bitch from her Medical Lab program. Kim was doing her best to pretend she didn't exist, but the other two girls seemed happy to find her working there.

"Who's your friends," Thumper eyed the strange girls, trying to decide if they were gay or straight. With this group, it was often hard to tell. Neither was his type, but he had learned early on that some of the sexiest women he knew had been frumpy nerds in their teens and early twenties.

"We just met a couple of months ago. They are in my English lit class. I mentioned I worked at the Pizzeria and they just showed up. Kim of course, you know already."

"So, you didn't invite them? They are simply customers? That might explain why Cooper is being so smooth." He grinned as Cooper showed the girls to an open booth, passed out menus, and took their drink order. He was smiling and flirting with the two obviously stricken girls. For the briefest split second, she thought about taking over the table, but realized the tiny bit of satisfaction she would get out of screwing up their order would not offset the amount of work it would require.

She had to hide a grin. Kelsie was chewing on the ends of her hair like she used to do in class whenever she was nervous. Joanna was pale as a ghost and looked like she would drop into a faint if Cooper bothered to look her way. Coop knew he was a hunk and he was turning on the charm. With his face and golden blonde curls, he looked like something off the cover of the latest teen fan mag.

Cooper knew how to play the game, so she sat back and enjoyed the final few minutes of free time. This way she could avoid Kim and give the odd couple a chance to be flattered by a cute guy that was way out of their usual circle. They didn't need to know he was gay. It would break their hearts to know all that flirting was an act to increase the size of his tip.

She finished off the last of the Mongolian Beef and Black Pepper Chicken, stole the last few bites of Thumpers egg roll and debated whether she had time to order a cheesesteak sandwich. Deciding it would take too long, she resigned herself to what she'd managed to glean from her friend's plates.

"You going to hang around for a while?" She realized it was already a few minutes later than she thought, grabbed her apron and slid toward the edge of the booth.

Thumper shook his head no. "Got a date. Some of us have a real-life, with real people, not imaginary friends in park bathroom stalls."

"Screw you," she said, then blew him a kiss. Thumper was only teasing but his comment was right on target. Since Katie, she had been avoiding any kind of relationship, preferring unencumbered hookups with women she met in the clubs or online. The online dates had been Cooper's idea, but so far, none of them had clicked. Of course, she still had hope. In the meanwhile, there were bills to pay. She needed to get to work. "Have a good time…but not too good. I'm certain you mother things I'm leading you down the path to hell."

"Hell? I passed the point of no return a long time ago. I think she's hoping you will rub off on me and save me from certain doom. Don't work too hard. See you tomorrow."

She was whistling as she cleared the table.

***

Finally, Andi thought as the last couple paid their check an exited the pizza parlor. It had been a crazy day and she had no regrets about shutting down the Pizza Parlor for the night before the regular closing time. The day had been a record series of mishaps guaranteed to make Murphy proud. Between the night in jail that made them late for work, the delivery truck not showing up until after the lunch rush was over, and then the water pipe breaking, that forced them to shut down the street so that no one could reach the building even if they had water to operate. It had been a crazy string of unusual events. Misty, usually a stickler for schedules, had sent everyone else home at four-thirty and had eagerly taken off for the evening. The baby was due in six weeks, so she saw an opportunity to prop her feet up and stretch out on the couch with a good book as an unexpected treat. Andi couldn't imagine how difficult it must be running a restaurant and being pregnant at the same time must be. At least Marco would be back home from his National Guard month of service in ten days.

Andi had stuck around with Jose, doing the kind of deep cleaning that wasn't possible during the usual operational hours. There had been enough water left in the pipes to fill the mop bucket and the carpet cleaner, and she had given both her full attention. Jose had concentrated on the kitchen, which was always clean; now it was spotless. Then she had helped him scrub out the walk-in cooler. Finally, they both began the routine prep work needed to open the restaurant the next day.

Andi always loved closing the restaurant at the end

of the day, when she could finish her side work with no pressure. Tonight, as she finished up the routine tasks, her inner demon really wanted Dawn to spontaneously appear at the door while the restaurant was empty. She had a work fantasy that involved her petite girlfriend, a can of whipped cream and a kitchen prep counter, and she often let that daydream carry her through the last hour of her shift. Of course, now that the opportunity presented itself, she hadn't heard a word from Dawn all day. Murphy must be laughing as another of his laws came to pass.

With a satisfying click, she flipped the sign on the front door from open to closed and turned out the lights, before making her way to the kitchen. Jose was almost finished shutting down the kitchen for the night. He was wiping down the last counter and getting ready to scrape the griddle. She rattled a few keys to let him know where she was going, and then entered the cold storage room from the kitchen, leaving the door open behind her. It still had the freshly cleaned baking soda smell from when they had scrubbed it out earlier. Once the water came back on and the road re-opened, they had opened the restaurant for business but had only sold a few takeout pies. There had been no reason to call Misty back in. She was certain the extremely pregnant woman was delighted to enjoy a rare night off.

Sometime during the last hour, Jose had made the pizza dough and set it inside the cooler for tomorrows lunch rush. She made a quick inventory of what might be needed for tomorrow and made a mental note to call Misty to tell her to pick up fresh bell pepper and mushrooms on way in. Jose had tossed the ones he'd sliced this morning because they tended to go bad quickly once they were cut. No one was willing to risk the restaurant getting a bad writeup to save a couple of dollars.

Andi smiled as she passed back into the main dining room. There was no need to run a vacuum over the freshly cleaned carpet, but it wouldn't hurt to get the spot in front of the counter. Once that was done, she was finished for the evening. There was a bulb out in the window display that needed to be replaced. She'd look in the supply closet while getting the vacuum, but she didn't remember seeing any of the small bulbs earlier.

"Seriously?" She muttered, passing shelves of cleaning supplies to find the vacuum missing from its usual spot. Someone had left it somewhere other than the storage closet again. Cooper was the chief offender, but Monday was his day off and he hadn't been around all day. Now that she thought about it, he hadn't come by the restaurant either. He was probably still catching up on the sleep they missed while incarcerated. If Cooper was the culprit; she had a good idea where to find it. Sure enough, it was sitting in the small closet beside the bathrooms.

Less than fifteen minutes later she was ready to lock up for the night. Jose called out from the kitchen that he was taking off, so she grabbed her leather jacket and headed toward the back door. She would stop by the bank and make the deposit on the way home. The bank night deposit drop was directly across the street from the dispatch room of the local police department, so she wasn't uncomfortable about carrying cash. One of the deputies, James, made it a point to swing through the area every night on his regular patrol route and that was common knowledge around town. Theft had never been an issue.

With the bank bag in her waistband and the key in hand, she used the other to arm the alarm system.

The restaurants' back door opened into a quiet alley lined by loading zones for all the shops on the block. Even though there were occasionally a few scavengers digging through the dumpsters, the cold weather had sent them all into some kind of shelter. She fought with the heavy metal back door, wrestling it into submission. Once it clicked shut, and after a few extra pushes and pulls on the handle, she was sure it wouldn't open until Misty unlocked it in the morning.

Her bike was parked outside the back door, under the streetlight, only a few steps from the door. Walking carefully so she wouldn't slide on the ice, she made her way down the steps and around the loading dock.

"Damn, damn, damn!" Some son of a flea-infested bitch had slashed both tires. Several times. There was no patching the rubber. The bike was not going anywhere until she bought new ones. She caught a brief glance of the taillights of Jose's truck just before he turned the corner and sighed. There was nobody around to offer her a lift home, and there was nowhere to get tires at that time of night.

She immediately dialed Cooper, swearing silently as the phone went to voice mail and the recording that confirmed he hadn't emptied his full mailbox came on. Praying he was just screening his calls, she hung up and waited for him to call her back. No such luck.

Of course, it would happen when Thumper was out of town; and there was no way she would ask Misty to come back out tonight.

Resigning herself to walking home she pulled a chain and lock from her saddlebag to make sure the bike was not stolen before morning—then she tried calling Cooper once more, hoping he would be paying attention to his phone. No answer. He was God knows where.

With no other option, she resigned herself to finding her own way home. At least she had her gloves in her jacket pocket.

A quick glance at her phone proved her timing was perfect. If she started walking now, the bus would be approaching the stop within minutes of her arrival. She reached for her wallet to make sure she had the right change, only to realize the only thing in her pocket was her keys. The wallet was lying on the nightstand at home, where she'd dropped it while reading the payment arrangements she'd made on her fine. Five hundred damn dollars for playing in a fucking fountain. And Dawn got to walk with a warning.

Her boots kicked through the slushy ice as she stomped her way toward the end of the alley. She was not looking forward to the long walk to her apartment, her teeth were already chattering, her riding boots were not waterproof, and even though her jacket was, she was wearing a thin tee shirt and black nylon pants that did nothing to keep the cold away. Life was just perfect.

Headlights signaled someone turning into the alley from the far end and she waved her hand, hoping it was James making his routine checks. With luck, he wouldn't be busy, and she could finagle a ride home. It was too dark to see what kind of car it was, but it stopped behind the first business and someone with a flashlight got out and walked toward the back of the building. That was a

good sign. Someone looking to break in would not be using a flashlight.

Slush slid underfoot as she began to walk carefully toward the car idling at the end of the alley. She hadn't made it more than a few steps before she thought she heard ice crunch nearby. She turned toward the sound. Nothing

Feeling slightly paranoid and even sillier for worry-ing, she began walking. The sound came again, this time it seemed closer. As she turned, she felt something heavy thud against the back of her head, followed by a sharp burst of pain. Her vision blurred. She threw out her arms trying to break her fall. There was a soft crack, followed by intense pain as she hit the ground. Someone laughed, and she caught movement from the corner of her eye. Then everything went dark.

***

"Andrea! Can you hear me? ---Andi? ---Andi? I need you to open your eyes."

She cracked her eyes and winced at the bright light. "Move that flashlight. It's giving me a headache."

"I doubt it's the flashlight. You took quite a wallop. At least they only hit you one time."

"Yeah, because they spotted you; I'm sure. Help me up."

"Lie still and let me check you out. Do you hurt anywhere else?

"Everything hurts," she moaned. "My head feels like it's about to explode." Her hand came away bloody when she reached back to touch the tender area. " Fuck! I'm bleeding!" Strong hands held her down as she struggled to sit up.

"No. Just stay where you are. You might have a con-cussion."

She figured she was lying in the back seat of James Patrol car. He had rolled up a sweatshirt and placed it under her head. " How long was I out?"

"Not long, a minute or two. You never really lost total consciousness. It was more semiconscious. Do you remember what happened?"

"Kinda. I was really pissed about some ass wipe slashing my tires. I figured it was some kid that was mad because we closed early, and they couldn't get a pizza. After I locked up the bike and decided to start walking; I saw you pull in and stop. I remember turning around and walking toward your car. That's about it."

"Yeah. All I could see were two shadows. Then one fell down and the other took off. I stopped to check on the one on the ground, found you and got you into the back of the car. By that time the person that hit you was long gone."

"So, no way to find out who it was? That sucks."

"The bank across the street from that end of the alley has outside cameras. We might get lucky and get a clear look at the face but I'm not holding my breath. People tend to wrap up in the snow, so making identification from a photo is next to impossible. You didn't see anything?"

"Boots. They were wearing designer boots. The real ones, not Wally World knockoffs."

"What makes you say that?"

"I was looking at the same ones in Neiman Marcus at the mall last week. They cost over five grand. Hand-tooled leather with crystal embroidery."

"Maybe we should get that bump checked out. I think you might have been hit harder than I thought."

"No. No hospital. Seriously, I'm okay. I think it was a woman that hit me."

"A woman in designer boots that cost more than two months' salary. In the muddy slush. In a filthy alley. In the middle of the night."

"When you put it that way, it does sound crazy." She squirmed uncomfortably as the ambulance pulled up, lights flashing. He talked to Karen Padgett, the EMT before she took a look at Andi's head.

"You're lucky you are so pig-headed about that pony-tail. It's probably what saved your life. There's a tiny cut, buts it's stopped bleeding. I don't think you need stitches. We can take you in and do an x-ray if you want to go." She paused as her two-way radio squawked. "James. Is there any way you can take care of this. There was a wreck over on the bypass and they are calling for a second ambulance."

"Yeah, sure. You go ahead. I will make sure she gets

home okay."

Andi nodded approval so Karen told the radio dis-patcher she was clear and heading for the auto accident.

"Look, Andi, I can't make you go to the hospital if you don't want to. I tell you what, let me drive you home. You already have a knot on the back of your head and it's going to be sore. Promise me you will get Doc Wallace to look at it in the morning."

"Deal. But I want to ride in the front seat. I never want to be in the back of a squad car again. Just thinking about it makes me shake."

"Heard you made the front page of the weekly '*Who got busted*,'" You can tell me all about it on the way home.

Chapter 19

"Coop! Pass me the OJ. You want any breakfast Dawn?" Andi broke an egg into the bowl of pancake batter and began stirring while she waited for the griddle to heat up. The sausage was draining on paper towels. They really needed to get a coffee pot, the instant was okay, but it fell far short of the fresh brew she got at the restaurant.

"No time. My taxi should be here any minute. I'm supposed to meet the parents for brunch at ten." She kept one eye on the clock on the wall as she gathered her things.

"Then why are we wasting time talking when I could be kissing you goodbye?" She pulled Dawn back into her arms, then lowered her mouth to hers. One kiss led to another, each growing deeper and more erotic. She groaned as Dawn used the tip of her tongue to trace the outline of her mouth before she pulled back and nipped at her bottom lip. Andi now had a different type of breakfast on her mind.

Finally, Dawn pulled away. "You've got to stop that. I really can't be late today. It's almost impossible to get them away from work on a weekday."

Andi couldn't deny that Dawn was always talking about how busy her parents were. There was no argument against that, so she went with cute. "Babe, you know I can never control the things my tongue does when I'm around you."

Dawn snorted. "Cooper is probably getting off watching two girls kiss."

Andi smiled. "I think him watching is getting me off, too." She grabbed Dawn's ass cheeks with both hands and lifted her up for another kiss.

Cooper put his hand over his mouth and yawned. "Oh, the things I am forced to endure for friendship," he said as Andi stepped away to flip the pancakes.

Dawn smiled and pushed her away when she tried for more. "I'll see you in class. My cab should be waiting. I'll see you in class. My cab should be waiting." She slid her arms into her jacket and reached for the door.

Andi stick out her tongue. "I guess it's a quick break-fast and a cold shower for me. See you in class." Her eyes stayed on the petite blonde until the door closed. It had been a crazy night, what with the early delivery scare and Cooper being in the wind. They had been at the hospital for several hours waiting to make sure it was just false labor. Afterward, Dawn had managed to keep her awake for the rest of the night. Now she was wide awake; so instead of heading back to bed and sleeping for a couple of hours, she headed for the bathroom. Fifteen minutes later Andi stepped out of the shower, towel-dried her hair and tied her tresses on the top of her head, covering the soggy mess with a hair scarf. She had just enough time to stack the breakfast dishes in the washer, and then take Chipper out for a quick bathroom break before leaving for class.

She looked for his leash. As usual, it was not hanging on the rack in the kitchen. Theta left two options. Either it was lying somewhere near the coffee table, of Cooper had it. After looking around the living room with no luck she headed for Cooper's room. Sure enough, it was lying on the nightstand beside his bed. She snatched it up, making a mental reminder to add buying an extra leash to the growing list of things she needed to do.

Tipper was waiting by the front door, but he was not waiting quietly. His fur was on end and he was growling. As she approached the door he began barking furiously.

That's strange. I wonder what's got him so riled up? She peered through the tiny viewing circle but there was no one standing by the door. Of course, they could be standing to the side, just outside the range of vision. It was probably the neighbor's cat.

Tipper kept barking and paced back and forth the front door as she squatted to pull her sneakers out from under the coffee table, and then pulled the sneakers on.

"Calm down Tipper..." Andi picked his abandoned leash up from the floor, snapped it to his collar and cracked open the door. The landing outside was empty. Since Tipper was in a hurry to go outside and practically dragging her through the door, she chalked it up to one crazy-ass dog and forgot about it.

Tipper jerked on the lead, looking around as if he expected someone to be standing outside the door. That's when she looked down and spotted the lumpy newspaper-wrapped bundle. They must not have had time to set it on fire. She looked down the front of the building toward the dumpster, catching a glimpse of a leg just before it vanished.

" Come back dipshit! You got something to say, I'm here waiting." No one appeared. No one was in sight in the parking lot outside the apartment. There was no way she was going door to door looking for the pranksters.

Tipper continued barking at the newspaper-wrapped package on the porch. She used her foot to carefully flip it open, expecting to find the usual piles inside. Instead, it was a dog. A dog that looked exactly like Tipper; except this dog was covered in blood from the gash across his throat. Panic took over; her legs began to tremble, and she was having trouble holding onto the leash.

She decided to go back inside and call the police. There was not much they would do about it. They would probably consider it a sick prank, but she wanted a report made.

This was not a prank.

This was a threat.

***

Officer Michael Lang shook his head sadly. "You are right, this is a bit more macabre than the average prank we see. The dog looking just like yours was intentional. Andrea, someone does not like you."

"You've known me since middle school. There's a lot of people who do not like me."

He let a brief smile crack before he resumed his neutral, businesslike expression. "I need you to think. Who might dislike you enough to do something like this? Killing a defenseless animal just because it looks like your dog is abnormal behavior. This is one of the signs we were taught to look for in the academy. It might be a dog today, but it could easily escalate into an attack against you."

"No idea. Maybe it was one of Coopers' crazy exes. You know what a Ho he is.

Michael made notes as she spoke. "I doubt this has anything to do with Cooper's taste in men. It's more than likely someone you pissed off at the restaurant. A pissed off teenager. You probably gave them the wrong pizza or something."

"I certainly hope so. If something happened to Tip you would have to reserve me a cell, because I would be hunting them down. They may not be dead when I found them, but I would damn sure make them wish they were."

Mike's face pinked. "I'm gonna pretend I didn't hear you say that."

They both began laughing.

"If you can spare a garbage bag, I will remove the evidence of the crime. Someone may be missing a pet. They will make a report down at animal control just in case."

She watched as Mike pulled on disposable hospital gloves and then gingerly slide the entire bundle into the plastic garbage bag. There was no blood on the stoop. Someone had killed the animal somewhere else and then carried it to her apartment. It was possible the figure by the dumpster had been the one, but it was also possible that was simply a tenant tossing out their garbage. Either way, it was not enough info for them to waste time or money investigating.

"You can pick up a copy of the report in a few hours. My gut feeling is someone is sending you a message. Unfortunately, there is no way to know what that message is. Unless they stepped in one of Tipper's fertilizer deposits. But I'm sure if that was if, they would have knocked on the door and told you about it."

The radio on his collar squawked and he muttered some numbers. "Got a domestic call. I need to take off. I wouldn't worry too much about it. Tipper would tear them apart if they tried to grab him. Got to run."

" Hope so. Later." She waved by and went back inside, shutting and locking the door behind her. It was better to be safe than sorry.

Lately, a lot of little things were bothering her. The truth was, she was aggravated with her life. Dating Dawn had turned out to be nothing like the perfect relationship she'd imagined. She had built this fantasy in her mind, a fantasy that would be difficult to achieve under perfect conditions. This was far from perfect. She really liked going out with Dawn but keeping her strange hours was starting to get old. Dawn had such quirky rules.

There was the never spend the entire night issue. Dawn would occasionally stay until just before daybreak but never later. Not once had she spent the entire night. Andi was tired of the odd interrupted sleepovers. It was a nauseating emotional roller coaster; make love, snuggle up in bed, sleep until five or so, then she would rush off. She claimed it was because she still lived at home with her parents. They were early risers and expected her to join them for breakfast. She seemed a bit too controlling to her but then again, Andi had been raised by a single parent who worked twelve-hour days. She really had no point of reference.

Dawn also refused to let anyone know they were dating. Especially Kim. Kim might be her ex, but she was also a friend. She claimed it had shattered her emotionally when they broke up. *So, what if she didn't want Kim to be hurt any more than she already was. Fuck her! Don't her feelings matter? And why couldn't they ride to school together?*

Dawn claimed it was easier that way. It didn't feel

easier. It was beginning to drizzle, and the fine mist of icy water felt like needles against bare flesh at fifty miles per hour. If it wasn't for her crazy two-vehicle issue, she could have left the bike at home and ridden in with her. Much warmer that way too. Instead, she donned her leathers and was riding the thin edge of legal as she rushed to reach the campus before the bottom fell out. She prayed she would avoid crossing paths with any of the local police department. Most of them knew her on sight and let her slide by with the occasional extra few miles per hour. There was no way any of them could excuse her running an extra ten to fifteen over the limit… in the rain.

Was Dawn ashamed for anyone to know they were a couple? Andi decided it was time that she talked to her reluctant girlfriend. They needed to lay out some ground rules and clear up a few misconceptions. After school today she was going to have a serious discussion with Dawn. Then she would know whether they had a future or not.

It was too late to go back to sleep, so she decided to head over to the school and get a jump on the essay she needed by Friday. She'd beat the rain but realized she didn't really have anything to do for three hours. The library wasn't open. The laboratory was empty, so she decided to get some studying done. There was a really comfortable chair they used when drawing blood samples, so she dropped down into it and opened her textbook. The soft buzzing of the lab equipment made a pleasant drone in the background…

***

"Wakee, Wakee."

Blinking stupidly in her seat, Andi looked up at the uniformed guard shaking her shoulder. As she shook off the last vestige of sleep she realized that she had been sound asleep slumped over the open textbook with her head lying on the open gym bag, She sat upright in her seat, ran her tongue over her teeth to remove the nasty film and wrinkled her nose up at the stern-looking woman in uniform standing in front of the desk, a shiny silver badge glinting on her chest. *Security… Didi… Damn.*

"You can't sleep in here," Didi said, maybe with too much satisfaction.

"I have literally been the only person in this room for probably a couple hours," Andi coughed, clearing her throat between words as she tried to wake up her sleep-deprived brain.

Obviously, Didi could care less about her opinion. She'd been carrying a chip on her shoulder ever since she'd hit on her in the locker room back in tenth grade. Andi had been polite when she turned her down, but there was not a large lesbian population in their school, so word had spread quickly. That had been five years ago and Didi had never gotten over the humiliation.

She glanced at Didi's crossed arms and caught the time on her watch. Late morning. It had been maybe two or three hours since she'd arrived, although she wasn't sure exactly when she'd fallen asleep. "I'm not bothering anyone."

Didi's expression softened. She turned and motioned with a hand for me to follow. "Some people here are a bit…"

"Like the south end of a mule heading north," I offered, picturing Kim clearly in my mind.

Didi barked a laugh that made me jump as I gathered my things and stood up. "I can think of at least one," she said, rolling her eyes. "…a mule heading north," she repeated, chuckling softly as she led me back into the drab corridor. "In the future, you might want to try the library. They don't like anyone in the classrooms between classes. Just check-in at the info desk. That was they know you are a student and don't call us in."

"Uh, thanks. I'll keep that in mind." She was surprised when Didi didn't disappear as soon as she left the classroom. Instead, she walked along with her as she headed for the student breakroom, chatting aimlessly about people they had known in school. They were almost there when the radio on her shoulder squawked, requesting assistance with a fight. They both walked faster.

The noise level rose as they turned the final corner before the main hall, but the crowd of students gathered nearby made it clear it wasn't due to the usual between class breakroom activity.

"You got to come to see this," Thumper said to Andi as Didi pushed her way into the crowded room. His eyes rested for a few extra seconds on the hot pink bag slung over her shoulder. Dawn's bag. He paused as if waiting for her to say something,

Andi shrugged it off and did not answer his unspoken question, her closely lidded eyes and stark facade making it clear he wouldn't like her answer if she had to give it.

Thumper was smart enough to drop it, moving to the side so she could squeeze in beside him behind the crowd of students filling the main hall outside the break area. They could hear peals of laughter coming from inside.

"So, what's going on," Andi pushing a loose strand of her hair behind her ear. The girl in front of her was shorter than she was but just tall enough that she could not see over her into the break room.

"Catfight."

Andi stood on tiptoe and tried to get a better look. She couldn't make out what was being said but she could hear shouting that cut through the laughter coming from the people watching—and she recognized both voices.

Dawn and Kim. Oh shit! Not today!

'It's hilarious. Kim keeps flip-flopping between screaming and calling her slut and whore, and crying hysterically while begging her forgiveness. Then she started claiming she did not want to lose her to some skuzzy slut. I have absolutely no idea why it matters so much to her. Dawn treats her no better than she treats any of the others; insecure women following her around like a puppy following its mama's teat. They kept it up for about fifteen minutes, then suddenly they went at each other like two cats tied by their tails and thrown over a clothesline. It was…" Thumper's shoulders tensed as he put two and two together and realized who they were fighting over.

As if by magic everyone around them stopped talking and moved to the side, allowing them access to the main breakroom. Others remained frozen where they stood, a small ring of people around Dawn and Kim, who lay on the floor, tangled together by both their entwined legs and their death grips on the other woman's hair. Neither appeared ready to release the other.

Andi wondered how long the two had been twisted

together. From the way the other students were react-
ing to her presence, it was evident that everyone in the
room believed she was involved in whatever the issue was
between the two women.

Someone had notified security, and Didi and Tifton,
a towering man with sandy hair and tense muscles, were
attempting to pry them apart.

Andi decided the best thing for her to do was to
avoid the ring of onlookers, many of whom were using their cell phones to record the event. She was sure it
would be streaming live at this moment. She turned to
leave just as the two guards pulled the women apart.

Kim's bright red lips were stretched into an impossibly thin line and her angry green glare could punch nails
through steel. With her naturally wild red hair knotted
and tangled from the scuffle, and her arms crossed tightly
over her chest to cover up her bare breasts, she looked
like a madwoman from some Irish war drama.

Dawn was equally out of sorts. Like Jack before the
Giant, she stood before the much taller woman with her

green eyes flashing angrily. One of her lips was busted and a trickle of red had rolled down her chin. Her slender hands were balled into tight fists at his sides.

Andi could imagine what was going through her head. The public fight was bad enough, but she was probably furious that the right shoulder of her favorite black jacket was ripped halfway off. She kept pushing it back into place while trying to maintain her belligerent stance.

Andi could see her body shaking from where she stood, whether from shock or anger she couldn't say. Her chest rose and fell with heavy breaths. It would have been incredibly hot, and sexy as hell if she didn't have to think the catfight had something to do with Dawn spending time with her. Obviously, their secret relationship was not as secret as she'd thought. Seconds later that was confirmed.

"Send your bitch away," Kim spat, a wet bloody splotch landing on the ground in front of her. " Tell her, tell her we are engaged. Show her the ring. The ring I put on your finger."

Andi instinctively took a small step toward her,

catching the attention of the security guard holding onto Kim's arms. Didi's eyes quickly signaled how bad a decision that would be, and Andi stopped.

A few of the Instructors were now entering the hall from different corridors to assist. There was no way she was going to get close to her now. Instead, she snapped, "We're not fucking dogs, Kim, and unlike you, no one gives me orders." It was a good effort, but Kim's words had cut to the quick. *Engaged? They were engaged?*

The second officer spoke up. "It's not an order, but I suggest you all move on to your classes unless you would like to join these ladies in the back of the patrol car. I'm sure we have room for a few more." His voice was a harsh growl that rumbled through the room.

A few of the onlookers close to him shrank back. Like ripple around a rock dropped into water, most started to scatter in different directions.

Andi decided to head for the classroom, her presence could not help Dawn and it might make things worse. As she walked away, she realized she was relieved it was all now out in the open. This wasn't how she preferred people to find out about her relationships. But now that the genie was out, it would be impossible to force it back into the bottle. One major problem loomed ahead…now she wasn't so sure it was really a relationship. Either Dawn was a blatant liar, or Kim was. Until she had a chance to find out which it was, she didn't know what to believe.

Dawn did not show up for class. Coincidently, neither did Kim. Her jealousy kicked in and all kinds of imaginary scenarios went through her head. She got the impression from several of the other students that the *not so well-kept secret* of their blossoming relationship was spreading amongst our classmates. No one came right out and asked if something was wrong, but from the expressions of a few faces, they were fighting the impulse to ask her outright. She risked a quick glance at her cellphone when the Professor wasn't looking, but there were no missed texts or calls. Thumper had just managed to slip into his seat without disturbing his lecture after spending an hour in dialysis. Now he was distracted by the class project.

It gave her a chance to think. Unless Dawn was in

jail, it didn't rate her not taking the time to give her a heads up. Since she had been sitting in a patrol car earlier, she decided to give her the benefit of the doubt.

Four hours and two classes later, she still hadn't shown up. Nor had she called or texted. Andi's mood was somber and dark, and the dreary overcast day fit it well. As she pulled the bike out into traffic, a brief smile broke through her depression. At least it had stopped raining. k

***

"So, who pissed in your little red wagon?" Misty always had her own way of putting things that pretty much summed up how Andi was feeling at the time.

"Who the fuck, do you think?" Andi wrapped her apron around her waist and began stacking the red plastic glasses we used for everything except coffee. Days like this made her happy they were unbreakable.

Misty held her tongue after she noticed Andi's blood-shot eyes and the dark circles under them. Andi rarely let anything that happened in the clubs affect her, so whatever it was that had prevented her from sleeping, it was something she felt intensely. She decided to word her answer a bit differently.

"Well, since Cooper has been in a great mood all morning, you two obviously haven't had a fight. Thumper is still at the clinic. That leaves Dawn. What did she do now?"

"Nothing. That's what's wrong. I'm probably jumping to conclusions. It's just…you know how she jumps up and takes off whenever she stays over. Well, this morning she did it again. Supposedly it was to meet her parents for brunch. Instead, I get to school in time for ringside seats to a catfight between my girlfriend and her fiancé."

"Fiancé?" Misty cocked her eyebrow, and Andi smiled as the cartoon owl in Nihm popped into her mind.

"Yeah. That's the way it sounded. Looks like I am the scum of the earth, the sleazy whore on the side."

"Andrea, you are a lot of things, but that's not one of them. It looks like Dawn has some explaining to do."

"I agree. I wanted to talk to her after class, but she never showed. Neither did Kim. I could handle that; it could be a coincidence. But she hasn't called or texted.

My imagination is running wild.

"That's only human. Well... it's normal to feel insecure when a relationship has never been defined. You just need to talk to her. There might be more to it than you overheard. Perhaps the other woman thinks you broke them up. She may not realize you have just begun seeing her. Get the facts and then get some kind of guidelines laid out, seriously. No one needs to feel the way she makes you feel."

Andi nodded her agreement but decided she was going to do a few investigations of her own. The only way she could be certain Dawn was telling the truth, was to know the answer to a question before she asked it.

Chapter 20

The restaurant was just opening when she walked in the next morning. It had been a restless night and Andi was still not ready to face customers. She seriously needed coffee. Lots of coffee. Her apartment lacked, a coffee pot, so she always came in early. Unless she placated her caffeine addiction before her shift started there was no way she could function.

"Ever gonna get a coffeepot?" a deeply accented bass rumbled from the kitchen.

Marco! He was back! Thank Heavens! It made life so much easier with him back home. Now she didn't need to worry about Misty all the time.

"Never! Why bother when I can get better coffee at work?"

She waited as he filled her cup, breathing in the intoxicating aroma of freshly brewed nirvana. Her mind began wandering as she dumped sugar and cream in the steaming brew. Between the break-up and the break-in, she wasn't in the mood for black coffee. She was so caught up in self-degradation she didn't see Cooper come into the restaurant.

As usual, he acted as if nothing was wrong.

"Long time no see stranger," he said sarcastically as he reached for an empty coffee cup.

"The military waits for no man…or baby. I just glad I was able to get my month in before he or she decided to make their appearance. I was just about to join Andrea for coffee. You want some?"

"Of course. Have I ever turned down fresh coffee?"

"What the hell, you left without me," Cooper demanded of Andi, plopping down in the seat across from her. "You should have known I would be home before time to leave for work."

Marco and Andi both rolled their eyes.

"You know I'm not one to butt in on your personal life but—" she stopped talking when it became obvious Cooper wasn't paying her any attention. He looked exhausted. It must have been a rough night. Her calls had gone unanswered all weekend. Once she had decided that her break-up with Dawn wasn't that important after all, she had wanted to go out. As usual, Cooper was nowhere to be found. Which of course, meant she was annoyed as hell with him.

"I'm perfectly happy the way things are. But thank you, for caring. Kiss, kiss." He took his empty cup and headed for the kitchen.

She glanced at the clock on the wall, knowing it would show about five minutes before their shift was supposed to start. Cooper was always late to work, and as usual, he slid in just before the restaurant opened for business.

As if on cue Marco yelled at them to flip the sign to 'Open'.

Andi shrugged, not at all sad to be avoiding that conversation. She brought her mug to her lips, swallowing the last of her coffee, wishing she had tome for another cup. Marco made an amazing cup of coffee.

She sighed and placed her mug in the dishwasher

rack and clocked in. Hopefully, the next few hours would pass quickly, and she could get over being irritated at Cooper. She never stayed mad for long and they had a lot to talk about. As the bell above the door jangled, she pasted a smile on her face, grabbed a couple of menus and followed the couple toward a booth. They were regulars and knew exactly what they wanted. She brought them their tea and headed for the kitchen to put in their order.

Dawn was sitting in a booth when she came back from the kitchen.

Andi ignored her, hoping she would take a hint and leave. It was soon evident she had no intention of taking a hint. Finally, she gave up and walked over to the booth, handed her a menu and asked, "Can I take your order?"

"Don't be like this. I need to talk to you." Dawn eyes brimmed with unshed tears,

Andrea wondered if she could cry on demand. She seemed to be an expert at everything else. "I heard everything I needed to hear the other day. Glad you lip went down, it looked awful with Kim's fist in it."

"Let me explain. I want to tell you what happened."

The tears were actually running down her cheeks now.

"The only thing you need to tell me whether you want thin crust or thick with your pizza. Have you decided what you would like, or should I come back?" She thought about tossing her a cloth napkin but figured that might be too cruel. Instead, she stood beside the booth with the pad in her hand, pencil ready.

"Did you mean what you said?" Dawn struggled to keep her voice from cracking.

Andi's face flushes for a moment as she eyes the pale woman before her. "I'm not in the habit of saying things I don't mean."

"So. we are through. It's over?" Dawn was crying now; claiming she did not want to lose what they had together.

Andi had absolutely no idea why it mattered so much to her. She was the one engaged to another woman, not her.

Dawn waited but Andi did not reply. "You didn't answer my question," she snapped, her voice quavering as she fought to regain her composure.

Andi looked at her and forced as much venom as she could into her voice. "Yes"

Dawn crossed her arms and glared defiantly back. "I don't believe you."

What could I say to get the idea through to her? If the facts hadn't worked maybe fiction would, but she couldn't understand why a lie seemed more damaging than the truth. "I'm seeing someone else," she replied, careful to keep her face neutral.

"Someone else?" Dawn's face fell. She paled and her hands were shaking as she reached for Andi's arm.

One day Andi hoped to learn not to engage her mouth before her brain kicked in. Today was not that day.

Dawn's surprise grew into anger and she reacted.

The slap was hard enough to turn her head. She wondered if she would have the outline of her fingers on her face in the morning. Had she made a big mistake? The other woman's viselike fingers were now clamped so tight that her arm was starting to turn hurt. She almost believed Dawn really cared.

"Just go away," Andi snapped.

Instead of the sharp retort she'd expected, Dawn took a step back, voice silent. Her taut face showed a momentary quiver, and then she walked away.

Misty appeared, coming through the swinging doors from the kitchen with two trays of hot pizza for the bar and transferred them to the steam table. When she noticed Andi talking to Dawn, she thought about interrupting but decided it might be best to keep her opinions to herself. Andi seemed to have the situation well in hand.

After Dawn left, her only comment was "Your break ended ten minutes ago, and I could use some help bussing the tables." She offered her a sympathetic smile and Andi knew she realized how much she was hurting.

"Sorry," Andi responded. She headed to the back to grab a dish bin.

***

The sun was still shining when she finished her shift. Time had flown by, and she hadn't really had a chance to talk to Coop about what had happened. Since she was scheduled to work a split shift today, she needed to decide about what to do with the extra free hours. She didn't want to go back to her apartment and stare at the walls for two or three hours. Instead, she headed over to the public library. She could drop by and pick up the book they were holding for her.

She had reserved the textbook two months earlier, after finding out she would need it for a class and that it cost over three hundred dollars. For less than twenty, she could photocopy the text. Another benefit, there was a small coffee shop on the first floor that served fresh bear claws and she was craving something sweet. The knowledge that Dawn would never be seen in a public library made it even more attractive.

Andi stopped, grabbing a cup of coffee before adding in the requisite three spoons of sugar and cream, and snatched up the last bear claw. Then she headed around the corner to the study area on the main level. She never had anything to study, but she loved scoping out the other women. She found an empty area near the windows, thumbed open her phone, and then her reading app. It had been a while since she'd read any of the books she'd downloaded. She debated between the latest serial romance or a fantasy world of fairies and dragons. Neither was particularly appealing. Nor were any of the women she'd spotted. After deciding she needed to give it up, she grabbed the book from the library and headed to the print shop. The clerk promised to make the copies and have it ready in the morning, so she headed back to the restaurant, hoping that Cooper would be up to a heart to heart before it was time to work the dinner crowd.

The smirk on his face said it all as she opened the door. He motioned with his eyes toward the redhead sitting alone at the takeout table by the window.

Andi almost didn't recognize her. Kim's kinky red hair was pulled back and tied with a leather cord, making it look like she had a giant pompom on the back of her head. Instead of the usual greens, she was dressed entirely in black; like some Goth kids' version of the Queen of Hell.

Cooper was nothing if not predictable. He knew that Kim was the last person in the world she wanted to see. At least Dawn wasn't with her.

Realizing she would be watching her, Andi strolled

nonchalantly across the main dining room and passed through the swinging doors to the kitchen. Once indie, she grabbed cooper by the arm, and pushed him into the storage closet, pulling the door shut behind them.

"What the hell! I can't believe you were laughing and talking with her. You know she just came to rub it in. Did you see how she looked at me? If she had her way, they would be holding my wake before the weekend."

"Calm down. Yeah. She's a bitch. But she buys a lot of pizza and this is still my family's business. I kinda feel sorry for her; she was the one that got cheated on. It hurts."

"It still sux." Andi hated to admit it, but Cooper was right. In the greater scheme of things, she was the bad guy. Not Kim. She almost felt bad for her as she finished her meal, paid her check and headed out the door.

Copper didn't make it any easier. "I wouldn't turn my back on her anytime soon." Cooper laughed out loud as Andi restocked the to-go cups.

Andi wasn't surprised at her attitude. She'd brought a lot of it on herself.

"Maybe you should avoid going out alone at night," he added as she stopped and looked back through the main window.

Andi wanted to be surprised, or even upset by what he had just said, but honestly, it kinda made sense. Kim had made her feelings crystal clear. It was war, whether she liked it not.

"The best thing you can do is not to have anything to do with her or Dawn."

"We don't have any classes together this coming semester, so that should be easy to do. We don't go to the same clubs. Dawn stopped calling... finally. I think she got the message and will leave me alone."

"Why in the hell didn't you tell me that someone broke into the apartment?" Cooper looked pissed as he slid onto the bench next to her. He stretched his feet, trying to release some of the tension built up after standing on them all day.

Damn, He's been talking to Thumper ...or maybe Misty. She shrugged. "Honestly, I didn't want to talk about it. I am not even sure someone did. Nothing was out of place,

Well almost nothing."

"I live there too, you know."

"It's not a big deal, I changed the locks and they didn't take anything," she said, making light of the situation even though it still gave her the creeps to be there alone.

"You still should have told me. And if you changed the locks, how does my key…." Cooper sighed. He was always losing his keys. Andi looked tired and he was pretty sure it wasn't because she had lost sleep worrying about him.

"Seriously Andi, you look like shit. How late were you up last night?"

Andi laughed, knowing she could easily reverse the question to focus on him. He looked like he might collapse at any minute.

"I think I got about an hour or two this morning before my alarm went off. How do guys do it?"

"For starters, it doesn't take me nearly as long to get ready, that guarantees me an extra hour or two," he smirked. "And I was in bed before midnight."

"And that is supposed to make me think you got some rest? You need to come home more often. Lately, you look like you have been sleeping in your clothes and wearing them again the next day."

"Hey, don't knock it, it worked back in high school."

She wasn't sure if he was serious or not. Finally, she shot him a look that said she hoped he was joking. She was never sure. They had been friends forever; Cooper had become the annoying little brother she never had. She was a tomboy, and he preferred to play dress-up with dolls. By seventh grade, she realized that she was more interested in kissing girls than being one of the boys. Less than a week later Cooper admitted the idea of kissing a girl made him queasy, but he thought Dylan, the boy on TV was hot. After officially coming out in Middle School they had faced the derision and public taunts together.

In High School, everything changed. Being different became the rage. Everyone thought it was awesome to be lesbian, queer or bi and wanted to hang with them. For a while, they were popular. Over the years everyone drifted apart, going to work or to college. A few joined the military. Now they limited their circle to a select few and were much happier.

About a month after graduation they had moved into their apartment. He was an ideal roommate…most of the time. Lately not so much. Copper had become a little too wild lately.

It had started out innocently enough.

Cooper had been crushing on Donovan since the first time he waltzed into Marco's Pizza parlor. His infatuation took over his life. He would drag her to the local bars hoping to spot him. If he did, he would insist we sit back by the wall so that he could watch him but never approached him. After a while he had friended him online, joining in a multi-player shooter games with him even though he had no idea how to play. Then he spent an entire weekend holed up in the apartment trying to get up to speed on the game he was playing. For months all his free time was wasted playing online with Donovan. She finally resorted to bribery; luring him away with shopping or food.

His scheme must have worked, a few months later he

was dating Donovan. Surprisingly neither was interested in playing video games. That relationship hadn't lasted but another had quickly taken his place.

Until now. Now he was still gone almost every night, but he was being secretive about the new man in his life, and this worried her.

"Earth to Andi!" Cooper snapped his fingers in front of her face, his fingers coming way too close to her nose for comfort.

"Sorry, guess I zoned out." I didn't want him to know I was worried about him.

Cooper shrugged but let it go.

By the end of the shift, she was looking for any excuse to sit down. Marco offered her a couple of aspirin, but she waved it away. "Think I'll wait until I can eat something. They usually go away on their own."

"Suit yourself. See you tomorrow." She stopped and took a look at the dark clouds gathering over the lake. It was going to be close. Scraping any thought of hitting the drive-thru on the way home, she gunned the bike and made a dash for home.

The fresh air helped. Andi rolled into her parking space and cut the motor, grateful to have beaten the rain to her apartment. At this time of year, you never know what the weather would be like. Lately, her timing had sucked, and she ended up getting soaked.

Suddenly nervous, she looked around, wondering if she was about to find another dead dog on her porch. Everything looked normal. Someone was working on his truck in the parking lot in front of the next apartment building in the complex. Another man was walking down the sidewalk after dumping empty boxes into the dumpster, but other than that, there was no one in sight. So why did she feel like someone was watching her? The hairs on her arm stood on end, and her hands trembled.

Stop being such a wussy. Removing her helmet, she searched through her pocket for her keys and then moved to open the side case. To keep calm, she held her breath and counted as she searched through her keys, looking for the right one. Hands shaking, she pushed it into the door lock, only to discover she'd grabbed the wrong key again. She quickly switched keys and slipped it inside.

After three tries, she managed to open the door. Stepping into the apartment, she immediately closed the door, slid on the backup chain and threw the deadbolt before running to the kitchen to make sure the back door was secure. Like a frightened child, she turned every light in the apartment on and checked under the beds and in every closet. It was only after she was berating herself for her fears that she realized if someone had been in the apartment, she had just locked herself in with them. On the way in, she had tossed her coat on the couch and her cell phone was in the pocket. She immediately got it out and held it ready in her hand, just in case. Tipper yawned, stood up and circled around in his bed like a cat, stretched his back and collapsed. Seconds later he was asleep.

Andi felt like an idiot. If there had been anything to worry about Tipper would have been barking. There was no one in her apartment. But that didn't mean no one was watching her.

Since getting smacked in the alley last week she'd become more observant. Now she was certain someone was following her. There has been a battered blue Ford van parked at the convenience store on the corner when she passed. That same van had been in front of the restaurant the night before last. She remembered the roadrunner decal on the back glass. It had pulled in behind her as she passed the store and followed her until she turned off into the complex. Unfortunately, she hadn't been able to get a look at the driver. It could be a coincidence; simply someone who lived in the neighborhood. But she could not afford to take anything for granted.

After a quick shower, she snuggled up on the couch in her favorite pajamas and the blue Sherpa throw Cooper had bought for her last birthday to watch a movie. Cooper must have stopped in long enough to change clothes; she'd found his leftover Kung Pao and fried rice in the fridge. That, plus a chocolate pudding cup had satisfied her immediate hunger, but she just couldn't focus on the movie. Switching the television to a music channel, she opened her laptop and began browsing through her messages. After a few minutes, she gave up pretending and opened her profile, unsurprised to find out Dawn had blocked her. It was the same on all of her social media accounts. She figured big Red had something to do with that, not wanting competition from the ex. She grinned and signed out, then signed in with a fake profile she'd established when Katie had disappeared. She was surprised to see that Dawn had not been posting. According to her main profile, the last post she'd made was the night before the fight in the breakroom.

Evidently, she'd gone dark. That surprised her. Dawn was a media hog; it was hard to imagine her going without posting. Too bad she could not close down the memories as easily as she closed the computer application.

She crawled into bed, exhausted. Between the stress from the breakup and the late nights watching movies, she had no energy. Against all rationality, she did a quick mental review of the apartment, reassured herself that she had locked the deadbolt and gave herself permission to relax. Tomorrow would be there all too soon.

An hour later she decided there was no way she was going to sleep. She flopped back against the headboard and pulled the latest stack of books. An avid reader, Cooper had drug them in for her to rifle through. She hadn't had much of an opportunity to relax with a book while dating Dawn, Now, it seemed like time was all she had.

The first cover brought a smile; remembering her conversation with Cooper at work about judging a book by its cover. As typical of Cooper, the heroes were male, cute, heavily muscled and dressed in skimpy outfits that barely cover their groins. Not that there was anything wrong with the idea of two handsome male strangers who fall in love while fighting the forces of evil. If you were into that kind of thing. It did absolutely nothing for her. Sighing, she put it aside and picked up the next book--- a mystery. Fifteen pages later she laid it back on the night table.

Everything Cooper had said about Dawn was true. When she made a fool out of her in front of everyone she cared about, she'd wished the floor would open up and swallow her. Now she realized how ridiculous that thought had been. Dwelling on her misfortune would not solve the problem. True, she had wished Dawn gone from her life; gone so that she would not have to see her face again. Now that she had dropped out of school, she wondered if anything she had said had anything to do with it.

Regardless of her own lies, Dawn blamed her for the fight with Kim. The sad part is that she kinda missed seeing her crooked smile and the way she would suddenly burst out in a braying laugh at the very worst possible moment.

Breaking up with Dawn had felt like someone had dropped an emotional bomb on her. Her psyche was blown apart and it would be a while before she could put it back together again. Even if she could find a way to overlook what had happened between them, there was no going back to what they once had. Her parents had proved you can't go backward, and it had almost destroyed them both. The relationship was never the same; it was impossible to get that feeling on innocent abandon again.

No. They could try to work things out, but in her heart, she knew there wasn't chance in hell they would ever get back together. It was time for her to come to terms with reality and move on. She needed to build her wall so high no one could ever hurt her again, not family, no friends, no one. She enjoyed being a player, and for now, that would be enough.

She sighed and picked the book back up; tapped her fingers along the spine absently, turning the book in her hands before she flipped it open to page one and began to read. She had never read a book by Agatha Christie, but she was a famous writer, so she expected it to be a good read. An hour later she had no idea what she had just read.

Cooper was right. It pissed her off to admit it, but she was not in love with Dawn. She was in love with the idea of being in love. She tried to force herself into a rela-tionship because she wanted that kind of life, the one her parents had before her dad had cheated and destroyed the fairytale. Until she came to grips with her own messed up emotions and accepted the idea that she was just as much to blame for what happened as Katie was, she would never be able to move on.

She flipped the book back open and began to read again. Several chapters into the book she must have fallen asleep.

***

Andi woke up suddenly, gasping and looking around. After a few seconds, her heart stopped pounding in her chest, and she was able to catch her breath. It had been a strange nightmare. She had dreamed about the first time she had been to Faces. The dream had started out exactly the same as she remembered the date...

She had scribbled a note for Dawn and pinned it to the front door before heading to wake a quick shower. The impromptu make-out episode outside the auto shop had been on her mind all afternoon and she was looking forward to seeing how close to her fantasy she could get.

Dawn was waiting when Andi finished her shower. She looked perfectly at ease, with one pillow behind her neck and her arm propped atop the other. "You look great," she said, noticing just how the soft black cashmere sweater followed the curves of her breasts. Everyone in the club will be hitting on you."

Andi raised her eyebrows and grinned mischievously

at her comment. She hardly ever wore black, not need-ing anything to help slim her athletic figure. Her breasts were about perfect for her body and she had a flat, but firm, stomach with slender almost boyish hips. The late fall days were still warm, but once the sun went down for the night, the temperature would drop dramatically. The sweater was her only concession to feminine fashion, and it looked great with her faded denim jeans.

"You look pretty damn hot yourself. You sure you don't want to stay home and cuddle up with a good movie?"

"Nope. Tonight, I plan on showing you off. It's just going to be you and me."

"You and me and about two hundred strangers. You know Faces is going to be packed. I didn't tell Cooper we are going to a new club. He'd be dying to tag along."

"Cooper wouldn't like Faces. I don't think I've ever seen a man inside the doors."

"That wouldn't stop Coop."

Dawn's face fell. "Are you going to tell him where you are?"

"No, I won't." I gripped her wrist. "But I really think I should. He's my best friend." Her phone was buzzing again, so she took a deep breath and answered the call. "Hi, Coop. What's up?"

"You tell me. You ducking me or something?" His voice had that peculiar whine he got when he was peeved.

"Nope. Was in the shower. Dawn heard the phone ring, but I had a head full of suds at the time. I knew you would call back." She managed to say it without skipping a beat, although her heart hammered in her chest. Could he tell?

"So, what's up? "

"Nothing much. We are heading out to grab a bite, then I hope to convince Dawn to shinny out of her dress and allow me to ravish that luscious body." That much was true. She simply left out the part about driving to the other side of Atlanta to check out the club.

Dawn was right, Faces would bore him silly since the only men in the bar were transitioning to women. Drag turned him off since he liked being the center of attention. His own preference ran to slim fitness model types.

Was she wrong to want one night out without him? Apparently, her efforts to discourage him worked.

"I guess I'm gonna go by and visit Thumper. Maybe he will feel up to shooting some pool. Pay nice, don't break your new toy."

She sighed as Cooper hung up. A bored Cooper was a dangerous Cooper. He got into trouble during the hour she was in class. Her being in college gave him the perfect excuse to hang out in the break area. He took advantage of the time; his social circle was expanding rapidly. There was always a party going on somewhere, and Cooper loved to crash them.

Andi knew he preferred her as his wingman, but Thumper had often been drafted into filling the vacancy her dating Dawn created. Without any set boundaries, the two tended to take things to the extreme. Too much alcohol. Too much pot. And lately, too many late nights with strangers that turned into breakfast in bed and occasionally dinner the next day.

Not that she had much room to talk, until Dawn came along, she was usually the one urging the others to go out. So why was she feeling guilty?

The drive to the Southside of Atlanta took a little over an hour. Faces had been built in the huge, auditorium sized basement of a once-famous hotel near the airport. Over the years the neighborhood had deteriorated as airport construction had relocated the entrance and exit to the airport away from Interstate 75. Newer, modern hotels had been erected near the new egress, and the only other business, an auto factory, had been moved to Mexico. With no customers to support it, the hotel had been closed and scheduled for demolition. The Thompson Brothers had swooped in at the last minute and saved the building, converting all but the basement and the first floor into apartments. A mini-mall, a health club, and a steakhouse now occupied the first floor and Faces had the Basement.

The bar was like something out of an old Eighties Disco movie, complete with hot wings, an outdated jukebox playing Burning down the House, and two the middle-aged bartenders doing tricks while pouring drinks. Not that they needed any help keeping my attention.

The middle-aged bartender tank top sat dangerously low, allowing more than a glimpse of well-rounded breasts inside a hot pink pushup bra. I could only hope to look that good at forty.

"You have got to be fuckin' kidding me!"

Andi turned to see what had gotten Dawn so agitated. Sitting at the bar talking to the bartender was one of the girls from her English lit class. Miko or something like that. "You know she was Gay?"

"I had no idea. Maybe she lives in the building and it's just convenient. Or maybe it isn't," she added as a tall, Amazonian type pulled the tiny Asian girl into her arms. Both women were giggling as they made their way to an empty two-top on the opposite side of the dance floor from the long mahogany bar. The waitress left to get their order and Andi relaxed, looking forward to enjoying her first time in an entirely lesbian club.

That's when things went wonky. She had gone to the bathroom. When she returned, Dawn had been dancing with Kim. And everyone was staring at her. Then one woman had pushed her. Then two others. Before long, she was being shoved from person to person around the club. When the big dyke with Miko had pushed her, she had fallen backward through a plate glass window. It felt like she was falling from a great height. Right before she hit the ground, she had screamed and woke up.

***

Andi sat upright in bed. She could feel her heart racing, her hands were sweaty, and it was hard to catch her breath. In the back of her mind, she could head a faint buzzing. It took her a few seconds to realize it was her cellphone vibrating on the nightstand. She snatched it up and looked at the screen. It was from Cooper. She hit redial. "What now?" she snapped.

She could hear him breathing for a couple of seconds, but he did not speak. Assaulted by guilt, she sat up on the bed and answered again in a more cordial tone.

"Hi, Cooper. Sorry about bitch mode." She took a deep breath, trying to let go of the frustration churning inside.

"I heard you scream. Wanted to make sure you were alright."

Heard me scream? He was calling from his bedroom. The bedroom on the other side of her wall.

"How long have you been home?"

"What time is it?"

"Two-thirty-four."

"What day?"

"Monday, no make that Tuesday. It's after midnight."

"Then I guess about 10 hours. I wasn't feeling good,
so went to sleep. I guess hearing you scream woke me
up."

Ten hours? That meant--- You mean you have been
here all day?"

"Yeah, I called Misty and told her I wasn't feeling
good. Are you okay?

"Yeah. It was just a bad dream."

"Still haven't heard from her, huh?"

"Not a word."

"Doesn't that imply Kim was more than a friend?"
he says.

"Discussing my ex-lover's secret fiancé with you
seems strange," she snaps, moving her hand toward the

end call button.

"Luv ya."

" Love you. Nite." The phone went dead.

Chapter 21

Andi maneuvered her bike around the group of teenagers dancing between the two parked cars just inside the Park entrance and looked for Thumper's black Chevy pickup. There were several black trucks in sight, but none of them was his extended cab 4X4.

Hmmm. No Thumper. Guess he got caught in traffic, too. There had been a minor collision about two blacks away and traffic was snarled in both directions.

She had no idea why Thumper wanted to meet her in the park to study for their chapter test. Usually, they made it a point to meet at Billings or one of the other restaurants in the area if he didn't drop by the apartment. He said he had business to attend to today at the park, so it would be easier to meet her there.

One place was as good as another to Andi. This test was a make or break requirement for the class. Flunk this one and it was all over. No more financial aid and that meant no money for school. Thumper insisted she would pass it with flying colors. Then why was her stomach doing loop-de-loops? She wasn't quite as confident as he was about her chance of passing. She picked a likely spot on a grassy knoll that allowed her to see the entrance, spread out a quilt, and made herself comfortable. The weather was perfect, 82 degrees, a gentle breeze and not a rain cloud in sight.

Dealing with Thumpers' idiosyncrasies could be trying. His mother, finding herself acting as both mom and dad after his daddy passed away in a motorcycle accident, had pushed him into situations requiring experimentation and imagination. Thumper was a change of life baby, born when she was in her forties. Andi had found this tidbit of information something of a surprise since Professor Anderson seemed so strait-laced in class. She taught him to think outside the box, to take chances and learn from his mistakes. Also. how to accept responsibility for his bad choices.

After three months in her classroom, Andi was

jealous of the family life he described. Not that his life was perfect. She could not imagine going to bed at night wondering if she was going to wake up the next morning. It had to be hell.

She glanced at her watch, wondering, where was he? They had arranged to meet at two o'clock and it was going on three. Thumper had never stood her up before, it wasn't like him. He would always text if there was a reason he would be delayed. It must be something he could not control, like traffic. At least it happened on a Sunday; a wreck in rush hour traffic could be impossible to get through. She sat back on her hands, stretching her legs out in front of her. *Too bad I didn't think to bring a pillow.*

Rolling to her side, she propped her head on her backpack and shifted her eyes to a group of bikers gathered at the bottom of the hill below the baseball field. After watching them for a few minutes she decided they were either drunk or crazy; possibly both.

One by one they tried to ride their motorcycles up the hill. One by one they slid back down. Some came rolling down before the bike did. Sometimes the bike rolled over them on the way down. This would have been dangerous enough on dirt bikes. These idiots were riding street bikes. Big ones; designed for long highway runs.

There had to be at least twenty people gathered at the base of the hill egging then on. Many were standing or sitting on the back of pickups; the rest lined both sides of the narrow stretch, cheering or jeering the brave but foolish men as they attempted the climb. A couple of the men had leather vests with club patches on their back, similar to what the men in the bar were wearing in Savannah. She expected to see someone seriously injured at any moment. They were tempting fate, and something bad was going to happen… soon.

She glanced at her watch again, noticing another fifteen minutes had passed. It was well past three and still no message. She began to pack up, gathering her books and folding the quilt. The loud thrum-thrum of a bike motor drew her attention. One of the bikers was riding her way. She kept her eye on the motorcycle, wondering what he wanted.

He pulled up next to her and shut off the bike. "You

Andi?"

"Yes." *How did he know her name?*

"Would have come up earlier, but we all thought Andy was a guy. It just clicked into Coondawg's head when you started packing up that it could be you. Thumper is in the hospital. No reason to wait."

"Uh, thanks." *Was he expecting a tip? Hope not, cause I'm broke.*

He cranked his bike and went back to his friends without another word.

She drove straight to the hospital.

Chapter 22

It was late when she left the hospital. She rode by the restaurant to let Cooper know but he had not shown up for work.

"I can't believe he just left you hanging. Hell, I can't believe he's not answering my call. Thumper is in bad shape. What if he had died. What if you had gone into labor? He's been acting strange lately, well even stranger than normal. He's hiding something and I intend to find out what it is."

"At least he sent a text," Misty said, "the last time he'd pulled a no-show he didn't bother."

"Sure, you don't need me to hang around?"

"No. I've got this, you have enough on your mind. I'm glad Marco is home; it makes things easier. This last week has been dragging by. I'm hoping the doctor has good news for me tomorrow; this baby can't get here soon enough to make me happy. My legs are killing me. "

"Yeah, the baby is due next Tuesday. It looks like the doctor got it really close." Andi was glad she had everything under control. Jose was closing up so Marco could take her home early. Monday's were typically the slowest day of the week.

Jose noticed how she hesitated at the door. "It still bothering you"

"Yeah. I wish I could forget but…"

It's enough to mess with anyone's head. Someone hurt you. Maybe even tried to kill you. You just go one home and study for that test." Even though it was still light outside, he stood at the door and watched as she walked to her bike, put on her helmet and swung aboard the motorcycle.

She waved and hit the ignition switch.

Jose remained at the door until she reached the end of the alley before going back inside the restaurant. Lois would keep an eye on everything and call him if she needed anything.

Turning right at the corner of the alley, Andi braked to avoid the same blue van that had been parked at the end of the alley the previous week. She figured it must belong to someone that works at the Chinese restaurant on the corner. Whoever it was, they could use a few lessons in street etiquette. It had been going the opposite way in traffic.

Her apartment was only ten minutes away from the pizza shop, so she hadn't bothered with a jacket. Now she was regretting that decision. The temperature had dropped at least ten degrees and her body temperature was following it. She scrunched lower to cut as much wind as possible, and ride straight to the apartment. Once she grabbed her jacket, she could decide what she wanted for dinner.

Luckily, the complex had assigned parking, so she didn't have to search for a spot. She rolled into the assigned space, cut the engine and got off the bike. The security light on the pole outside was out. She made a mental note to call maintenance in the morning. The barking of the Jacksons beagle drew her attention and she looked to see what had gotten him so upset. He had been attacked by an irate possum a few weeks earlier, and the wily beast was still raiding the cat food put out by the widow Stone for her dozen or so cats. The door opened and closed, and the barking stopped.

Girl, this is getting ridiculous. No one is following you.

Chipper looked up from his spot on the couch as she passed through the door, yawned, and immediately went right back to sleep. Her jacket was hanging by the door. She started to reach for it, then changed her mind and decided to stay home.

A coke and a can of chili quieted her rumbling stomach. Watching Chipper gulping down his dinner relaxed her, even the tiniest bit of normalcy was welcome. She was not the paranoid type and very few things scared her, so why was making excuses to stay home? No one was stalking her. No one was hiding in the shadows waiting for their chance to attack.

Once she calmed down, she began to wonder where Cooper was? It was a weeknight, so it was doubtful he had gone clubbing. He rarely dated during the week, but it did happen. She quickly typed out a *where r u* text and waited. It only took seconds.

Bad time. Ttul8r.

Typical. Cooper was not much for details. It still made her feel better knowing he was okay.

Since there was no reason to wait up, she headed to bed. She was sick of studying. Last year she could stay up all night partying and grab an hour or two of sleep before going to work. Now she preferred snuggling up with Chipper, turning the sound off on her phone, and zoning out for eight to ten good hours. She could lay around, snoozing under the covers until noon, grab a quick brunch and be ready for her test.

Then the phone rang, and every thought of sleep vanished.

***

Andrea listened to the dial tone on her phone for a few seconds before she realized the call had ended. She collapsed down onto the sofa, covered her face with her hands and let the tears that welled in her eyes fall. She screamed and threw the sofa pillow at the television. Why wasn't Cooper home? She needed to hit someone, anyone, just to make someone understand the pain she was experiencing. Despite the short time she had known

him, Thumper had become an important part of her life.

She ached from the loss with every iota of her being.

There was no way to know how he would take the news.

He could buckle down and be a rock-solid shoulder for

her or wimp out and become a blubbering mess. But

she needed her bestie, there was no way she could get

through the next few days on her own.

She grabbed her phone and began texting SOS over

and over to Cooper's phone.

***

Cooper arrived home within half an hour. She was

still sitting on the floor by the sofa. He took one look at

her face and knew what had happened.

"Thumper?"

She nodded and broke into tears. Cooper dropped to

the floor and pulled her into his arms while they cried.

She had no idea how long they stayed there. Some-

time later Copper had pulled her to her feet. Like a

zombie, she followed him into the bathroom where he

used a wet cloth to remove the salty tears from her face. Her reflection in the mirror was a stranger; eyes red from swollen veins, lids puffy. She took a deep breath, mentally fortifying her resolve and walked into the living room. Her phone was still lying on the sofa where she'd dropped it earlier.

With no hope of relieving the depression they'd slid into upon hearing the news, Andi broke out the liquor leftover from New Years and they got smashed on Black Jack and Tequila. Two hours later they were sprawled out on the living room floor, doing their best to come to grips with the senseless death of their friend.

"I can't believe he's gone," Cooper said. Then he grabbed the tequila bottle from her grasp, took a large swig and began coughing until she slapped him on the back. She could feel him trembling beneath her fingers. When he lifted his eyes, they are wet with unshed tears.

"I know. It doesn't seem fair. He was only twenty-three. What happened to the three-score-ten years my parents were always talking about?"

"Fuck God. No, I didn't mean that. Not really. It just

sucks. Do you really believe he's in a batter place now?"

"Yes. I know people say I shouldn't because I'm gay, but I can't see God holding that against me. Besides, Thumper wasn't gay." She had to believe he was in Heaven because it was the only way she was going to be able to accept the idea that he was gone.

"He was a ho. Hell, he probably smashed more than you and me together."

"Yeah. He was a sexy asshole."

"He was so hot. Just the kind of man I love. You know, I may have had a bit of a crush on him."

"Naw. I would have never guessed." She tried to look serious, but it didn't work.

Cooper tossed a sofa pillow at her head which missed and knocked over a lamp, blowing the bulb and throwing the room into darkness. They both erupted into a round of giggles.

" You think was happy when he died?"

"You mean was his life better because we were in it? Yes. He told me being late for class that day and getting stuck with you as a lab partner was the best thing that could have happened to him."

"Damn."

"Yeah… Damn."

Chapter 23

The morning of the funeral it was raining. The dreary weather matched her feelings completely. Even though it had stopped raining by the time they needed to leave for the funeral, it was still dray and overcast. It was as if heaven knew it wasn't fair that he had died so young.

After the viewing, Abdi walked around the funeral home in a daze. It hadn't seemed real, seeing in lying in the casket that way. Instead of the usual black tee and jeans, they had dressed him in a pale gray suit. His hair had been cut short and someone had removed the earing he wore in his left ear. Gone were the rings he wore on almost every finger and the Turquoise and silver medallion he was so proud of. His face was carefully made up and they had tinted his lips a pale pink that gave him an almost delicate appearance. It was impossible for her mind to reconcile the body lying in the casket with the brusque alpha male she knew Thumper to be. After a few moments, she couldn't bear to remain there. She decided to go outside and see if Cooper had arrived.

She stood alone on the front porch, just outside the misty rain. Through the window, she could hear bits of conversations. One, in particular, made her pay attention. Three teenage girls were talking about her and Cooper.

"…believe that woman had the nerve to show up here. If he hadn't been hanging around people like them, he might not have got AIDs."

"Yeah, I hear his boyfriend is coming, too. I can imagine how that's going to make Aunt Caroline feel. She almost fainted when she heard they were going to be pallbearers. At least she was able to convince his mother to let her take care of the body. Can you imagine him arriving in heaven dressed like a reject from a bad vampire movie?"

"A Lizzy and fag; I'd be afraid God would strike me dead for entering into his house. Let's go see if there is anything to eat in the kitchen."

The other two girls giggled, and the conversation faded as they moved away from the window.

Andi fought back the impulse to go and show the

little twits what a Lizzy could do. Mrs. Anderson deserved better than that. Thumper wouldn't care. In fact, he would have been right beside her. She was just glad Cooper had not been standing there to hear the girl's words. He was just pulling into the parking lot. He parked near the funeral home and walked towards his Andi; whose temper flaring over what she had overheard. *How could they say his mother blamed us? He was exposed to the virus years before they met him. We did nothing except to be his friend. How could anyone think it was our fault?* The idea that she might be to blame, even in some small way, for the death of her friend, was tearing her apart.

Cooper could tell she was upset about something, so he asked her what was wrong.

"I heard these girls talking shit and it upset me. I'll tell you about it on the way home. I took a cab instead of riding my bike, so I'm catching a ride with you."

"Good. I didn't want to be alone anyway. You want to go find a place to sit?" He gestured toward a pew near the back of the chapel.

"Cant. We have to sit with the other pallbearers.

They want us together."

Then I need to make a quick pitstop before we go sit down. She headed toward the back of the building.

On her way back to the chapel after leaving the bathroom, she could hear melody and song lyrics sifting effortlessly through the air. She stopped and peeked into the room, puzzled to find Diane Martin playing the piano. She didn't know the song she was singing, but she sounded great. Diane must sense her presence because she stopped playing, she turned in her direction and motioned her over.

"Thumper picked the song. I hope I can do it justice."

"It's beautiful. I didn't know you two were friends."

"We weren't now, but at one time we were very close. He's my cousin. I'm not sure what happened to the family. My mom and Caroline and Libby were so close. Like the sisters, you see in the movies. Then one day everything changed. They stopped handing together. Mom went back to school, Aunt Caroline became active in the church, and Aunt Libby devoted the rest of her spare time to making the remainder of Thumpers' life the best possible."

" Yeah, I can imagine it wasn't easy on anyone. It's hard to believe something as simple as a tattoo could do so much damage."

"A tattoo?"

"Yeah. Thumper got sick from a bad tattoo."

"I wish that was what happened. Thumper got sick after my uncle molested him. He was ten years old. Aunt Caroline refused to accept what happened even after he pled guilty. He died in prison, of Aids."

"So that's why that girl called Cooper his boyfriend. Thumper was straight. But he claimed it came from a bad tattoo needle."

"Caroline's daughter and her flock of sheep? Yeah, sounds like something they would say. She always blamed Thumper for her daddy going to prison. As if a ten-year-old boy could seduce a grown man. No, Albert was a pedophile. She stopped playing and closed the piano cover. "Looks like it's time for us to go inside. Its times like this I wish I did not play. She smiled, a soft winsome smile that reflected all the pain she was carrying inside. "I'm glad you came. You really made the last months of his life feel normal. I didn't want to let him go, but I am comforted by knowing he died happy."

Cooper was waiting by the door when they walked up. He arched an eyebrow but didn't ask.

People were making their way into the chapel for the service, so we headed for the front.

Neither looked particularly happy as they walked up the aisle toward the pew reserved for pallbearers. The weight of the eyes upon them grew heavier the closer they were to the pew. Andi did her best to relax, and act like she wasn't concerned with the scrutiny, but it was all she could do not to squirm in her seat. The time passed quickly, and before it seemed real, they were carrying the casket toward the small private cemetery next to the church. The rest of the service was a blur, a memory she wanted to tuck safely away for a day in the future when she could look back on her memories and be happy, knowing he no longer suffered.

***

Cooper searched the apartment, not really expecting to find her there after the funeral. He had to work and hated the idea of her being alone. Andi was a creature of habit. When she was upset, she did the same thing. He knew exactly where to find her.

Sure enough, when he reached the top of the ridge, he spotted her motorcycle. In the distance, he could just make out quiet sobbing. The overlook was an enormous flat rook that jutted out over the Chattahoochee. There was Andi, sprawled out on her back, her eyes squeezed shut, a half-empty bottle of Jack Daniels clutched in one hand.

When she noticed him standing beside her, she opened one eye, groaned and then closed it again.

"I'm very drunk, now go away," she slurred, then rolled over onto her side. It was too dark to see her face, but he didn't need to see it, to know how swollen her eyes were.

"You are wasted. That means I'm going to need to drive that damn terror machine down this trail, in the dark, without spilling you off. That's not likely to happen the way I want it to. So, come on and try to hang on."

"I can drive."

"You can barely stand up. I need to get you home and sober you up. So, get on." He cranked the bike and started to pull off. Then stopped and opened the side case on the bike, removing two bungee cords. By hooking them together it was long enough to reach around them both. He worked the bungee up as close to her arms as possible, fastening it around his own chest. It wasn't much, but even that little bit was enough to keep her balanced. Creeping along as slowly as he could and still remain upright, he worked his way down the trail.

She was openly crying by the time they reached the apartment.

"But really, I was just enjoying the peace and quiet…" That was a lie. I was hiding from my emotions. It had been harder than I'd expected to see him in that casket. "I'm a horrible person."

"You are not a horrible person. It's not your fault Thumper died."

"But he didn't trust me. He told me it was a tattoo

needle."

"He didn't want to disillusion you. You're a lot more sensitive than people think you are. Thumper knew it. That's why he didn't tell you. He didn't want you to feel sorry for him. The needle story made it seem like an accident. This way he knew you were his friend, and that you hung around with him because you wanted to, not because you felt sorry for him."

"You knew, didn't you?"

Cooper looked directly in her eyes. "Yes."

" I miss him already."

"Me, too."

Chapter 24

Life sucks. It was simple, and it summed up the way her life had been going lately.

First Thumper died. He was twenty-four fucking years old. Now Misty was lying in the same hospital, and the doctor had that same damn look on his face. She was in labor, but it was still in the early stages. Hopefully, they could slow her contractions, the baby wasn't due for another week and Marco was stuck at the restaurant until he could get someone to hold down the fort. It would happen on a Friday. She wasn't too worried about the baby; they had an excellent NICU. Of course, anytime the mother suffers preeclampsia, it endangers its life. And possibly the mothers too. It didn't look like Marco was going to make it on time, but if Cooper hurried, he could get there before they took her down to the delivery room. Andi kept her eye on the clock the entire time, realizing it was a race. Her stomach was rolling, and she felt nauseous herself. What was taking him so long?

Her phone beeped, signaling another incoming text. Marco again, wanting an update. He had finally gotten the last customer out; Jose was delivering the Pizza and then he was going to come back and close up for the night. She sighed. Marco was on the way. Thirty more minutes, she only needed to hold out half an hour.

A familiar voice caught her attention. Cooper was pale and shaking when he ran up to the nurses' station. "How is she?"

"She's in good hands…there's been some complications. The doctor has decided to move up the labor and deliver the baby by an emergency cesarean. His heart rate is erratic, and the obstetrician is afraid they may lose them both if they try a traditional delivery." She did her best to appear calm, knowing Coop was about as far from a solid foundation as you could get right now. His personal life was in shambles and he had not been taking care of himself. Even now, he looked rough, as if he had been up all night partying again.

The nurse standing at the desk smiled at his harried expression. "You need to scrub up now and get into your greens. Your wife is adamant about you being them when your child is born to cut the cord."

"She's not my wife." Cooper snapped irritably. "She's my sister. Her husband is about a half-hour away. He had to close the restaurant before he could get away." Cooper took a deep breath and swayed, then turned almost as green as the gown she passed him to wear. "So, her baby brother gets to stand in for daddy," Andrea said as she helped him slip it on and then tied the back laces closed for him. There was not much anyone could say. Misty had held on this long because she wanted her husband there when the baby was born. She was out of time. The doctor needed to deliver the baby and she was going to have to be satisfied with Cooper.

Andi hoped that the delivery was going to be easy, that Misty and the baby were going to be okay. Lately, it seemed as if Murphy's Law had been written just for her. Looking back, she now knew everything Cooper had surmised about Dawn was true. After she made a fool out of her in front of half the school, she had wished the floor would open up and swallow her. Despite her humiliation, she had survived and now she realized how ridiculous that thought had been.

Dwelling on her misfortune would not solve the problem. True, she had wished Dawn gone from her life so that she would not have to see her face again. Now that she had dropped out of school, she wondered if what she had said to her that day had anything to do with it. Regardless of her duplicity Dawn had refused to ac-knowledge her own involvement in the fiancé fiasco, she blamed her for the fight with Kim. That was just one of the red flags. Now she knew it was one of many. The girl had issues. Major issues.

The sad thing was that she still kinda missed seeing her crooked smile. She even missed the way Dawn would suddenly burst out in a braying laugh at the very worst possible moment. Some little part of her heart wanted to try to work things out, but in her more logical mind, she knew there wasn't chance in hell they would ever get back together. Andi sighed and walked back toward the waiting room. It was time for her to come to terms with reality and move on. She needed to build her wall so high no one could ever hurt her again, not family, no friends, no one. She enjoyed being a player, and for now, that would be enough. Not to mention she will be busy being an aunt to the new baby. She couldn't wait to find out if it was a boy or a girl. Misty had refused to allow the doctor to let her know the sex, not wanting to spoil the surprise. It had made buying gifts a bit of a challenge, but considering how nontraditional her friends were, the baby ended up with a great balance of things anyway.

She remembered the last time they were at the hospital and realized her memories had a habit of invading her thoughts her at the worst possible moments…they jumped from the hospital to the baby, to the baby shower in seconds. Tears filled her eyes as she thought about the baby shower. Thumper had helped her with the shower, going shopping with her and picking up the cake and decorations. The next week he had gotten sick and gone to the hospital. This hospital. He had died in a room on the fifth floor.

Once the baby arrived, she would go upstairs and tell him all about it. If she could, she would drag Cooper up there with her. He hated hospitals as much as she did, so that may not be possible, but in her mind, if Thumper's soul was hanging around, it would be in the place he died, not where they had buried the body.

He would appreciate being the first one to know if it was a boy or a girl. Well, the first beside Cooper. If Cooper didn't faint. The thought made her smile.

Chapter 25

Her phone had been buzzing while she was in the cab, and she had a good idea who it was. Cooper realized she was probably on the bike, and that she would answer once she parked it, so he wouldn't be expecting an immediate answer. Figuring out the best way to tell him was the problem. She had to tell him the truth, but somehow, she needed to tell him what had happened without him getting upset. There was no easy way to do it and she was not going to sugar coat it. Lying to her best friend would hurt her more than Cooper. Just knowing she'd gone out to a bar without him was going to piss him off. She remembered the last time she'd done that. She'd gone to the same bar with Dawn. Omission wasn't exactly lying, so why was the guilt creeping into her conscience?

Within minutes of her flopping down on the sofa in her living room, the phone buzzed again. She took a deep breath to steady her nerves and answered the call.

"Hi Coop, what's up?" Gawd, her voice sounded so fake. There was no way he wouldn't know she was hiding something.

"Where are you? I've been trying to get in touch with you all night, "

"I'm at home. So, what's up?" She needed to get his mind off her disappearance long enough to come up with a decent excuse for her absence. He probably thought she had hooked up with Dawn again. She hadn't, but it wasn't for lack of trying.

"I'm on the way home. Don't go anywhere." She didn't argue. There was a beep and then a dial tone. He hadn't even said goodbye. That was new. He always said *Love ya.*

He hadn't asked where she had been, and she wasn't going to press her luck. Something had him stressed. She could tell that from the high-pitched tone of his voice. It always went up a few octaves when he was upset. But he hadn't sounded angry, so she was reasonably certain it wasn't her secret excursion that had set him off. She decided to make something to eat. The one certainty she had in her life was that Cooper was always hungry. It only took a minute to confirm her choices were limited.

Cooper was fuming when he entered the apartment ten minutes later. He tossed his jacket across the back of a barstool and looked around from Andi.

"Andi?"

"Be there in a minute Making popcorn." She opened the fridge, looking for butter seasoning for the popcorn. She kept digging around inside the refrigerator, hoping to stall long enough for him to settle down on the sofa. It didn't work, he marched straight into the kitchen to confront her.

"Why didn't you answer my call?"

He sounded strange. Angry. This surprised her. It wasn't as if he hadn't vanished for days at a time. It hadn't even been twenty-four hours since they left the restaurant.

"Sorry. I was on the bike. What's up?"

His eyes were dark and full of concern as he took in her appearance; the baggy clothes, the scraggly pony-tail, the swollen hand. He took a step toward her as she turned away from the refrigerator, then froze as his eyes locked in on her face. He immediately began shaking. By the time he reached her, his eyes were wet.

Andi tried to remain nonchalant. Cooper was like that, he always cried when he got mad. It was obvious he was pissed. She waited while he examined her face, then waited while his eyes make a quick scan of her body. She knew what he would see. Vicious shades of purple and greens intertwined with puffy flesh around her left eye. There was also a nasty cut above her eyebrow. It had taken three stitches to close it. Her bottom lip was purple and swollen. Beyond the swollen hand was a neon pink cast. There was a hairline fracture about an inch above her wrist. She was glad he could not see her stomach and back, the doctor had shown her photos that clearly displayed at least two different boot size bruises. She was lucky; x-rays had shown no major damage to her kidneys, and other than a few days of slight pink tinge in her urine from the blood, she should have no lasting effects.

"A little early for Halloween, don't you think," he chuckled, in an unexpected attempt to make her feel better. He pulled her tight against his shoulder. She turned so her face landed against his chest, so her crying was muffled by his sweater--- the desired effect. "What the hell did you do to deserve this?"

"I went back to Faces. Looking for Dawn."

He stepped back and looked at her. That was Cooper, the only man she knew that could make her feel like an unruly child without saying a word. He stayed that way for a moment then pulled her back into his arms. "I don't know what is going on in your head lately. You haven't been yourself. Somethings not right and I'm going to find out what it is and fix it. But first, I want you to lay down on the sofa and rest. I'll grab you a pillow. Then you can tell me everything."

She took the bowl and left him standing in the kitchen, his hands on his hips and an exasperated expression on his face. Not that she blamed him, she had been kicking herself ever since she was lucid enough to remember she'd brought it all on herself. What the hell was she thinking, walking into Kim's favorite hangout alone? She might as well have been wearing a *kick me* sign.

He had her settled, resting against her favorite pillow, and covered with a thick throw in minutes. Then he flipped through the channels, looking for something she might want to watch. There was a Dr. Who marathon on, she loved sci-fi. He grabbed a coke and joined her, shifting the pillow to his lap, so she could recline against him. He could tell Andi did not feel like answering his questions, but he didn't care. "What were you thinking, going to Faces by yourself. You know what that place is like."

She pursed her lips into a tight smile. There was nothing she could say that would make sense to him. In his mind, what's done is done. Over. Kaput. Shove it in the never do this again file and forget it. It wasn't that easy. This time she was the one who screwed over the faithful girlfriend. She had hated the woman Katie had run off with. Now she wondered if Katie had been totally honest with her. She may not even know another woman was in the picture. Or like her, she may be filled with guilt. It was a miserable feeling.

She'd tried to explain how she was feeling but the

conversation kept going around in circles: She would express her reasons for her interest in talking to Kim. Cooper would shoot her reasons down, although not as passionately as he could have. He was really worried about her getting hurt. She decided to give it one more try. "I want to talk to Kim, too. It's hard to explain. I need to explain I didn't know about her. I need closure."

"So, you think you are still in love with Dawn?" He had a strange look in his eyes. He was hiding something.

"No. I never did love her. I'm not even sure why I started dating her. She's nothing like my usual type. Maybe that's what it was, something new and exciting. I should be angry about her lies, but I'm not. I wanted answers. I needed to understand the lies."

"Me too. Explain the part where you avoided telling me where you were going before I get angry because you let yourself get screwed over again by someone you gut warned you against?"

"There's nothing I can say that will prevent you from being pissed off. I screwed up going to the club. She wasn't even there. No one I recognized was there. This is where the story gets screwy. I think someone spiked my drink."

"Oh please, you're a lesbian. Who would spike your drink? Can't you think of a more convincing excuse to getting your ass whooped that that?

"It does sound odd but it's the truth. And believe it or not; I wasn't looking for Dawn, I was looking for Kim."

"Kim? Why would you go looking for that bitch?"

"I don't know. I just damn, I don't know what I was thinking. I wanted to see if Dawn was really missing or if she was just avoiding everyone. I figured Kim might know. My gut told me she wouldn't tell me even if she knew; but if I was looking at her, I thought I could tell if she was lying."

Cooper relaxed. In her own crazy way of looking at things, it made sense. "So, did anyone try to take you home with them?"

"Nope. But I did get jumped by three of Kim's buddies on the way to my car."

She filled him in on what she could remember about the assault. She was walking from the club to the parking garage. She heard someone call her name and turned to look. That's when one of them hit her from behind. Before she knew it, she was on the ground, with one sitting on her chest while getting kicked by the other two. Things were a bit blurry after that. She vaguely remembered when the bouncer from the bar pulled them off. He sent her to the hospital in an ambulance, so her bike was still sitting in the parking garage downtown. That was another lie she would need to make better once he forgave her for going to the club without him, not answering his calls when she was not on the bike.

"And you tried to fight all three." He shook his head at the idea. That exasperated tone was back.

"It wasn't as if they gave me a whole lot of choice in the matter." The nerve. As if *she* never had a right to be exasperated by *him*. Cooper was more emotional than anyone she knew. He probably had more estrogen than most women. He wasn't a bodybuilder like most of his boyfriends. Tall and naturally thin, almost feminine, and lightly muscled like a fashion model, he disdained any-thing that brought up a sweat.

Now that she thought about it, he was basically a male version of Dawn… at least in appearance. They were nothing alike in personality. Dawn expected to be taken care of, she had to feel protected at all times. Cooper was like a bandy rooster; he had never backed down from a fight…even when the odds were stacked against him. He would whip the entire bar if he thought some-one was trying to hurt her. It would never cross his mind that she was stronger and probably a better fighter than he was.

"Want some?" She passed him the bowl of popcorn she'd been nibbling on and he took a handful.

"I was worried about you. I thought something might have happened to you."

"Something did happen. I'm certain someone fol-lowed the cab home last night from the Hospital. I think it was the same van that was following me the last time I went out with Dawn."

Coopers' eyes darkened. He shifted uncomfortably.

Then he pulled a rolled-up section of the paper from his back pocket. "Andi, I think you out to read this."

"What is it, another article about the engagement? Don't you think I got the message the first time?"

"Just read it," Cooper's hand dropped the folded newspaper on her lap.

She picked it up and let her eyes drift over the page. There was a photo of Kim and Dawn. Beneath it was a two-inch-long announcement of their engagement. Visible documentation of her stupidity. She scanned the first couple of lines and shrugged. "So, I'm a homewrecker. The other woman. I screwed up."

"Just keep reading."

"Why, so I could learn all about what a naive fool I was? Not interested."

"Naïve, yes. A fool never, your gut kept telling you something was wrong the entire time you were going out with her. If you will just lis—"

"Save it, Cooper. You've done your good deed. She's no longer a part of our life, she can go screw with someone else's head."

"I don't think that's going to be a problem. Andi. Read. The. Damn. Paper." He turned her head with his finger, looking right into her eyes. "Dawn is dead."

Andrea jumped. "Jesus Cooper, that's not fucking funny."

"Language, kiddo, and I wasn't trying to be funny. You need to flip the paper over and read the story below the photo." He held the newspaper so Andrea could read the headlines too. BODY FOUND NEAR MARINA IDENTIFIED.

Andi snatched the paper from his hands, reading quickly. Her eyes welled with tears as she read the name of the deceased, Dawn Worthington. According to the article, Dawn's body had been discovered early yesterday morning. She was assumed to have lost control before going into Altoona Lake near the Dam. The article went into detail. Daughter of Craig Worthington, the head of surgery at Northwest Hospital and Doctor Evonne Dixon Worthington, renowned Child Psychiatrist. Fiancé of Kimberly O'Rourke daughter of one of the city's premier Neurosurgeons, Doctor Devon O'Rourke. The family was not available for comment. The initial report was that she had been dead for over a week, however, the exact time of death was contingent on the coroner's report. That would not be available for a couple of weeks.

Well, that explained why she hadn't been in school. Probably why she'd been jumped too. They think she had something to do with it. Andi was surprised at how little the news affected her. A week earlier and she would have been heartbroken, or least she would have thought she was. Now, even though she felt sad at the news, she didn't have the gut-wrenching pain she'd expect to experience over the news that a woman she thought she'd been falling love with, was dead. Despite her best intentions, there had always been something about Dawn's behavior that had prevented her from letting her guard down. Her feelings had been hurt when she found out Dawn was engaged to Kim, but it had not pushed her into the deep depression she'd experienced when Katie had run off with Mikki.

Maybe she was growing up. Not like Coop. Cooper could be so gullible at times. One day that pretty face was going to get him into the kind of trouble he can't walk away from. Not to mention, it wasn't as if he'd never gotten himself into a disastrous relationship. Like the baby scare. That had been a crazy one. It hadn't been that long ago, last year, right after Donovan embarrassed him at the bathhouse. She could still remember the panicked look on his face…

"You what?"

"I'm going to have a baby." After making the announcement, he flopped down on the bed beside her, reached into her can of mixed nuts, and began tossing the shelled meats into the air, trying to catch them with his mouth as if he was still six years old.

"I know you like to dress in pink, but last time I checked, it was still physically impossible for that to happen."

"Ha. Ha. Ha. Stop being facetious. I know I'm not pregnant. Lissa is." He stacked a few pillows and then leaned back against the headboard, a smug expression on his face.

"Who the fuck is Lissa? And how does that make

you …" Her eyes opened wide. " Don't tell me. You're bi now?"

"No. I'm definitely a man's man. It was a onetime thing, more curiosity than anything else. Well, curiosity and a who lot of peach schnapps." He began grinning, a wide-open, cat got the canary grin that made his announcement even more of a ludicrous statement.

"No. This is a joke. You're fucking with me. You and a girl? No way."

"No joke. I'm gonna be a daddy. Or a mommy, depending on who you ask. Melissa is going to give me the baby; she's eighteen and is not ready to be a parent. I am."

Andi decided to keep her opinion on that to herself. She loved him dearly, but the idea of Cooper as a parent scared her. Not that he wouldn't be a caring parent, he had a heart of gold. It was more the idea of the bouncy playboy settling down to a day of diapers and dribble. She could not imagine him as a homebody. She closed her eyes, picturing him in a pink gingham apron, covered in flour, one hand on the rolling pin, the other on the baby on his hip. It was all she could do to keep the laughter under control.

"Well, I was going to suggest we drive down to Masquerade for the Freak Fest tonight. But since you are pregnant…"

"Bitch, you better get that mouth under control. I've only got seven more months to find a baby daddy. That seems like as good a place to start my search as any. Maybe I will get lucky."

He had been so excited. Then three days later he found out Melissa had lost the baby. She still had her doubts about the miscarriage, wondering if there had ever been a baby at all, but since she didn't know the girl, she kept her mouth shut and gave him a shoulder to cry on, even though he never used it.

Now, finding out about Dawn dying left her feeling the same loss. Unhappy…but it was not the life-ending earthquake she imagined it would be. Only a distant sense of sadness. And just enough relief to make her feel guilty. Then another thought hit her….

"What the hell should I do? According to this report, she died last Friday. That means I was one of the last to talk to her."

"You mean text her. Last time I head, you can't kill someone through a phone."

"Never mind any of that. All I'm sayin' is, if I was investigating a murder, I would be going through her phone records. They must know we were having an affair. That makes me a suspect."

"Do you want me to hang around here today? Now that Marco's back I can take a day off and stay with you."

"No reason to drag you into this mess. Go to work. I may need your help paying for an attorney." She kissed his cheek and thanked him for being there for her. When the door clicked shut behind him, her smile fell, and she slipped to the floor beside the door. Her brain had yet to wrap around this new reality. *There were things she should do, weren't there? Should she contact Dawn's parents? Or would they blame her?*

The threat of tears stung her eyes, so she relaxed and let them flow. She would deal with the police if they showed up. Make that *when* they showed up. There was no way they would not come and talk to her. She would figure it all out. Right *now*, she needed to go on as if everything was normal. If that was possible. What had happened the night before suddenly didn't seem so simple.

Then Tipper began to bark, and the doorbell rang. She resisted the urge to peek out the window, somehow knowing it was the police. Instead, she forced her face into a halfway normal expression and opened the door.

Chapter 26

Andi penned Michael up in the back dining room the next afternoon when he came into the restaurant. "Have they found out anything else about Dawn?"

"On the record or off? You know we are not supposed to talk about this stuff. And you are listed in the file."

"Mike, stop playing Cop for a minute. I don't want any major information. I just wasn't to know if there are any new clues. Talk!"

"The only thing we were able to find out was that her brakes had failed completely."

"Her brakes? The car isn't even a year old yet."

"Which is why we've had a couple of officers look under the hood. It seems like there had been some serious tampering with the braking system."

"On purpose?"

"Enough to make us fear that someone wanted the brakes to fail."

"What do you mean by that?"

"It wasn't heat damage. The brakes have metal line hoses full of fluid, the only wires are for speed sensors or brake lights. The metal lines were contorted and crimped in a very strategic way. Whoever did it, knew a lot about mechanics. There was even a sensor that had been yanked out."

She shook her head. "That doesn't make a lot of sense. Dawn doesn't know much about cars, but she was fanatical about maintenance. She wouldn't have driven there if the light was on. She calls a wrecker for a blown fuse."

"We have an expert mechanic taking a look into it as we speak. But as of right now, this is not considered an accident."

"What? Someone tried to kill her?"

He glanced down at his damn notebook again. "Did Dawn ever mention anyone she was afraid of? Or anyone that might want to hurt her? Do you recall anyone she had been fighting with? Someone who might've gone too far trying to get even?" He kept his eyes on her face as he asked the questions, watching for unspoken signals that she might know something.

Andi shook her head. "There's only one person she's been fighting with lately besides me. That is Kim. At least as far as I knew." The whole idea that someone had purposefully tampered with the brakes was absurd.

"Hmmm. Do you think that Kim would try and hurt her?"

"No. I don't know. I don't know Kim well enough to say. Me? Yes, she does not like me. But I have no reason to think she would ever hurt Dawn."

"How about anyone who drives a Black truck or Van. A big one, not a small one like Toyota."

"You mean besides you?" She tried not to smirk. "No, not really. Marco drives a White Ford, and ol Man Nelson had a navy-blue Chevy. That's about it. Why?"

"There was paint on one side of the car. Black paint. It's a shade that hasn't been used in a few years, so we figured it was maybe an old farm truck."

"There's enough of them around. But I haven't seen any lately."

"It may not be related to the accident. But keep your eyes open. Let me know if you spot one."

She promised to keep looking as she walked him toward the door. Two new customers came in as he was leaving, and she was soon too busy to think about it.

***

Andi shoved the final prep tray into the cooler with a deep sigh of relief. Sometimes she really hated working at a restaurant.

Jose had to leave early, one of his kids was sick and he was at the local emergency room. He had been brought the States as an infant and grew up in the area. Unlike most of his family, Jose was legal. He had his driver's license, Social Security number, and paid taxes. His kids were born in the US. But Juanita his wife wasn't, so whenever one of the kids got sick, he had to take them to the doctor since she was afraid of being deported.

That left Andi to do his nightly prep work before

leaving. It was too much for Marco to do in the morning with Misty having to stay home with the new baby and they couldn't afford to pay another kitchen helper.

Today had started out bad and gone downhill from there. The police had kept her at the station until three in the morning asking questions about her relationship with Dawn. Most of the answers had been simple, she went to school, from school to work and usually worked until closing time. Of course, she had no way of proving that she went straight home after work, but Michael had been able to back up her alibi during working hours and knew what time she usually left for the evening. The police wouldn't explain why, but Mike said since she rode a motorcycle, they did not really think she had anything to do with Dawn's accident. They had to satisfy protocol and ask her everything anyway. This had pretty much ruined the first half her day. Cooper had a date, so he left at nine. Jose's baby getting sick was just the sour cherry on the melting ice cream. At least it wasn't raining.

Quickly she ran a mental list of everything she needed to do before locking up and checked all the boxes.

Finally! She was past exhausted. After switching over to night lighting, she grabbed her jacket, typed in the security code on the pad by the exit, and locked the back door of the restaurant, noting that someone had busted the security light on the pole again. Immediately paranoid, she looked up and down the alley, but nothing appeared out of the ordinary.

She wished they would leave the lights alone. Mike claimed there was a growing problem with homeless transients, but she was certain it had been broken by one of the teenage street gangs that were popping up around town. The homeless were always looking through the dumpsters for usable items, and they needed the light to see. The teens simply didn't care. And they would steal anything that wasn't nailed down. Knocking out the lights gave then the cover of darkness.

Normally she would just toss her helmet in the saddlebags but lately, she had thought it might be best to lock it up. She searched through her keychain for the keys to her saddlebags, unlocked the clamshell, and then pulled her helmet out and laid it on the seat. The screech of an angry cat over by the dumpster caught her attention, and she turned to see what was causing the racket.

The slight flash of moonlight reflecting off the knife was the only warning she received. The razor-sharp blade sliced deeply into her forearm, cutting across the muscle down to the bone. There was a brief pain as the knife cut through the soft tissue, but the pain ended almost as fast as it began.

Unfortunately, the attack didn't. Whoever it was, they seemed intent on doing the most damage possible in a fairly short time period. The knife-wielder was swinging wildly but putting a lot of force behind the blade. It was obvious the assailant was not an experienced blades man however Andi knew even an accidental stab to the right spot could do lethal damage. The odds were not in the attacker's favor, but she could not risk a lucky blow. She screamed and jerked away, scraping her face on the brick wall. Blood began dribbling down her face. Now frantic, and beginning to feel the effects of lost blood, she began scanning the alley for anything she could use for cover. There was nothing in sight, so she grabbed her helmet off her seat and threw it as hard as she could. It missed but it did distract the assailant.

Twisting right away from her attacker, Andi kicked out with her foot, somehow managing to land the blow and knock the unknown person backward. It threw the assailant off balance, and she managed to avoid a direct hit in the side. She winced as the tip carved a narrow furrow along her rib left. The cut wasn't deep, but it hurt like hell.

She began to back away, knowing there was no way she could avoid the next strike. Unless she maintained pressure on her forearm with her hand she would bleed out. There was no way she could use her arms for balance, so, outrunning them was out of the question. She still wasn't sure how many there were in the alley.

The amount of blood she was losing scared her. She could feel it, warm and sticky in-between her fingers. She wondered if she was dying. Her hand was not big enough to cut off the flow. And there was no way she could not take her eyes off the shadowy figure long enough to search for something she could use to slow down the bleeding. Instead, she screamed, "Help!" as she backed slowing up the alley.

No one noticed. Not even Avi's pitbull and Kujo usually went crazy at the slighted hint that anything out of the ordinary was going on in the alley. As if the attacker could read her mind, he announced, "Don't look for the dog to bark, I packed the meat with tranquilizers."

The voice sounded familiar. Andi couldn't see well enough to recognize her assailant, but she could hear his heavy boots crunching on the crushed pea gravel as he moved slowly around in the alley darkness.

Then the shadow stepped into the light and Andi gasped.

"Not who you expected, am I?"

"No, a psycho bitch from hell never crossed my mind."

"I'm sure you didn't. That would require you to use your brain, and we all know how difficult that is for you." She somehow managed to smirk while laughing. "Dawn always was attracted to dumb blondes. Her finding a brunette to play with was new." Kim took a step closer to

Andrea. "Not that getting rid of you will be any harder than any the others." She began laughing loudly, it was an odd braying wheeze that sounded like an asthmatic donkey.

Others? For a second, Andi simply stared, silent, not knowing what to do. She did not have time to waste talking to a crazy woman. Her heart was pounding. She was already feeling woozy. Despite the freezing air, beads of warm blood slid down the side of her face onto her shoulder and her hand was growing numb. Would she be able to keep it clamped around the cut? Somehow, she needed to get help before she passed out from loss of blood.

Kim had no intention of allowing that. "Don't even try it. There's no one working nearby, and I put enough ketamine in the meat I fed that damn dog to kill it. Either way, it's not going to be making any noise. You made a big mistake. I'll make you regret not walking away from Dawn when you had the chance. You may have thought she loved you, but I'm the one she agreed to marry. She promised she would love no… one… but… me." She used her finger to emphasize her words as she spoke.

"Son of a bitch., it was you! you killed her!" Everything that had happened flashed through her mind. It all became so clear. The tire, the attack at the bar, even the way the police had acted.

Kim glared at her; her pale blue eyes cold and full of hatred. "Like I said, She's mine. If I can't have her, nobody will. It was easy. It was pure luck that she stopped at that station to get gas. My best friend works there and said she often stops by to fill up. You know Jeffery, he's in the automotive class? He definitely knows you. He has a great video of you and Dawn making out behind the shop. It didn't take me a minute to slice the brake line. All I had to do was follow her until she was crossing the water berm, and then shove her over the edge. Didn't even dent my bumper."

"You are crazy!"

"Crazy like a fox. It was perfect. I paid cash for the old truck and it's not registered in anyone's name. I simply parked it at the station ahead of time. Then I established my alibi by driving down to the club in my Lexus.

I made sure everyone saw me. Then I waited until the band started playing and told Jeffery I needed to go to the bathroom. I doubt he ever thought to check the time. Between the Crown Royal and the Extasy he took, he was so fucked up he probably hasn't realized I've left the club. He was in the mosh pit when I left. I will just join him and start dancing. My car never left the lot, the attendant clocks them in and out. Rock-solid alibi. Simple."

For a brief second, Andi felt a burst of hope. There was a car with turn signals on passing the end of the alley, but it went past the alley without turning in. There was no way they could have seen her in the dark. She tried screaming once more. "Help. Fire! Fire!" Someone had told her that would get someone's attention faster than anything. It didn't work. All the nearby businesses were closed; there was no one to hear her cries.

"You know, I was beginning to wonder if I would ever catch you alone again."

Again? Denial was hitting her hard. She couldn't believe what Kim was saying, but she knew there was no reason she'd be making it all up. She started replaying what she'd said, trying hard to comprehend was she was trying to tell her.

"I thought you were onto me that night you almost caught me following you," Kim confessed. She began circling slowly, trying to find an opening. "I hated scrapping the truck, but the police are looking for an older vehicle that color. It was crushed in another state, so no one will find it."

Andi knew she needed to keep her talking as long as possible. There was a slim possibility that Michael would come by the restaurant again. Very slim. He had just made his rounds. She was starting to feel so weak. "So, you *were* the one who cut my tires?"

Her breath fogged in the cold air for a moment before she spoke, "I've been doing everything I could think of to keep you two apart, ever since my cousin told me about you and her dancing at the bar."

"You were spying on us?"

"Of course. It was ridiculously easy. Dawn drove the same route every time she went to see you."

"What about my apartment—how'd you get in?"

"Picked the lock. My grandfather was a locksmith in New York. He was able to do a lot with his money after he sold the house and business. Money goes a lot farther in Georgia."

Andi felt her stomach roll and realized she was shivering. "I'm going to be sick."

Kim laughed again. "You are going to be dead. That's one of the signs. You are losing a lot of blood. Soon you will be too weak to hold your grip." She grinned as Andi went to one knee.

Andi tried to remain focused and alert. She kept her eyes on Kim's face. It seemed to blur in the darkness, resembling the skull in the painting of the Grim Reaper she'd seen in Underground. Blacky had taken a photo with him. So, had she. Now she wished she hadn't.

Kim seemed to know what she was thinking. "It shouldn't be long now. Once you pass out, you will bleed out in minutes. But I've been told it's a painless death. Much better than drowning. You will be seeing Dawn soon enough. Give her my regards." The mocking tone in her voice was hard to ignore.

Andi knew Kim wasn't worried about confessing, she intended no one would be alive to testify against her. She had planned this out meticulously, even arranging her alibi ahead of time to ensure no one would question her whereabouts.

Kim seemed to realize Andi was stalling. She looked around, making sure they were still alone. Then she began to laugh.

Andi knew it was just a matter of minutes now. She was already beginning to feel faint. Her vision was so blurry she didn't notice Kim moving toward her until it was too late.

Kim grabbed both her arms and pinned her against the door once more. The sharp edge of the knife she was holding sliced a shallow line across Andi's good palm, adding to the blood loss.

"Get away from me," she yelled, doing her best to wrestle out of Kim's grip. The redhaired woman's eyes were wide and wild, and she seemed stronger than Andi thought one person could be. There was no way she could free herself. Her fingers were slick, and it was becoming harder to keep her grip on her arm. The two women went back and forth, rolling against the door a few times, Kim's grip getting tighter and tighter around Andi's wrists. She grunted against her, but it was no use. With only one arm, it was impossible to keep her from landing another blow with the knife. And it was becoming harder to concentrate on two things at once. She could block a blow, but that would mean she had to let go of her arm. As weak as she was, it wouldn't be more than a few seconds before she passed out from blood loss.

Then Kim jerked her hand up and drew back the blade.

Andi screamed as Kim swung at the side of her head.

Chapter 27

"Where is she? Is she okay?" Cooper rushed into the emergency room, spotted his sister talking to a strange woman beside the soft drink machine and ran that way.

"She's resting now, but yes. She'll be fine. She lost a lot of blood, they had to give her plasma, but the doctors say she will make a full recovery. There might be some rib damage and a possible concussion. There's a lot of bruising on the left side of her ribcage where the bitch kicked her when she passed out. Luckily, Maggie arrived in time. She used her bra to make a tourniquet and kept the pressure on her arm until the paramedics arrived."

"Why didn't someone call me? I had to find out from Jose."

Maggie winced at his words. Her adrenaline had been flowing so strongly by the time she arrived at the hospital that she hadn't even considered the possibility that her roommate might be worried about why Andi wasn't home. When Misty showed up, she assumed word had gotten out to everyone.

"I'm sorry, Cooper," Misty said. "We were busy with the police. There was a lot of paperwork to be done. The only reason I found out, is that I'm listed on her medical records as the emergency contact."

"But she's okay?"

"The doctors seem confident she will make a full recovery. They called a specialist in to reconstruct the cut muscles and tendons. She may not be able to lift weights, but her arm will be fine for normal use. Thank God Maggie showed up at the restaurant."

Maggie? Why did that name seem familiar? "I assume you are Maggie," he said to the unknown woman.

"Yes, that's me. I'm glad I was there to help. To be honest, it could have been a lot worse considering it looks like someone was intentionally trying to kill Andrea. Some woman named Kim."

"Kim! That's Dawn's ex-girlfriend. Or maybe her current fiancé. Fuck. We aren't sure what the hell she was.

With Dawn dead, it's kind of hard to find out the truth." He paused as the possibility of Andi being dead too, sunk in. He looked at Maggie. "I guess I owe you a big thank you. I don't know what I would do if something happened to Andi."

"You and Andi are close?" Maggie looked puzzled.

"Of course. I love her," Cooper said.

"But I thought she…" she hesitated, unsure how to say it. Maybe Andi was not out. There hadn't been time for a lot of conversation in Savannah.

Cooper saw the question in her eyes and quickly answered her unspoken question. "No… I love her. I'm not *in* love with her. Andi's like my sister. Besides, I prefer slightly different equipment when I play games." He grinned. "Don't let me stand in your way."

Maggie looked at him and had a small revelation. "So that's why you were so rude to me when I called the restaurant earlier?

"Was that you? Sorry. I thought it was a friend of Dawn's wanting to lay another guilt trip on Andi."

Maggie didn't understand what e meant, but she

decided to leave it for another time. She noticed the nurse beckoning from the entrance to the curtained enclosure surrounding Andi's hospital bed. "Looks like we can go back in."

Andi was sitting up in bed when they walked in. She smiled at Cooper and Misty but appeared surprised to see Maggie. "Hi. I never expected to see you again."

"I was offered an apprentice position at CASA and decided to accept. I could not turn down the chance to work at a five-star restaurant like Bacchanalia. And Buckhead is not that far from here. After I got settled into my apartment, I decided to drive up and surprise you. I think I was the one who got surprised."

Misty laughed. "According to Driscoll, she slammed into Kim like a linebacker. Hot her a couple of times and she ran off. Then she stopped most of the bleeding and called for help."

"But how did you find me?"

"It was luck. Or maybe Devine intervention. I had called the restaurant earlier but got cut off. So, I decided to try in person. When I arrived, the closed sign was up, but I remembered you saying you often worked in the kitchen after the restaurant closed. I decided to walk around to the back and see if your motorcycle was still there. I could see there were two figures struggling and then I heard someone call out help and fire. I called 911 and ran toward the struggle. To be honest, I thought someone was getting raped. I was astonished to see it was you. There was so much blood. I just reacted." Maggie kept her eyes on Andi the entire time she was talking. It was strange, how the idea of losing her was so intense. It felt as is no time had passed since that weekend in Savannah. She searched her face, looking for any sign that she might feel the same way about her.

Then Andi reached out and took her hand. She smiled up at her. There was a twinkle in her eyes as Misty and Cooper silently slipped out of the room. "You know, I have never eaten at a five-star restaurant. Never could afford it. I'm looking forward to trying out all the new recipes."

Maggie grinned. "Get well. Then we can see what we can cook up…together."

www.ingramcontent.com/pod-product-compliance
Lightning Source LLC
Chambersburg PA
CBHW020910110726
47900CB00001B/87